THE DEADLY WEED

THE DEADLY WEED

Cora Harrison

**SEVERN
HOUSE**

First world edition published in Great Britain and the USA in 2023
by Severn House, an imprint of Canongate Books Ltd,
14 High Street, Edinburgh EH1 1TE.

Trade paperback edition first published in Great Britain and the USA in 2023
by Severn House, an imprint of Canongate Books Ltd.

severnhouse.com

British Library Cataloguing-in-Publication Data
A CIP catalogue record for this title is available from the British Library.

ISBN-13: 978-1-4483-0982-5 (cased)
ISBN-13: 978-1-4483-1029-6 (trade paper)
ISBN-13: 978-1-4483-1022-7 (e-book)

Typeset by Palimpsest Book Production Ltd.,
Falkirk, Stirlingshire, Scotland.
Printed and bound in Great Britain by
TJ Books Ltd, Padstow, Cornwall.

This book is dedicated to my sister, Eleanor, a lover of the beautiful and historic seaside town of Youghal in the county of Cork.

ACKNOWLEDGEMENTS

A sudden bout of illness when I was in the final stages of this book has meant that my usual gratitude to those who help to bring a book out has been very much increased. To Jo Grant, my publisher; Peter Buckman, my agent; Anna Harrisson, my editor; and all at Severn House, thank you so much for all your generous support and editorial help.

ONE

When the telephone in the Cork City Police Station rang just before nine o'clock of the evening of the 27th of July, Inspector Patrick Cashman was alone. 'Barrack Street Police Station,' he said.

'Is that the police. I want to report a murder,' said a quavering female voice.

There was a young constable, also on night duty in the outer office, but otherwise the building was empty. It would, Patrick had thought hopefully in the minute before the telephone rang, be a quiet night. No ship had docked that day and it was a Tuesday evening, so there was no spare cash for drinking until wages and meagre dole payments came on Friday afternoon.

Nevertheless, he was, as always, meticulously prepared for any emergency. A murder, he thought resignedly, was unusual these days since peace had arrived in Ireland, but a murder would be relatively easily dealt with. A riot would have been more difficult with only two men awake in the Cork Police Barracks. Now he might have to rouse another sleepy and resentful constable from his bed, but if it had been a riot all the Barrack Street police would have been needed, and he might even have to call in the army from the hill-top Collins Barracks.

Almost ten years had passed since the war for Ireland's independence had been followed by the bitter fighting between two factions: those who followed Michael Collins, who still called themselves the Irish Republican Army, the IRA, and those who followed Eamon de Valera and wanted peace even if it came with a price. Even after the post-ceasefire talks led to the signing of the Anglo-Irish Treaty on the 6th of December in the year of 1921, trouble in the shape of assassinations and riots erupted from time to time. The IRA and Sinn Fein, Patrick knew, were still very strong in the city of Cork, nicknamed

the Rebel City, and the police were always on the alert, night
as well as day, for fighting to break out.

'Who is this speaking?' he asked cautiously. Though he was
sure that he recognized the voice, he was cautious by nature.
That, he felt, was one of his main assets. He had been born
in the slums of Cork, born to a mother who, like many of the
poor in the city, had been deserted by her husband, the father
of her son. She had, Patrick often thought, done her best for
him, but her best had been very little. He had been, he guessed,
looking back over his childhood, not much for her to boast
about. He had been shy, quiet, and had avoided other boys of
his age. He had been neither good-looking nor clever. School
was a puzzle to him in the beginning but after a while he had
learned a valuable lesson – that hard work made up for any
lack of quickness. If he didn't understand something, then he
did not give up until comprehension dawned. And that tenacity
of purpose, perhaps inherited from his missing father, had
served him well as he worked his way through the early years
of the Christian Brothers' school and then, when he was
thirteen years old, to everyone's astonishment, he won a scholarship to the North Monastery School, which meant that he
did not need to leave school at the age of fourteen, but could
carry on until he was eighteen years old, could get himself a
good job and dig his mother, as well as himself, out from the
soul-destroying poverty of their existence.

By the time that Patrick was sixteen, he had concluded that
he was not clever enough to win another scholarship and attain
the dizzy heights of a university degree, but the newly formed
Irish national police force was looking for recruits and he set
himself to gain a place within the ranks. It had been a good
choice. Despite the renaming of the Royal Irish Constabulary
with the new Gaelic title of Garda Síochána there was a taint
of the conqueror about the police force and clever boys who
could look for a good job disliked the idea of becoming a
member of what was still called the 'Peelers'. Patrick, with
his respectable Leaving Certificate results, was welcomed
immediately he applied and by dint of hard work rose through
the ranks from constable to sergeant and from sergeant to
inspector and now he had an even more dazzling prospect in

front of him. The superintendent, a relic of the old days when the police force was known as the Royal Irish Constabulary and was formed almost exclusively from those with English origins and of the Protestant rather than the Roman Catholic faith, was due to retire and Patrick had hopes of inheriting the title and the responsibility. His prospects, he knew, depended very much upon the reference that he might receive from the man who had been his superior since the days when he had joined the force. He could not afford to put a foot wrong during the next few months, he thought, as he braced himself for what the night could bring.

'This is Mrs Maloney and I want to report a murder,' said the voice.

Patrick tightened his lips and bit back a sigh of exasperation. Everyone in the police station knew that name. Mrs Maloney loved to report any breaking of the law. This, at least to his knowledge, was the first time that she had reported a murder, but she was a regular patron of the telephone box on St Mary's Isle and did not hesitate to report children stealing from the back of horses and carts and other such misdeeds, as well as drawing the police's attention to fights and attempted burglaries.

'Yes, Mrs Maloney,' he said.

'Oh, it's yourself, Inspector Cashman. Well, there's a man been murdered, burned to death.'

'Burned to death,' repeated Patrick trying not to sound too disbelieving. This, in his experience, was an unusual report from this wretched woman. Mainly it was shoplifting, small boys hanging on to the back of lorries and, of course, fights in the street and outside public houses.

'Have you called the Fire Brigade, Mrs Maloney?' he asked, and was not surprised when she told him that she had and gave him the precise time of her call to the Fire Brigade on Sullivan's Quay, and also the precise time of their arrival. She was, he had to admit, a conscientious citizen.

'They've taken him away, but I could see that he was dead. Covered his face they did, just like they do at the pictures down in the Savoy Cinema!'

'I see,' said Patrick. 'Well, thank you, Mrs Maloney. I'll

see to this matter immediately.' Quickly and firmly, he replaced the receiver and when it almost immediately rang again, he bit back an exasperated curse. However, one never knew what the night would bring and so he picked it up and gave his name, this time.

'This is the Fire Brigade from Sullivan's Quay, Inspector,' said the voice on the other end of the line. 'We were called out to a fire on St Mary's Isle and I'm sorry to report a casualty.'

'St Mary's Isle!' So, the meddlesome Mrs Maloney was right. 'Not the convent,' he said quickly.

'No, not the convent, that wooden building they call it "The Cigarette Factory", but it's just a wooden shed. Not much of a fire either. More smoke than fire.'

'And the casualty?'

'Smoke inhalation,' said the man. 'Dr Scher is here. Everything is in order. Only rang you because of the dead man. The woman who gave the alarm was screaming about a murder. I told her that I would phone the police, just to get rid of her while we made sure that everything was safe. She's been on the phone to us a couple of times since. I thought I'd better let you know, but you will be getting the report tomorrow morning.'

'I see,' said Patrick. 'Well, thank you for letting me know.'

And then he settled down to making notes about the phone calls, checking his watch for accuracy against the clock in the reception office and nodding at the sound of the cathedral's bell on the stroke of nine p.m. just as he signed his name.

He then went to place the account on to the superintendent's desk and, once he had returned to his own office, put the matter from his mind, turning to doing some work on updating court reports and checking his meticulous filing system. The rest of the night, he thought, was, hopefully, going to be one of those rare quiet ones and he would sleep well when he went to his own quarters in the barracks at nine o'clock in the morning, once the day staff arrived. As for the accusation of murder, well, the day staff could deal with that. If Mrs Maloney had her way, half of the children of Cork city would be in prison for one crime or other.

He had just finished clearing his desk when the phone rang again. Too early in the morning for trouble. It must be Mrs Maloney once more, he thought.

'Yes,' he said, somewhat impatiently.

'Is that you, Patrick?' the voice sounded astonished and slightly irritated, and Patrick hastened to explain.

'Yes, this is Patrick Cashman, Superintendent,' he said. 'Sorry for that. I've had Mrs Maloney on and off the phone all through the night. I thought that she was back again.'

'So have I!' Luckily the superintendent sounded friendly, quite sympathetic. 'How that woman got my private number I just cannot understand, but she was on to me a few minutes ago. Was afraid that you were not taking her seriously. A fire apparently. And a man murdered or burned to death, she thinks it's the same thing, apparently.'

'Well, there has been a fire on St Mary's Isle, a fire at the cigarette factory. Not a serious fire, but there is a casualty, no burn injuries, smoke inhalation, Superintendent. I've made a note of everything that has happened. I've left it on your desk.'

'And this girl who started the fire?'

'I know nothing about that, Superintendent.' Patrick frowned at his notes. There'd been no mention of a witness to him. 'The Fire Brigade said nothing about arson, Superintendent.' Patrick could hear a defensive note in his own voice and felt irritated with himself. He'd need to look into this claim of a witness straight away, before the superintendent took the mention of it too seriously.

'But there is a man dead, is that right?'

'That's right, Superintendent.'

There was silence from the other end of the line and then that peculiar sound which meant that the superintendent was clicking his tongue against the roof of his mouth. 'You know, Patrick,' he said, 'I don't think that we can ignore a report by a respectable member of the public if a death has taken place because of that fire. Apparently, according to Mrs Maloney, the factory girls arrive for work at eight o'clock in the morning and work until six in the evening and she says she saw one of the girls leaving later than the others. I think you need to talk to them, see if they know anything about this fire. The police should be present when these girls arrive at their work-place this morning and they should be questioned. Of course, Mrs Maloney should be seen as well and encouraged to tell her side of the story. And unless that girl has a satisfactory story to tell, you should bring her back to the barracks, I think. Will you manage that, yourself, Patrick? I know you will be tired and want to get some sleep, but I would appreciate it if you can handle it. And, of course, give you the extra time off whenever it suits you.'

'Certainly, Superintendent,' said Patrick rapidly. 'You are quite right. It would be best if I were to deal with it myself. Don't worry about the time off; I've had an easy and peaceful night.' The superintendent had made up his mind; he knew that. He might as well, he told himself, give in with good grace.

'Good lad,' said the superintendent. 'As soon as Joe arrives, get it over and done with. Bring him with you. No harm in arresting the girl, even if we let her out tomorrow. I don't want the newspapers to get hold of this business and have them implying that the police are not doing their duty. You can bet that Mrs Maloney will be giving interviews and it makes a better story for the *Cork Examiner* if they imply that there is a suspect, and that the suspect is still at large. They love saying "still at large" in the newspapers. That would never do, espe-cially today. You remember that the big boss, the Chief Superintendent of all Ireland police force, will be here by mid-morning, all the way down from Dublin. Coming to look us over. I was going to ask you if you could have a quick rest and then come back so that he sees us all working away. Do you a spot of good, too, Patrick, otherwise I wouldn't dream of asking it of you.'

And, with that, the superintendent rang off. Patrick went and washed his face in cold water and combed his hair. Time to rouse the young constable who always, sensibly, took a camping mattress into the reception office whenever he was on night duty. He too, would have to stay on duty, thought Patrick. This was a tricky and difficult matter and Patrick had already decided that he would need the constable as well as Joe to come with him so Colm would have to stay on duty until that business was taken care of. He looked at his watch. Seven o'clock. Not too early to phone the owner of the so-called factory. He leafed through the telephone book, cursing the amount of people with the surname of Murphy who lived in the city and county of Cork.

'Good morning, Mr Murphy, this is Inspector Cashman from Barrack Street,' he said, thankful that the man was one of those people who announced their name after picking up the receiver. 'You've heard the news from the Fire Brigade, I hear,' he went on.

'Just on my way up to Cork, Inspector.' Mr Murphy sounded as though he had something in his mouth. Having his breakfast, doubtless. 'I'll come by car. Quicker than the train,' he said speaking more clearly now.

By the time that Joe arrived, Patrick himself had breakfasted on strong black coffee and a cheese sandwich. He had, without compunction, taken the money from petty cash for Colm's breakfast, leaving a note for the superintendent as well as a memo in the cash box itself. And then he despatched the young constable to the pub in Tuckey Street to buy himself some breakfast and bring back some of their famously strong black coffee for Patrick.

'Brought you a sandwich too, to take the taste of that stuff away from your mouth,' Colm had said. 'Timmy the bar man wanted to know if you had a hell of a hangover and I said that you didn't drink but that you were up all night working hard to keep the city safe and so he threw in the sandwich for nothing. Said that he had made it for a man who passed out before he could eat it.'

Patrick had looked rather dubiously at the sandwich, but it had been a kind thought by young Colm and the bar man, so he had eaten it and felt very much the better for it. The coffee was a shock to the system, but he certainly felt wide awake and ready for action by the time that Joe, punctual as always, arrived through the door just before eight a.m. Once the full staff of the police station had arrived, Patrick was able to switch the phone back to the reception desk and take his time over telling Joe, his next in command, what had happened during the night. First, though, he sent a couple of young policemen over to St Mary's Isle to keep an eye upon the cigarette factory and make sure that no looters could strip the place before its owner arrived.

'I'll tell them to open the door and the windows and get the smoke out of the place, but not to touch anything else,' Joe had said when despatching them. It might, thought Patrick, be possible to interview the girls there to save having to take them back to the barracks.

'A sure-fire place for a fire if you'll pardon my attempt at a pun,' said Joe, when he came back. 'I've seen that place and so have you, I'm sure. Just think of it, Patrick. There are all those dried-up tobacco leaves lying around the floor and then all those boxes of cigarettes piled up on the shelves. I'm not a smoker, myself, not even a pipe, but you know, Patrick, between us two, if I found myself alone there, I might well be inclined to grab a cigarette and try it out – and perhaps, if I were to be very careless, drop the match upon the floor. Perhaps that was what happened.'

'That's if you had matches – I doubt if they leave matches out on the shelves, also,' said Patrick, 'but I agree that if a fire did start then it would spread rapidly. Better hear the official report.' He lifted the receiver of the phone upon his desk and said: 'Just get me the Fire Brigade Barracks, Tommy, will you?' and then replaced his receiver rapidly before Tommy could embark upon one of his interminably long conversations and line by line accounts of the contents of the morning copy of the *Cork Examiner* newspaper.

He had just begun upon an explanation to Joe about the superintendent's instructions about interviewing the factory girls and arresting the girl accused by Mrs Maloney when the phone rang again.

'Inspector Cashman, well, you're an early bird,' said the voice on the other end of the line and Patrick grimaced. He would get little out of this fellow. Just arrived, doubtless. Obviously had not even read the report of the overnight duty officer if he didn't know that Inspector Cashman had been on duty all through the night.

'I'd like to speak to the officer who was in charge during the night, if that is possible,' he said curtly. 'I won't keep him long, but I have a couple of questions if you will be so kind as to fetch him.'

There was a silence at the other end of the phone and then the sound of the receiver slamming down upon a desk. Patrick waited and then a tired voice, suppressing a yawn, said, 'Yes, Inspector Cashman.'

'Just a quick question about Mrs Maloney, the lady who reported the fire – I understand that she lives quite close to the cigarette factory?'

'That's right, Inspector. Just a minute. Yes, I've got the piece of paper now. I'll read you what she said, Inspector, and then I'll send a lad over with a copy if that would suit you.'

'Perfectly, thank you very much.' An efficient man, thought Patrick with relief. His testimony will be reliable. The offer to send over a copy was welcome, nevertheless he held his own indelible pencil poised over a piece of paper and began to rapidly write the words as they came. 'Many thanks! Have a good rest,' he said when the man had finished.

'Well, Joe,' he said once he had replaced the receiver. 'It looks as though our old friend Mrs Maloney has ambitions to be a member of the police. Not only has she decided that this fire, a very small fire, more smoke than flames, apparently, was arson – a deliberate attempt to burn down the building, according to Mrs Maloney, but she says she saw a girl with bright red hair leaving the factory later than all the others yesterday evening. She saw her popping into the girls' privy, newly built, that, and attached on to the timber shed apparently, and then, according to Mrs Maloney, started a fire there. The fire smouldered so the building itself was hardly injured, but the man left inside, presumed to be drunk, inhaled the smoke, was made unconscious by it, I suppose, but was dead by the time that the Fire Brigade had arrived.'

'Presumed to be drunk?' queried Joe. 'By whom and why?'

'Apparently Mrs Maloney told the Fire Brigade, when she phoned, that she had seen the girl run away after she started the fire, but she thought the man must have been still inside and she guessed that he might be drunk, dead drunk – these were her words, apparently – she told them that he was dead drunk every night when he locked up and went off staggering

down the road in St Mary's Isle. Anyway, the superintendent
wants her, the girl, I mean, brought in.'

Joe's eyes widened. 'Arrested?'

Patrick winced. 'Brought in and detained for questioning,
but as he wants us to question Mrs Maloney and any other
witnesses as well, and then go back to her, she might have to
go in the women's prison if she is not cooperative. We should
have something here, some sort of a cell, but, of course, we
don't and so suspects, who might prove to be quite innocent,
must be taken off to prison.'

'Does them good, most of the time,' muttered Joe, 'but this
girl, well, I think these girls working there have just left school
this summer. She must be very young.'

'I was thinking that if she has a mother, she could go with
her . . .' Patrick's voice tailed off. He wasn't sure that he
wanted to question the superintendent's orders, not on a day
like this with the Cork barracks full of all the bigshots from
the police headquarters in Dublin. 'Let's go,' he said curtly.
He had to obey orders, he told himself as he unlocked one of
his drawers and pulled out the smallest pair of handcuffs that
lay there.

'Better take the car,' he said aloud.

At least, if they had to bring the girl back for questioning,
they would not have to walk her through the streets and expose
her to the curiosity of the populace. And if they could lay their
hands upon a mother to the girl then they could pick her up
and allow her to stay with her daughter – that's if she agreed.
Mothers of fourteen-year-olds in these slums usually had six
or seven younger children to care for, or even more. Or else
there was no mother and that might prove to be the likeliest
situation.

He would, also, he thought, have a word with the Reverend
Mother. She, after all, had had these girls in her school for
more than ten years and would, he hoped, know all about
them. He would have to break the news gently to her. No
doubt but that she would be upset and worried.

TWO

B ut it was Sister Bernadette who brought the news to the Reverend Mother.

She came in, as usual, with the Reverend Mother's meagre breakfast on a tray, but for once the *Cork Examiner* did not repose upon the tray, but was carried by Sister Bernadette, rolled tightly, and held in one hand. The tray was carried by the newest recruit to the lay sisters, a fourteen-year-old child, named within the convent as Sister Eithne.

The lay sisters came from families of modest means, usually from the country and usually had had a limited education. They were, in effect, servants who dedicated themselves to the same life as what were known as the choir nuns, but instead of teaching, they worked in convent kitchens, laundries and gardens. Reverend Mother always entrusted the new lay recruits to kind-hearted Sister Bernadette as she mothered them and taught them useful skills in cooking, laundering and cleaning so that the girls were employable if they decided not to take their final vows but to return to the life which they had tried to renounce when still only children. Sister Eithne was a recent recruit, and the Reverend Mother was pleased to see a happy smile upon her face.

'You'll never guess, Reverend Mother, who made your breakfast this morning!' exclaimed Sister Bernadette. 'Yes, it was this little lady, did everything, toasted the bread beautifully and now, Reverend Mother, she would like you to drink some tea and try the toast while we are still here.'

Something was undoubtedly wrong, thought the Reverend Mother. Why was Sister Bernadette still clutching the *Cork Examiner*, instead of handing it over with a quick résumé of the news? And why the insistence on drinking some tea and eating some toast? Certainly, the fourteen-year-old novice looked slightly bewildered to hear that she was supposed to want to watch the Reverend Mother consume her breakfast.

Indeed, the child looked now as though she couldn't wait to retire from the room. As rapidly as she could, the Reverend Mother swallowed a cup of tea and munched her way through a half slice of toast.

'That was delicious,' she declared. 'Perfect tea and perfect toast. Thank you, Sister. Now could you take the tray back to the kitchen while I have a little chat with Sister Bernadette.'

Still with the *Examiner* tightly scrolled and tucked under one arm, Sister Bernadette slightly shook her head to her assistant who having stretched a tentative hand towards the tray, then withdrew it, staring in a puzzled fashion at the piece of toast remaining upon the plate. Sister Bernadette put a firm hand upon her most recent recruit's shoulder, steered her across the room, opened the door for the child and then closed it with a gentle click behind her. The tray, with its unfinished meal, was left behind – undoubtedly there was some bad news which would have to be absorbed by the comfort of tea and toast. The Reverend Mother waited calmly while Sister Bernadette came back and poured out another cup of tea and handed it to her Mother Superior, placed the scrolled newspaper on the mantelpiece and started to deal with the fire.

'There's some bad news in the *Cork Examiner* this morning,' she said, as she heaped a shovelful of coal on top of the smouldering sods of turf. Sister Bernadette believed in tea and warmth when there was a crisis and so the Reverend Mother obediently sipped from the cup and moved to the seat beside the fire.

'There's been a fire out there last night,' began Sister Bernadette. She glanced towards the closed curtains of the window overlooking St Mary's Isle and then back at the Reverend Mother before continuing: 'That cigarette factory went on fire yesterday evening. You can't see anything; the fog is too thick,' she added as the Reverend Mother's glance, also, went towards the window.

'Any casualties?' Sister Bernadette would have read every word of the news item and would then have reread it. The Reverend Mother replaced the cup of tea carefully upon the small table by the fire and then gripped tightly the fingers of her enfolded hand. Ten bright happy faces sitting in a semi-circle, enveloped in snowy white aprons, were in her mind's eye and she breathed a prayer.

'The newspaper says just one casualty, one body has been recovered. That's all it says, Reverend Mother. They won't say any more. They will have to wait until the relatives are informed. That's the way that they do deaths like that on the *Cork Examiner*. The building is all right,' she added. 'They think that the fog might have helped. The mist would have travelled in through the cracks in the door and window. There was a burned hole in one wall, but not a thing was destroyed, not even the dried leaves, the wall just smouldered. That was the word they used in the *Cork Examiner*, "smouldered", not "blazed", nor nothing like that,' she added, looking anxiously into her superior's face, and then pouring some more tea from the pot on top of the stove.

The Reverend Mother sipped it gratefully, conscious that her mouth and throat were dry and that despite the heat from the fire in her grate, she was beginning to shiver.

'What caused the death?' she asked. and, in her mind, she sent up a prayer to the Holy Mother of Jesus: '*O Mary, Mother most divine, have pity on all mothers.*' And then, deep within herself, the words seeming to be listed in a scroll across the fog-besmirched window, she prayed: '*O God of mercy, not one of my girls! Not one of those children burned alive!*'

Sister Bernadette unfurled the morning's copy of the *Cork Examiner* newspaper and passed it across. 'Death is thought to have been caused by smoke inhalation,' she read, and a certain measure of thankfulness came to the Reverend Mother. The death of a child was always a terrible thing, but when it was relatively painless, then it was more bearable. There had been, she remembered, that primitive outside toilet erected at her request for the use of the girls. Smoke inhalation, she thought, might have made a girl, taking a few minutes away from a boring tedious work, drop off to sleep and the smoke would drift into that doorless, roofless shack and the sleeping child would continue to breathe in the poison. Otherwise, why just one casualty?

Smoke inhalation was not too bad a death, she thought. She had known worse even among small children in her charge.

Smoke inhalation could be smoothed over during the breaking of news to an anguished mother.

'I wish that they had never gone to that place,' she said suddenly. It was, she knew, an illogical thought, but Sister Bernadette nodded in agreement.

'I was just thinking the same thing, Reverend Mother. It's so sad, isn't it? It seemed such great news that day, I've been thinking about it this morning. Thinking about the gentleman, Mr Murphy, coming and talking to them, wanting to test them to see who was neat-fingered. Nice man he was, of course. He was your cousin, wasn't he, Reverend Mother? – *is* your cousin, I should say. Came from Youghal, didn't he, by the sea? I remember going there by train when I was a little one. An aunt of mine took me for a treat.'

'That's right, Sister Bernadette, my cousin, Mr Murphy. He is a great man for getting ideas for making money and when he found some tobacco plants growing in a field, tobacco that had been planted a long time ago, hundreds of years ago, by a very famous man, called Sir Walter Raleigh . . .' The Reverend Mother thought about explaining to Sister Bernadette all about Sir Walter Raleigh and the gift of land in Youghal from Queen Elizabeth, but then decided it was of little importance put alongside the tragedy of a death.

Sister Bernadette, however, knew all about it. Remembered everything. Had been dusting the corridor and heard the Reverend Mother teaching the girls about Walter Raleigh and how he had crossed the seas, found new lands, and she had heard the gentleman, the Reverend Mother's cousin, tell the story to the girls about how Sir Walter Raleigh had grown his own tobacco down in Youghal, only thirty miles away from their own city of Cork and how he had been the first man to smoke a cigar. And Sister Bernadette had laughed to herself at the story of the servant throwing a jug of water over Sir Walter's head because she thought that he must be on fire. Remembered all about how the fourteen-year-old girls being tested to see who had neat fingers and then the excitement when every one of those ten girls in the sixth form of the school had been deemed worthy of a place. The kind lay sister wiped her eyes at the memory and the Reverend Mother felt tears prick her own eyes and compressed her lips as she fumbled for the comfort of the string of rosary beads in her pocket and breathed a prayer to Mary, the mother of Jesus.

'They were so happy, Reverend Mother,' said Sister Bernadette sadly. 'There was I hoping that they wouldn't be too upset if they were not picked. I had thought that it would be just Maureen McCarthy, you see. She was always such a smart girl. I could hear her asking questions while I was polishing the bench outside the classroom and then you took them into the parlour, and I got a sheet from the airing cupboard and there they all sat in a circle, and it was then that I was sure that Maureen would get the job when I saw how she filled the little tubes so fast with the crumpled pieces of tobacco leaves.'

'I was sure, too,' said the Reverend Mother. 'I asked to be the first to try, knowing that I wouldn't be too good at that sort of thing and that it might comfort those that failed if they saw what a mess I made of it. I did think that we would have tears afterwards, though.'

Sister Bernadette shook her head sadly. 'And then the excitement when your cousin said he'd give every one of them a job, said that he'd decided they'd work well in a group of friends; that they could chatter together while they were filling the little tubes with the dried tobacco leaves; do you remember, Reverend Mother? God love them; they were so excited. When I think of their little faces . . .'

Kind Sister Bernadette wiped her eyes, and the Reverend Mother felt a lump come to her throat. One of these fourteen-year-old girls was now lying dead in a mortuary, she supposed.

'Started in the girls' toilet; the postman said that.'

Sister Bernadette had a news-gathering service appearing at her back door six days in the week in the form of the local postman, and she was seldom wrong. Ironic, though, thought the Reverend Mother, thinking of how she had telephoned her cousin Robert only a few weeks previously and furiously demanded that some sort of a privy for her girls be erected immediately. And now, perhaps, that had proved to be the death knell for one of them.

She got to her feet and stared bleakly through the window,

remembering her last visit to that wooden building which housed the cigarette factory. She had been uneasy, had not liked the atmosphere. Had felt suspicious of her cousin's manager, and his manner towards one of the girls. She had been, in fact, worried about all ten of these girls who, so recently had been under her care. She sighed heavily. And then she felt a touch upon her arm.

'You did your best for them, Reverend Mother. No one could do more than you do for the children in this school.'

'Thank you, Sister Bernadette,' said the Reverend Mother gratefully. 'Thank you for your care of us all. Now I must go and see if I can talk with Dr Scher. He will know the details. Do tell Sister Eithne that I thoroughly enjoyed my breakfast and that I think she will make a very good cook. How is she getting on?' she added, aware of her responsibilities for these children with often poor backgrounds and little education who came to join the lay sisters in the convent, to serve the choir nuns and to dedicate their life to Christ, at far too young an age, she always thought.

Sister Bernadette beamed happily at the change of subject. 'She's a great little girl. Only just fourteen years old. Eldest of ten children, would you believe it, Reverend Mother? Not had too much mothering, I think, so I give her a few little treats from time to time. You'd be amazed to see how she loves a spoonful of sugar!'

Reminded of her responsibilities to the convent community as well as to the pupils, the Reverend Mother took a sweet from the jar on her desk – kept there to reward good work from her pupils – and handed it to Sister Bernadette with instructions to tell Sister Eithne that the toast was just as she liked it and then set off down the corridor towards the telephone.

THREE

After a sleepless night Patrick was beginning to feel a little drowsy and so he assigned the car-driving role to Joe, put the notebooks and indelible pencils on the back seat, positioned himself in the front passenger seat and opened his own window widely so that the damp early morning air might have a chance to sharpen his wits, but then closed it rapidly as fog poured into the car.

Habit, he thought irritably, though useful, was proving a nuisance this morning. He had trained himself to sleep as soon as he came off duty and fell into his bed in the police quarters at the barracks. He had found by experience that it was only by a strong effort of will after some eventful nights could he banish the morbid tendency to go over his decisions and his words, so he had disciplined himself to blot out the night, as soon as he left his office, and shutting his eyes and occupying his mind by counting the cottages on Barrack Street. He had tried sheep, but sheep were not real to him – he could take no interest in them – and so he had turned to the Barrack Street cottages, forcing himself to visualize each one of them before moving on to the next dwelling.

This morning he forced his mind away from all such thoughts, blotted the line of similar cottages from his mind's eye and focused on making comments about the morning traffic. No point in any discussion about the case until the facts were fully established. Joe, as always, fell in with his mood and did not allude to the fire and the death until they arrived at St Mary of the Isle.

Once there, Joe wound down the window to signal to the cars behind him that he was turning and the usual damp, foggy air poured into the car through the open window. No smell of smoke, noticed Patrick, or, at least, nothing different from the usual stinking early morning air in this flat, riverside area of the city. Not much of a fire, probably. Patrick found his tired mind making notes as if visiting the scene of a crime and then he sat up very straight. There they were, ten girls, walking along, not laughing and pushing each other as girls of that age seemed to do all the time, but heads together, grouped together in twos and threes. And one girl alone, straggling behind the others. Red hair. This must be the girl Mrs Maloney saw leaving the factory the previous evening.

'Slow down,' he said to Joe. 'Park the car over there. We'll walk the rest of the way. We can take the notebooks and the indelible pencils in my briefcase.' The car would be useful for driving the girl back, would save her from too much scrutiny, but they didn't need it just now. The building looked undamaged, he thought as he got out of the car and scrutinized the scene. Not much of a fire, even less than he had been prepared for after reading the report from the Fire Brigade.

'Good morning, girls,' he said as he joined them. They giggled a little at this formality. One or two muttered a 'good morning', but most of them were filled with embarrassment. All except one.

The red-headed girl was stony-faced and tight-lipped. Brave girl to turn up, he told himself. She must know. The voices of newspaper boys on South Main Street reporting the news of the fire, reached even here on St Mary's Isle.

'You've heard the news,' he said.

There was a moment's silence and then one said: 'Yes, sir.' And the others echoed her words. All except the red-headed girl. She looked straight ahead and seemed to ignore the glances of her friends.

'Good,' said Patrick. Joe, he noticed, had walked briskly ahead of them and he could see that the door to the wooden shed was wide open. Young Colm and the other policeman had done a good job, he thought when they arrived. Nothing had been touched, but the window had been opened to its outmost and a piece of wood had been jammed into position to make sure that it did not slam shut. And the door had received the same treatment. There was still a slight smell of smoke from the sacks of dried tobacco leaves and from the burned section of the wooden wall between the workroom and the privy where the fire had been started, but it would be possible to use the room to interview the girls initially and then, if necessary, if anything significant emerged, they could be taken back to the barracks to make a written statement.

'I'll do them one by one with Colm keeping an eye upon the others and making sure that they can't have a chat when they come out but are sent straight home once I have finished with them – what do you think?' asked Joe in an undertone.

'Good idea,' said Patrick. 'Of course, they will all chat together later on, but at least you will get a fresh account from each before you release them. I think I'll deal with the red-headed girl and take her back to the office when you are finished. In the meantime, I'll make sure that she says nothing to the others.'

He watched as Joe took his notebook and indelible pencil from his case and then went across to have a word with the young policeman. Patrick took some steps forward and beckoned to the red-headed girl.

'What's your name then, young miss?' he asked.

'Maureen McCarthy,' she replied. She sounded sullen and angry, but that was not to say that she was guilty of anything. She probably knew that the local busybody was keeping an eye on the factory and had seen her there the previous evening. He felt sorry for her, but orders were orders, and it wasn't for him to criticize his superior officer.

'Perhaps you could show me around then,' he said quietly. 'Let's walk outside the building. Is it all made from wood?'

'You can see that for yourself,' she said with a grimace. Dramatically she raised her eyes to the sky as though incredulous of his stupidity. She had plenty of courage, he thought. It wasn't a good idea for someone in her position to sneer openly at a policeman. He would, he thought, ignore this. He would talk to her now, but not make any notes until they were back in the police station.

'I wonder why Mr Murphy had this building made from wood, instead of from concrete or stone,' he said aloud, and she looked at him swiftly, in quite an appraising manner, almost as though she was speculating about whether he was trying to trap her.

'Dunno,' she said briefly and then added, 'None of my business. Why do *you* think he did it?'

She had placed a heavy emphasis on the word *you* and there was a note of scorn in her voice. Once again, he admired her courage.

'I suppose it might be cheaper,' he said, and he watched her face.

She shrugged. 'None of my business,' she repeated.

'Or warmer. Did you find it warm?'

'Dunno! Didn't care!' She shrugged again.

Patrick had a moment of self-congratulation that he had decided against being a teacher. His Leaving Certificate results, though not good enough for university, were just about good enough for teacher training. However, he had decided against it. He didn't think he would have been any good at it and boys were probably worse than girls. Being a policeman was a better life, he decided.

'Show me the girls' privy,' he said.

'Men are not allowed in it,' she said defiantly.

'I'm a policeman,' he said quietly. 'That makes a difference.' She was, he knew, trying to make him lose his temper. He half-smiled to himself. She must be stupid if she didn't realize that he, when dealing with drunken sailors, faced a lot worse than a cheeky little girl.

She gave a short laugh at that but didn't comment as he followed her into the roofless and doorless space.

'So, you went in here before you left to go home yesterday evening,' he said.

She stared at him defiantly. 'Mind your own business,' she said, and he was taken aback. Fourteen years old and she was fighting back. This was unexpected. He was never going to get a proper account of the evening if he allowed her to answer him like that.

'Anyway,' she said, 'I'm not going to talk to you. I don't like rozzers.'

Patrick wished that he had kept Joe with him, but his assistant was already beginning on his interviews with one of the policemen marshalling the girls into a line. He beckoned to Colm.

'Walk that girl to my car, Constable,' he said in such a peremptory fashion that Colm, already tired after his night on duty, looked at him with alarm. Nevertheless, the youngster took a firm grip upon the girl's thin arm and frog-marched her over to the car. He had an efficient way with him, thought Patrick and resolved to keep an eye on young Colm. After the superintendent retired, and if he managed to inherit the role of superintendent, there might be other promotions for him to consider, as well as Joe's, of course.

'Come with us, Constable,' he said aloud. It was, he guessed, useless to ask the girl for an address in her present mood, but he was pretty sure that he had seen her on Barrack Street so, without saying a word, he efficiently swept the car around and headed back towards South Gate Bridge and then swung across to the steep hill of Barrack Street, noticing, as he passed the police barracks, that the superintendent's car was already parked by its front door.

'Ask her address,' he said curtly over his shoulder. 'If she doesn't know it, then one of those women there will tell us.' He would, he decided, put up with no more nonsense from this stubborn girl. Her testimony was of the utmost import-ance, and she should not be allowed to waste valuable police time and make a fool of him. For the sake of his dignity, he was pleased that he had thought of taking Colm with him. Let him do the battling with this obstinate girl – it would be good practice for him.

'There's a good parking place there, Inspector, plenty of people around that can give us information about where she lives,' said Colm, picking up adroitly on the necessity of impressing upon the girl that they could easily find her address if she chose to withhold it. Patrick slowed the car and put it into a low gear as though in readiness to stop and heard Colm ask the question in a teasing fashion. 'It's number three thou-sand, that's right, isn't it?'

She didn't laugh at that. Tense and frightened, perhaps, he thought.

'Number seventy-one,' she said in a low, sulky voice and then added viciously, 'and if you're looking for my mother, you'll be a long time looking. She's gone off with her sailor man and not a sinner knows where they went. So, put that in your pipe and smoke it, Mr Bighead.'

Patrick grimaced. It was a story that was all too common. Still, it might just be invented so, without comment, he accelerated to tackle the steep hill and roared the engine of the Ford so that it could reach the height. He knew every single one of the cabins on this street. Had spent the whole of his boyhood climbing its elevation while weighed down with a bagful of books.

'Won't do you no good,' came the girl's voice. 'She's not there, I tell you. Blind drunk and in bed with a sailor lad, somewhere or other. I don't care. And don't think you'll get anything out of me. Don't care what you do to me. I'm tough, I'll have you know.'

The door to the cottage numbered 71 stood open and there was a crowd of women around it. His arrival in the police car caused a sensation and they quickly dispersed.

'Mrs McCarthy,' he said curtly to the woman who was left. A cluster of very dirty children hung around her skirts, and she had a toddler in her arms. Every one of the children had a tangled mass of dirty and uncombed red hair. Patrick felt a moment of pity, and respect, for the girl in the back of the car. She, out of them all, had a clean face and her bright red curls bore the traces of a comb and were tied with a ribbon.

'Nah, she's not here,' said the woman in an irritated fashion. 'Gone off. Asked me to come to see her and soon as I arrived, she skedaddled with her fancy man. Me in the front door and off she went through the back door. Left me holding the baby.' She gave a mirthless laugh, nevertheless she followed it up with a kiss on the baby's dirty face and Patrick felt a certain liking for her and a reluctance to add the burden which was none of her making. However, she was the only adult in the house and was the girl's aunt.

'I wanted to have a word with Maureen's mother, but . . .' he said.

'What's the trouble? What's she done now?' she asked, and her eyes went again to the girl in the back of the car. 'That fire!' she exclaimed, and he knew that the group of women who had been clustered around her would have told her all the news from the *Cork Examiner*.

'She's being questioned about the fire up at the cigarette factory last night,' he said in a low voice.

The information was not new to her. She shrugged her shoulders.

'Wouldn't put anything past that "*wan*",' she said, and he realized that although the baby had evoked her compassion, this Maureen, a brazen-faced fourteen-year-old, was probably nothing but a nuisance to a woman who had troubles of her own. The other children had disappeared into the cottage at the sight of a policeman at the door, but he guessed that there could have been as many as eight or nine of them. They were thin and pale and had a hungry look about them.

Patrick felt in his pocket. There was half a crown there, but then he removed his hand. She might spend it on food for the children, but she might not. Alcohol was a curse in these poverty-stricken districts. It made life temporarily bearable for those whose lives were so hard. But if he wanted to do something for the children it would be better to give her a few loaves of bread.

'Any chance that her mother or you could be with her while I question her? If she refuses to answer my questions, I may have to hold her in a cell,' he explained.

She gave a mirthless laugh. 'Don't expect to see her mother until that sailor man runs out of money. And as for me, well you can see I have my hands full.'

He nodded. Nothing more was to be said. He could not ask it of her. Someone had to stay with these young children. No point in dumping them all into an orphanage. Those places were overflowing, and the children were better off in Barrack Street, where neighbours had a custom of helping those worse off than themselves. He returned to the car. The girl, Maureen, was still sitting there, looking out of the window. It was hard to see from her defiant face whether she was worried or frightened. He climbed back into the car and passed the half-crown over to Colm.

'Buy some bread and bring it back. We'll stay here,' he said. He waited until Colm had gone up the hill towards the small shop attached to the public house there and then he turned in his seat and looked at the girl.

'What's the name of the baby?' he asked in a conversational tone and noted that her eyes widened.

For a moment he wondered whether she would tell him to mind his own business, but then she shrugged her shoulders.

'Patrick,' she said, and added: 'He's called after the last baby that died.'

Patrick's heart stirred with pity, but he kept his voice casual. 'That was sad,' he said. 'What did the little fellow die of?'

His question took her aback. He could see that. After a minute she said: 'I dunno!' and shrugged her shoulders. It might be, he thought, that she imagined that babies died without a reason. He had vague memories of his youth where announcements were made about deaths of babies. He had been left with an impression that it was a frequent and an ordinary event.

When Colm came back with the bag stuffed with loaves of bread and with a bag of sweets peeping out from on top of them, he sent him in with it. If he could have trusted her, he would have liked to give Maureen the pleasure of presenting the bread and sweets to her little brothers and sisters, but he did not trust her. And he could not forget that a man had died last night, and this girl was the last person to have seen him alive.

'Lots of excitement in the house,' said Colm when he came back. He said it, not to his superior, the inspector in the front seat, but in an undertone to the girl in the back seat beside him. She shifted position; Patrick could see that with a glance into his mirror, but she said nothing in reply to the lad, not too many years older than herself. Going to be difficult, he thought, but no point in planning until he could see how things were going.

'Must teach you to drive some day when we are not too busy, Colm,' he said aloud. 'I got driving lessons from a fellow in a garage, but there is nothing like practice. No rushing, just a bit of practice every day. But I'll take you out to a quiet part of the straight road one day and show you how to manage the gears and after that it's just practice.'

'That will be great,' said Colm. 'Just wait till I tell my Mam. She will bake a cake to celebrate.'

Patrick flicked a glance at the rear mirror. The girl was

sitting very upright, staring out of the window beside her, ostentatiously displaying her lack of interest. He pulled the car into the forecourt of the Garda Barracks and got out quickly.

Not quite quickly enough. Maureen had been sitting as far as she could from Colm, and she must have been ready for his movement. As soon as he had closed the driver's door, he saw her and swore under his breath. She had taken Colm by surprise and slammed the back passenger door in his face. A fast runner but she had the ill luck to meet a woman with a crowd of ragged young children on the pavement, at the same time as a donkey and cart came down the steep slope of Barrack Street.

In a moment Patrick had caught up with her and grabbed her arm. He would put the handcuffs on her as soon as the woman passed, he told himself. She had almost made a fool of him, and he was determined not to lose her again. Holding her arm firmly, he fastened the handcuff to one thin wrist and then pulled both hands behind her back and clipped on the second handcuff, automatically testing both before handing her over to Colm.

'Take her into the barracks, into my room, Constable,' he said to the scarlet-cheeked Colm. He would have to reprimand the lad, he supposed, but he was more annoyed with himself. She had fooled him, too. Acting so quiet and almost as though she had no interest in the proceedings.

He let them go ahead of him, determined this time to keep a careful watch upon her. Colm was doing everything by the book, now, and he resolved to make no official note of the near escape and just give a few friendly words of advice to the lad. It was only then that he realized that Tommy, the door policeman, was holding out a note to him.

'Dr Scher on the phone for you,' he read. As soon as he had closed the door to the reception area he pocketed the note that Tommy had passed to him with one hand, while holding the phone with the other hand. Tommy, though an old nuisance, had been well trained in his youth by Royal Irish Constabulary. He had spotted the handcuffs and knew that this was a serious matter. No mention of police business in front of a suspect was how he had been trained and he kept to that.

'I'll take it here, Constable. You two take the prisoner down
to my room.' A quick inclination of the head and Tommy took
the girl's other arm and together they marched her down the
corridor. No harm in being careful, thought Patrick.

'Yes, Dr Scher, Patrick here,' he said into the phone once
the outer office was empty.

'Got Mr Robert Murphy here, he's the owner of the
building where the fire was kindled, Inspector,' said Dr Scher.
'He's here with me at the morgue this moment. He would
like permission to remove the body of the dead man back to
Youghal. I have no objection if you don't, once I've finished
the autopsy, with the help of some of my students, and
everything has been written down. I imagine that'll be some-
time this afternoon.'

Patrick had a quick moment's thought. He would have liked
to have seen the body and he certainly would like to have a
word with the owner of the business. It wasn't far to the
hospital, and he could take the car. A short time cooling her
heels would do the girl no harm. Give a bit of experience to
Colm, and Tommy would be delighted to lend a hand if he
had any trouble.

'Be with you in three minutes,' he said. 'Won't keep Mr
Robert Murphy long, tell him, Dr Scher, will you, and then
we can release the body to him. He can make his own arrangements with the undertakers.'

He replaced the receiver and went down to his own room,
saying curtly to Tommy: 'I've switched the phone through to
this room, Constable, so that you can answer if anyone phones.'
Tommy was an old pro and would understand that he was to
stay and assist the young policeman who might be deadly tired
after a night on duty. And then to the girl he said: 'I'll be back
soon. I'm leaving you with these two policemen and when I
come back, I will ask for a report on your behaviour and if it
is good, I may not place you in a cell for the offence of trying
to escape when in police custody.'

She made no answer, but he hoped that the threat would
alarm her. And so, he left her to Colm and went off to have
a quick word with the owner of the factory and with Dr Scher.

FOUR

'This is Mr Robert Murphy,' said Dr Scher as soon as he came into the hallway of the hospital. They were sitting upon chairs there and Patrick guessed that the man, the owner of the business, had not liked the atmosphere of the morgue.

Nevertheless, Mr Murphy wasn't a relative of the dead man and Patrick was conscious of the need to work fast this morning. He had to get back to the barracks as soon as possible, solve the problem of interviewing that stubborn girl and be ready to help the superintendent to greet the visitors from Dublin – all of which he had to get through before being able to put his head down upon a pillow and catch a few hours of sleep.

'Good morning, Mr Murphy,' he said. 'This must have been quite a shock to you when the Fire Brigade telephoned you.' Always a good idea to start with some sympathy, he had found from experience.

'Yes,' said the man. And then, almost instantly, 'Well, no, not really. Wasn't a shock. I had already been phoned by a Mrs Maloney, who lives nearby. She's on to me from time to time.'

Patrick bit back a smile. Trust Mrs Maloney. Where did the woman get all these phone numbers? His own superior was furious about that. Did she, perhaps, have a friend at the telephone exchange, he wondered. He would, he thought, have a word with the Reverend Mother about it. She might be able to throw some light on the subject.

'Let's go down and get the formal identification over and done with – just for police records, Mr Murphy,' he said and without waiting for an answer he led the way to the morgue. Just one body there, he noted, as he held the door open for Dr Scher and Mr Robert Murphy. It had been a quiet night after the alarm about the fire and the discovery of the dead body.

The man winced when he followed Dr Scher through the door. Nothing strange about that. Patrick ignored the instinctive recoil.

'You've already identified the body as your manager, Mr Timothy Dooley, I understand, sir,' he said to him, notebook at the ready.

The man nodded, looked a little sick. Not a young man, but young to be a cousin of the Reverend Mother, who was, he had always thought, as old as the hills. Perhaps this Mr Murphy was a second cousin or something. Patrick produced a form and took pen and ink bottle from their place in his briefcase and then wrote with practised ease the words needed for an official identification, noting that the man was aged forty, more than he would have guessed – easy life, probably.

'How long have you known the deceased, sir?' he asked with pen poised.

'Many a long year,' said Mr Murphy. 'I'd have to think. About ten years – it might be more. He worked for me when my wife was alive.'

Patrick held the pen poised above the paper. 'In what capacity – doing what?' he amended, seeing the man looked a little bewildered.

'Bit of this, bit of that, he was a very useful fellow, could put his hand to everything. I was running a small farm at the time when I first employed him and he could see to the animals, mend the tractor – very good mechanic – fixed up a link between an old plough and the tractor. Ploughed the fields in half the time that the horses used to do the job. Very useful fellow, Tim Dooley,' he repeated.

And then when Patrick said nothing, he said, for the third time, 'Very useful fellow!' adding, 'He took like a duck to water to this new business that I've set up here, turning the tobacco plants on my farm into cigarettes.'

'Got on well with your other workers, did he?' Patrick told himself that he was wasting time. There was no likely reason why there should be anything suspicious about this death, but he felt in his bones that there was something odd about this. St Mary's Isle was a quiet spot – not an island, but a patch of land which had the river on two sides of it.

The convent was built upon a patch of rocky ground which kept it reasonably dry, but the rest of the land was sodden from one end of the year to the other. Not a place where you would expect to find an accidental fire. No pubs there, not a place where drinking alcohol would take place and the place was so very marshy, so wet and very open on all sides, that it would not prove a popular place for vagabonds or malicious troublemakers.

'Well, enough, well enough,' said Mr Murphy. He had taken a few long seconds to reply to the question about relationships between the dead man and his other workers so Patrick, almost automatically, found his wits sharpening and his sleepiness disappearing.

'A few problems?' he queried.

'Bit of trouble about a girl.' The answer was muttered in a manner that fired his curiosity.

'Yes,' he said. Automatically he fished a notebook and indelible pencil from his pocket. 'Would you like to tell me about it?' he invited.

The man shrugged. 'On second thoughts, there was nothing to it. Nothing of interest to you.'

Patrick slipped the notebook and pencil back into his pocket. No point in pushing a reluctant witness until he got a few more details. Not the time and the place perhaps, he thought, looking across at the dead body. He turned towards Dr Scher.

'Death by smoke inhalation, is that correct, Doctor?' he asked. Keeping everything very formal, going through mechanical steps, often helped relatives and friends he had found from experience. He needed to go back a few steps now and to find proof for his instinctive impression that there was something slightly odd about this death in the swampy precincts of St Mary's Isle.

'Death by smoke inhalation. That is correct,' said Dr Scher. He was suppressing a yawn. Up all night, just like myself, thought Patrick.

'But no fire should have been lit in or outside the building, is that correct, Mr Murphy?'

'Certainly not. Certainly, there should have been no fire.' The man was stumbling over his words. Still upset by that morgue! Took a big gulp before continuing. 'There was no fireplace in the building, and no fire should ever have been lit on the premises. The building was made from wood and, of course, was full of sacks of dead leaves. I had men working there, making a double wall, stuffed with sheep's wool, and none of them were allowed to smoke. Everyone who worked for me was warned of the danger and told that a fire could blaze up very quickly with all those sacks of dried tobacco leaves.'

'So how would you account for the fire, then? Did someone deliberately set the place on fire? Have you seen the premises?'

The man nodded. Still looked a little sick. 'Someone might have disobeyed orders, smoked a cigarette in the girls' toilet, might have been a tramp, looking for shelter. Perhaps for a sleeping place . . .' His voice ebbed and he averted his gaze from Patrick's face and then catching sight of the corpse again, he shuddered and thrust his hands deeply into his pockets.

'Not a possible sleeping place,' said Patrick abruptly. 'I've seen that girls' privy. It's attached to the main building with two walls screening the place from the road and an old leather curtain instead of a door. A very deep hole inside with a wooden seat upon it and a pile of wet sawdust, that's no place for a homeless person. There is not enough room to lie down, just room for one person to stand and then sit upon that makeshift lavatory, and no roof so that the whole place is soaking wet. People sleeping rough in this city choose shop doors or beneath flights of steps, or in bus or railway stations, somewhere dry, even if they can't be warm. No, I don't think it would be a homeless person in this instance,' Patrick concluded.

The witness had, of course, said that it was the girl who lit the fire, but Patrick had no intention of saying this in front of the owner. Let the facts be properly established first.

He left a silence for a moment to allow that to sink in and then said briskly. 'Now, sir, could you think of anyone that might have wanted to harm your manager, who, apparently, was well known for staying late on the premises? There was a bottle of whiskey and two mugs upon the table and our witness gave testimony that she had observed him throwing empty bottles of whiskey out on the waste land around the St Mary's Isle on many nights so his habit of staying late and of drinking to excess may have been well known. A drunken man is slow to react so might not notice smoke seeping into the room where he dozed over his bottle of whiskey. Could you think of anyone that might have wanted to harm your manager?' he repeated. 'Did he get on well with other men who worked for you, men who were working on constructing the double wall and filling it with sheep's wool?'

'There was some trouble between himself and my gardener, the man who was superintending the work.' The sentence came out rather slowly and rather reluctantly, but that was normal. Most people, in Patrick's experience, did not want to report any bad feeling amongst workmen, friends, or relations when it came to a possible murder. This man would probably prefer if the affair was going to turn out to be an accidental death, caused by a match dropped in that outdoor privy, but, nevertheless, it was important to dot all the *i*s and cross all the *t*s. Having seen the place, having seen how wet everything was, he had already dismissed the possibility of a fire being caused by an accidental dropping of a match. And if the fire was not accidental, it was indeed possible that it had been malicious, had been meant to cause the death of a drunken man. The more information that he could get from the owner of the premises, the easier it would be to solve the problem of this dead body in front of him.

'Tell me about it?' he said, notebook in hand.

'Well, there was trouble over the gardener's daughter . . . these things do happen from time to time . . .' The man sounded reluctant, and Patrick suppressed a yawn and wished that the man would come to the point.

'Got her pregnant, did he?' said Dr Scher.

'That was it.' Robert Murphy turned with relief to the doctor. 'You know how it would be. The one was crying "rape" and the other was saying that it had been her choice as well as his. Made for a bit of bad feeling among my workers. Some took one side, and the rest took the other side. I thought of getting rid of him for a while, but he's good man, very valuable to me, so then I decided that it would be best to give him the job up in Cork and get him away from the trouble in Youghal.'

Patrick made a note and then nodded. It looked as though he might have to take a journey to Youghal before he shut the case, but for now he felt that the most likely verdict of the court would be death by misadventure.

'Just a minute,' he said curtly. 'Dr Scher, could we have a quick word? Perhaps, Mr Murphy, you would wait outside the door?'

'Well, what do you think, Doctor?' he asked once the owner of the building had thankfully gone through the door.

'It would be quite a clever way of disposing of someone, wouldn't it?' said Dr Scher thoughtfully. 'No violence in it. No risk to any bystander. It would have been known to everyone because Mrs Maloney would have told the world and his wife about the man staying late drinking – I'm sure that you know Mrs Maloney – she even rings me up – last time was about a woman selling some pills I gave her! Anyway, Patrick, from how you describe it, any fire in a wet place like that would have just been a lot of smoke and that fits with my diagnosis. The man definitely died of smoke inhalation. He had no hope of surviving even if the Fire Brigade had got there five minutes earlier. The lungs were coated in black soot.'

'Well, I don't really think that the fire could have been accidental, not in that soaking wet place. It might have been vandalism, but, again, why light a fire in such a soaking wet place?' said Patrick. 'There are a few flat slabs placed along the front of the building and a few leading towards the road. It looks like a footpath in the making, built so that someone could walk with dry feet from the door of the shed to the road where a car or a van could be parked. Why not light a fire upon that if vandalism or destroying the place was the object? But if you want to kill someone, perhaps killing by smoke inhalation is a clever method – new to me, anyway,' he finished and then felt annoyed with himself. He was breaking his own rule of evidence first and then speculation. He would go back to his own office and to his painstaking notes and approach the matter in a sensibly methodical way.

He would check on the name and address of the owner and then allow him to go back down to the seaside town of Youghal. At the moment, the police investigation had to concentrate upon that damp land of St Mary's Isle. But when he came back to the barracks, everything had changed. Outside the door was the rusty old police van with blackened-out windows which they used for riots. It was bigger than an ordinary van, completely empty of seats except for two in the front for driver and companion and equipped with two solid bars which held chained handcuffs down each side of the van with, in front of both bars, a wooden bench bolted to floor and van sides. In the case of a riot at least ten of the ringleaders could be piled in and secured to the sides with these handcuffs. Today there was only one occupant. A fourteen-year-old girl and she was handcuffed and shackled. Defiantly she had not sat down, but was crouched, with her back to the bar, and glaring out of the back door. The superintendent slammed it shut.

'Carry on, Sergeant,' he said in an angry voice to Joe and Joe obediently swung out of the yard and made his way towards South Main Street. He would be on his way to the women's gaol, guessed Patrick.

It was, he thought, best to say nothing – to ask no questions or to make no comments. He leaned into the back of the Ford car and spent a few minutes opening his briefcase and sorting its contents. From behind his back, he heard the superintendent give an angry snort, but Patrick did not move. The two young constables were there, Tommy, the duty officer, went back to his glass-fronted entrance booth and after a moment's hesitation the constables followed him. Patrick waited for a moment and then went to his own room and looked at the clock. Half past nine. The visitors from Dublin were due at ten o'clock he remembered. His hand hovered over the telephone. He could summon Colm and ask what had happened, but he decided that was beneath his dignity, so he occupied himself with making notes of his interview with the owner of the cigarette factory. Joe would be back soon. The women's gaol was not far from Barrack Street. Five minutes by car, he reckoned and five minutes to deliver the prisoner. With an iron

self-discipline he kept writing and did not lift his head when
he heard the superintendent giving some orders to Tommy
about the refreshments for the guests when they arrived.
Tommy would be responsible for uncorking the bottles of
whiskey and it appeared that O'Brien's of Princes Street would
be delivering fresh cakes and sandwiches. The superintendent
had probably spent a sleepless night worrying about the
arrangements.

The minute hand of the clock on the wall had just jerked
on to the figure eight when Patrick heard the noisy engine as
the police van was driven past his window and into the shed
at the back of the barracks. He occupied himself even more
concentratedly as he heard Joe's voice talking to Tommy.
Something about the traffic. And then Joe's footsteps passing
his door. A sharp double rap upon the superintendent's door.
A few minutes' tension. Then the door was clicked closed
again. Cheerful voices from the outer office. That would be
one of the O'Brien family delivering the cakes and sandwiches. Patrick blessed them. The superintendent had heard
them also. His heavy leather boots came rapidly down the
corridor, passing Patrick's door. A minute later Patrick's door
slid open, and Joe came in.

'She spat in his face, right in his eye,' he said as soon as
he had carefully shut the door behind him. 'He told her what
Mrs Maloney said about her being seen last evening at the
factory, after everyone else had left. He had to do something,
Patrick, and, of course, he's been in a bit of state waiting for
the lads from Dublin.' Joe, Patrick noticed, was looking at
him with concern. He passed his hand over his jaw. He had
shaved badly in the barracks' sink. He could still feel the
stubble upon his chin and a terrible wave of tiredness came
over him. He wished that he could just climb the stairs to his
room at the back of the barracks and sleep for a couple of
hours.

But he couldn't do that and so he shook his head vigorously
and then went to the window, opened it, and sucked in some
damp morning air.

'I see,' he said, as he brought his head in again. 'What was
the charge?' he queried, when he had found a new page.

Joe grimaced. 'Assault and battery of a police officer,' he said, and Patrick wrote the words without comment.

'Tough little girl,' continued Joe, after he had waited for a minute to see whether there were any questions. 'Didn't cry or anything.' He said nothing further, just walked out of the room, and Patrick was left feeling uncomfortable and conscience-stricken. Joe, he guessed, felt that he should tackle the superintendent, but Patrick decided that this morning, when the Superintendent of all Ireland was arriving from Dublin, was not a good time to tackle his own superior. Let her cool her heels in the gaol for a couple of hours. He had plenty to do.

First on the list was to visit the Fire Brigade and hopefully have a chat with someone who knew what he was talking about.

Upon arriving at the fire station, a familiar voice greeted him warmly, 'How are you, Patrick?'

One problem solved, thought Patrick. He and the head of the Fire Brigade on Sullivan's Quay had been friendly over a case a few years ago, and had been on first name terms then, but he had been unsure as to whether he would be remembered, and his practice would be to use surnames if in doubt.

'Well, thank you. And you, Chris,' he said thankfully as they shook hands and Chris ushered Patrick through the public area and into his office. Brushing aside the Cork practice of small talk before business, Patrick went straight to the point after being offered a seat.

'I wanted to have a word with you about the victim in that smoke inhalation case on St Mary's Isle,' he said. 'Do you have any notes about the victim, or did you see him yourself?'

'I was there when Dr Scher arrived, handed over the body to him. Didn't go to the autopsy, though, as we had another alarm – a ship with a fire in the hold. Not surprised to get a visit from you, Patrick. Had a feeling that there was something strange about the business. Why would anyone light a fire in an outside privy? Doesn't make sense, unless someone wanted to burn down the whole wooden building and then it was a clever idea. An excellent chance of getting a good fire going before it was discovered but, of course, that load of wet sawdust that had been dumped in there a few days earlier changes things. When I had a good look around, I thought that it looked as if smoke, not flames, might have been the object – you would want to be quite stupid to think that you could make a blazing fire with all that wet stuff around. Nothing better for making a fire smoulder than dumping wet sawdust on top of it. I was thinking that I might have a word with you about that, but I thought that I'd give you a chance to see what you were making of the whole thing before I stuck my oar in.'

'Wet sawdust?' queried Patrick, making a note. He had already noted that the sawdust had been delivered a few days earlier, at the request of the owner.

'No roof on that privy, no door either, just two walls, a heap of sawdust and a hole in the ground, somewhere for the girls to be private, so I understand, but in this weather the sawdust was probably damp or even wet when it arrived and you know yourself, Patrick, it would have got wetter and wetter with that mist and fog during the last few days. No need to keep it dry. Was just there so that it could cover over . . . well, you know – keep the smell down, I suppose.'

Patrick nodded hastily, hoping that his embarrassment did not show. 'Could you make a guess at how long the fire would have had to be burning to generate that much smoke?' he said.

'Well, we were called soon after eight. Lady who lives nearby, a Mrs Maloney, went down to the post office, I understand, and telephoned us – phoned the owner, too, I understand. Very public-spirited – or so the judge will say,' he ended with a grin. 'We know Mrs Maloney well here. She's on to us from time to time, especially around Halloween, of course.'

Patrick allowed this to pass without comment and waited for the answer to his question. Chris, he thought, might have been born and reared in Liverpool, but he had picked up the Cork habit of inviting a gossip on virtually every subject.

'Anyway, the man was dead when we arrived,' went on Chris. 'Can take as little as ten minutes for smoke to kill, as you probably know, and that place had no window open, and the door was shut quite tightly. He was quite a big man, burly

type, good lungs perhaps, so you might want to put another
five minutes or so on to that, but no more, in my experience.
Let's say fifteen minutes to kill him.'

'So, the fire was lit in the privy,' said Patrick, thinking that
he must remember that word 'privy' when giving evidence in
court. It had a dignified respectable sound to it. 'It burned
through the wooden wall,' he said, adding, 'there's quite a
hole in the wall, but it didn't really spread, just began to
smoulder, is that right.'

Chris, he noted, was frowning and he did not press for an
answer. It was important to give the man time to think. Chris
was an expert in this field; he had learned a lot about Chris at
the time of that explosion in the convent cemetery. There was
his training as a bomb expert, but, more importantly, there
was those years of experience, of turning up at fires in various
buildings, households, and businesses. The IRA, he knew,
were experts at burning down the premises of those hostile
to them. Chris would have had plenty of experience of deliberate as well as of accidental fires.

'It's odd, you know, Patrick,' said Chris, after a minute.
'Now not for a moment do I think that this was an accidental
fire – not for one minute. Even if you dropped a cigarette or
a cigar or a pipe in that outdoor privy, the chances would be
that any little fire would fizzle out almost immediately. The
place is soaking wet. No roof and the weather that we've been
having. So, the thing that is puzzling me, Patrick, is how that
hole was burned in the wall of the factory, as they called it,
burned just in the one place, just a couple of feet above ground
level, ideal to allow the smoke to seep through even if the
wall didn't burn down.'

Patrick felt a slight rush of pleasure as he silently congratulated himself. He had done the right thing in coming to see
this man who was an expert in fires. He said nothing, though.
Let him think it through without any harassment.

'But hole there was,' continued Chris. Suddenly and quite
unexpectantly, he jumped to his feet. 'Let's go and have a
look at the place, Patrick. We'll walk. Not so noticeable.' He
took down a plain gaberdine raincoat from the wall and
picked out a cap from its pocket. 'Give me a moment to tell

my number two,' he said and then he was gone, returning a few minutes later with a similar gaberdine raincoat for Patrick.

'No point in getting a townful of idlers following us – nothing like parading the streets in uniform to attract them. Leave your police cap here; you can pick it up on your way back. We'll walk past the convent, that won't take too long.'

FIVE

The convent seemed very quiet without the noise of the schoolchildren, chanting lessons, or playing in the yard, thought Patrick when they arrived at St Mary's Isle on the first day of the summer holidays.

'You know the Reverend Mother from that school, don't you?' said Chris. 'I remember her from that time of the explosion in the convent orchard cemetery. Very sharp lady, so I understand. Did she notice anything strange; do you think?'

'I haven't spoken to her, but I'd say that the nuns were at church during the time when the Fire Brigade arrived,' said Patrick. 'They would have been singing. The organ would have drowned out the sounds. Very wet night, too.'

'Don't suppose that the siren was going, either. The woman, Mrs Maloney, the person who phoned up, said that the place was empty. Was very sure of that. I saw the note, checked it afterwards. Said that everyone had gone home by then. She had counted out nine girls and she saw the tenth one come out, a couple of hours later. And, of course, the manager, as we know now, didn't leave the premises – would have been dead drunk, judging by that bottle of whiskey. Mrs Maloney explained afterwards that she couldn't be sure about when he left as sometimes he went out around the back, by Sullivan's Quay side. She was sure of the girls, though. Quite certain, she said, as they crossed St Mary's Isle in front of her window. They all came from Barrack Street, apparently. Most informative lady, this Mrs Maloney, but like all gossips, likes to embroider her message. I suppose you've heard from her from time to time,' said Chris with a grin.

Patrick made no comment. Mrs Maloney had, indeed, been informative to the police, also; but he thought that he would keep her various surmises to himself.

'So, you didn't go yourself,' he remarked.

'Don't usually go unless it's something serious. Didn't sound

like much – probably some tramp lit a fire and then went off
– that's what my second-in-command guessed. Went off to
make sure that it was out.'

'And discovered the body,' commented Patrick.

Chris said nothing for a moment.

'It's a bit of a lesson to us,' he commented after a moment.
'Of course, the door was closed and there was no window
open in the place . . .'

'You did everything that you could,' said Patrick. 'You
couldn't have saved him, could you, even if you had been
told the man was still inside, you wouldn't have been able
to get there any quicker and I doubt they lost more than a
minute or two before they discovered the dead man. He may
well have been dead by the time that Mrs Maloney got to
the phone box at the post office and summoned the Fire
Brigade.'

He understood this mood of self-recrimination that had
overtaken Chris, but he knew from experience that it was no
use to brood upon the past, and so he quickened his pace to
a speed that made talking uncomfortable for the next few
minutes. This was a city of needless deaths, and while it was
essential to remind oneself that every one of those deaths
was of importance, it was also necessary to keep a sense of
proportion. The Fire Brigade had come out on a specific
mission and had found a dead man. Now it would be important
for them all to keep their minds on finding the truth about
this fire. Important for the police, too, but especially for
himself as the thought of that fourteen-year-old girl shut up
in prison once again came to him.

What if she were innocent? Could he forgive himself if an
innocent fourteen-year-old was sentenced to life in prison?

'Here's the place,' he said after a few minutes of fast walking.
'Not damaged in any way,' he said. 'I have a key to the door
of the workroom, so we'll go in there first.'

'Taken everything away, haven't they?' said Chris when
they came into the empty room. 'Bare sort of place, isn't it?
Chair, desk and a few shelves on the wall. My men reported
sacks of dried leaves and boxes of cigarettes on the shelves,
but they have taken them away, also.'

'I believe that the girls sat in a semicircle on the floor and the manager sat on the chair and supervised them. The shelves held the made-up cigarettes and there was a barrel there in the corner full of dried tobacco leaves. The owner asked my permission to take them away as he wanted to get the smell of smoke from them and was going to lay them out in the sea air down in Youghal where he lives. My officers, including my second-in-command, Joe – you'll remember Joe from that time at the Orchard Cemetery? Well, he had already checked over the place and had made notes, so I was happy for the owner to salvage what he could.' Patrick spoke absent-mindedly as his eyes and attention were on the patch of burned wood that formed a gap in the wall at the back of the wooden shed.

'Odd shape – that burned section,' said Chris with a note of interest in his voice.

Patrick said nothing. He would never interrupt a man who was thinking hard, and he could see from Chris's face that something strange had struck him. He stood well back and allowed the fire chief to examine the hole.

'Let's look at it from the other side, from the privy,' said Chris after a minute and still without speaking Patrick followed him outside and around to the privy.

The privy smelled, but not too badly. Someone had dug quite a deep hole, built a small bank of earth around it and then covered the bank with a sheet of wood which had a hole cut out in the middle of it. The heap of soaking-wet sawdust was beside it, probably put there to keep the smell down.

'Something funny about that hole in the wooden wall,' said Chris abruptly. 'Look at it, Patrick. What do you notice about it?'

Patrick grimaced slightly. He had noticed nothing and even when his attention was called to it, he still saw nothing particularly strange.

'Not a very big hole,' he ventured and then had a brainwave. 'I've been thinking about the fire. What about if one of the girls sneaked out a cigarette from the pack, smoked it out here in the privy and then stubbed it out on the wooden wall

between the privy and the shed? Perhaps the whole thing was
an accident.'

The idea was not a success. He could see that immediately.
Probably, now that he came to think about it, the place was
too wet for an accidental burning to occur. Chris was thinking
of something else, running his finger around the hole in the
wall and upon the blacked timber around it. And then he did
something strange. Held his finger to his nose and sniffed.

'Funny thing, you know, Patrick,' he said, 'but you would
think that with all the smoke that I have inhaled during all
those years that I wouldn't have a good sense of smell, but I
do, and do you know what I smell?'

'As well as privy smells, smoke and burned wood,' said
Patrick cautiously.

'*To be sure; to be sure*, as they say here in Cork,' said Chris
buoyantly. There was a glint in his eye which interested Patrick.
It reminded him of Joe when he was on the scent of something.
He shook his head when invited to sniff the wood. He was in
no mood for games.

'I'm listening,' he said.

'No guesses? Well, since you are a busy man, I'll tell you
what I smell from that wood around the hole in the wall, and
it is petrol. Real petrol. It's had a couple of days to evaporate
so I'd hazard a guess that the wood there was soaked in the
stuff. And not just that. Have a look at the wall. Surprising,
isn't it, that one section of wood, almost a square, isn't it, is
burned out? Burned out completely, leaving a big square hole,
and the rest of the wall is untouched. What do you make of
that?'

'Deliberate arson, no accident,' said Patrick and Chris
nodded agreement.

'Whoever did it,' he said, 'wanted to start a fire without
being seen, not even by Mrs Maloney. Luckily for the owner
everything was so wet that the wooden building didn't catch
fire, just the section that had the petrol spilled upon it. Easy
enough to do. Buy a can of petrol, pour it over the wall, heap
up the sawdust so that the whole thing would go up in flames.
Not too bright, of course, given that the sawdust was so damp,
but there you are. Not everyone knows how to light a fire

properly, especially some of those very poor people who must spend every penny on rent and on food. Not looking too good for your little girl in prison, I'm afraid,' he finished, and Patrick's heart sank. He rubbed his fingers over his mouth but said nothing.

'Let's go and have a word with the local gossip,' said Chris cheerfully. 'Who knows, but she might have seen a suspicious character lurking around. And, you know, in the case of lighting a fire to burn down a business, you'd think it might be a rival businessman, wouldn't you? She might know something about that.'

Patrick thought hard. 'I think that the owner is the person to ask about that, but personally I don't know of anyone who might benefit if he goes out of business. Cork businesses are mostly about eating and drinking – meat market, beer brewing, that sort of thing. Everybody must have meat and beer, but cigarettes – well, they are a new fad and I'd expect shopkeepers to buy their cigarettes from England. Somehow, I don't think that he would have a rival. And, you know, he grows his own tobacco plants in Youghal. I don't think that they grow it anywhere else in Ireland, or in England, either. Anyone else trying to make cigarettes would have to import the dried tobacco leaves and that would cut a big slice off the profits, not to mind the publicity he gets from talking about Sir Walter Raleigh.'

Patrick glanced up at the sky. Time was getting on and he wanted to be back in his office at the barracks. He was sceptical about Mrs Maloney. Gossips were, in his opinion, a nuisance because if they didn't have anything of interest to say they tended to make it up. Nevertheless, Chris had been very obliging to come out with him and had spotted an important point that this fire was no accident but looked like a carefully planned piece of arson. The least that he could do would be to go along with him and listen to what Mrs Maloney had to say.

Mrs Maloney was pleased to see them. Didn't ask them in, but came out, shutting the door behind them and, no doubt, revelling in a sense of importance as every passer-by would see her in conversation with a police inspector and the head of the Fire Brigade. To give the woman her due, she certainly kept a close eye on what was going on around the neighbourhood. Apparently, according to her, it was the gardener from Youghal himself who drove the horse and cart with the load of sawdust. Mrs Maloney had all of the details.

'I can see that you are the sort of lady that remembers everything that you see,' said Chris. 'Now shut your eyes and tell me if you can remember the gardener going off at any stage.'

Obediently she shut her eyes, mimed intense thought, and then shook her head.

'Not him,' she said and there was a note of drama in her voice and an emphasis upon the word *him*.

'What do you mean: "not him"? You don't mean to say that he left the other fellows loose around the city?' said Chris. 'Don't tell me that he wasn't keen to get back home to Youghal with his lads. I know what gardeners are like. Never want to be away from their flowers and their potatoes and a few strong-armed helpers. I'd take a bet on that.'

'Well, you would be wrong, then, wouldn't you?' she snapped. 'He sent them off as soon as they had shovelled the sawdust off the cart and into the privy.'

'Sent them off? What for?'

'How would I know? Didn't bring back anything. I can tell you that. I happened to be putting out my milk bottles when they came back. Gone a good ten minutes, I'd say.'

Chris thought about that for a moment. 'And what was the gardener himself doing while the two lads were missing?' he said. 'Smoking his pipe, I suppose.'

'I don't know,' she said firmly, and Patrick looked at her with interest. She was a gossip and a troublemaker, he knew from experience, but she hadn't troubled to make anything up on that occasion. He could see that the thought had occurred to her that she could not remember what the man had been doing. And that, he thought, was of interest. It was time for him to take a share in the questioning.

'Take your time,' he said quietly. It was the first time that he, himself, had spoken with her, although he knew that the sergeant and constable had often had reports of various wrong-doings from her, and he could see that she was keen to impress him. Deliberately he said no more. She was, he knew, waiting for a lead from him, but he was determined not to give her that satisfaction. He wondered how many of the pieces of evidence that she fed the constable with were based on a strong hint of what was desired from her.

'I know,' she said after a minute's silence. 'I remember now. He was talking with the fellow from the garage down the road.'

Patrick gave a perfunctory nod. It was very much against his training and his usual practice not to immediately take a note of evidence, but this time he thought that he would get more out of Mrs Maloney if he refused to show much interest. He could see now that she was scanning his face to see whether that was of interest to him, and he was pretty sure that she was disappointed by his lack of reaction. It was Chris that broke the silence.

'Bought some stuff to kill the weeds from the garage man, did he?'

She shrugged. 'That would be it, perhaps,' she said. 'Petrol, I suppose, in a can, anyway. Looked like petrol to me.'

Patrick drew in a cautious breath. He had got there. Now was the moment for the notebook. He wrote rapidly for a couple of minutes – no need to ask her full name and her address; he had read through so many reports from this lady during the last few years that both were seared upon his memory.

When he had finished, he read it aloud to her.

'I, Mary Maloney, of number three St Mary's Isle, saw that gardener from The Grove, Youghal, receive a container from the owner of St Mary's Isle's petrol garage. It appeared to be a petrol can.'

She had her hand out for his indelible pencil and signed with her usual flamboyant cross – well known in police statements. If her evidence was to be of any use, he would have to get the whole thing typed out on the correct piece of police station headed paper, and then get her to sign that it was correct, but it might be worthless. It all depended upon the garage man, whether his account corroborated hers or whether there was a completely different explanation.

'You don't seriously think that the gardener had anything to do with lighting that fire – why on earth should he plan to burn down the shed? They weren't interfering with his job down in Youghal,' remarked Chris as they walked back together.

'You'd be surprised to see the number of written statements – most of them useless and most of them signed with a cross – that we collect after every murder in the city,' said Patrick, feeling rather pleased with himself that he had neatly ducked the question. Chris was a good fellow and probably quite trustworthy, but Patrick had not the slightest intention of betraying the fact that the police were quite interested in the gardener. He remembered being told by Mr Murphy about the rape of the man's daughter and the implicating of the manager in that. Such a violent act would not be easily forgotten by the gardener, and so he would be the prime suspect if the police decided that Maureen McCarthy had nothing to do with the death of the manager.

'I want to trace that can of petrol,' he said aloud. 'It may have been bought for some purpose and that damp outdoor privy would have been a safe place to store it. After all, no fire would ever be lit on the premises so if they wanted to store some petrol, then that would have been an ideal place. Now don't let me walk away with your coat and cap. Make sure that I collect my stuff before I make my way back to the police station.'

He would, he decided, collect his belongings, and then go straight back to the station. Aloud, he said: 'You've given me a lot to think about, Chris. I don't think I would ever have noticed that stain of petrol on the wall if you hadn't pointed it out. Obvious, once noticed, but I didn't! Someone lit a fire away from all that wet stuff and made sure that it burned a hole in the wall which had been soaked in petrol – just a small section of it, and of course, as soon as it spread, it met those piles of wet sawdust. Smoke, not flames, was what was wanted by our arsonist.'

'Someone waiting to see you, Inspector! Been waiting some time.' Tommy, the constable on duty at the door, always liked to be the first with fault-finding. 'I had to tell him that I didn't know where you had gone and when you would be back,' he added.

Patrick frowned. 'I hope you told him something more than that,' he said angrily. 'I should hope that you told him that Sergeant Duggan would see him.'

'In with him now, in your room.' Tommy jerked a thumb and went back to his newspaper and Patrick reminded himself to look up the man's age and make a secret count-down calendar. If he were lucky enough to be appointed as superintendent, he would do his best to get early retirement for that man. Tommy was a leftover from the previous regime of the Royal Irish Constabulary, but several of the old brigades had been allowed to stay in office to await retirement. Some had fitted in, but others, like Tommy, had cherished a feeling of superiority because of his RIC origins and his Protestant religion, both of which he shared with the present superintendent, and had never adapted himself to the new personnel.

Joe rose from his seat when Patrick came into the room and the visitor did the same. There was, noticed Patrick, a strong aroma of petrol from the man and he was not surprised when Joe, always, efficient, said: 'This is Mr O'Callaghan, Inspector. He owns a garage on St Mary's Isle, and he'd like to have a word with you.'

'Certainly,' said Patrick. Tommy, he noticed, had summed up his visitor's clothing and appearance and had not bothered to offer the usual cup of tea and a copy of the *Cork Examiner*.

'I thought I should come and see you, Inspector, because one of my lads was passing St Mary's Isle and he overheard Mrs Maloney talking about me.' The visitor was coming to the point quickly and Patrick appreciated that.

'Not saying anything injurious about you, Mr O'Callaghan. Just that you brought a can of petrol to the manager of the cigarette factory,' said Patrick, 'but I'm very glad to see you as it appears likely that some petrol was poured on the wall between the outside privy and the shed where the cigarettes were made.'

'Is that a fact?' The visitor seemed more interested than alarmed. A countryman, thought Patrick. *Is that a fact?* was

a very country expression and the burly figure before him had
the look of a man reared on a farm, not half-starved on the
city streets.

'You remember bringing that can of petrol to the cigarette
factory.'

'I do indeed.' A laconic man. Another pointer to a country
origin. Cork city people never used one word where ten would
trip easily off their tongues. Country people were more
restrained. This man was waiting for the next question.

'You knew the man who died in the fire,' Patrick hazarded
a guess.

'I did; indeed, God have mercy on his soul.'

Patrick seated himself upon the chair which Joe had
vacated. This promised to be a long business. His visitor sat
down also and stretched his legs.

'Perhaps you can tell me about it,' suggested Patrick. And
then a sudden idea came to him. 'You lived near to him, did
you?'

There was, he thought a wide range of accents in the
countryside around which bore no resemblance to the sing-
song speech of true Cork city people, but Youghal accents
where the letter 'O' was invariably turned into the letter
'I', were distinctive. The way that this man had pronounced
the word 'soul' showed his origins immediately.

'We were in school together. My girl was friends with his
girl when they were growing up.' The thought appeared to
arouse memories and once more he added: 'May God have
mercy on his soul.'

'So, when he needed some petrol he had a word with you,
down in Youghal, and . . .'

'Wasn't him. It was the gardener. Met him when he was
taking up a load of sawdust to the city, met him on the road.'

'Did he say what he wanted the petrol for?' asked Patrick.
His voice, he hoped, sounded quite casual.

'No, he didn't,' said the visitor. 'Just met him on the road,
no time for a chat. He had a lad with him and there was a
tractor, one of those new Ford tractors, on the road trying to
squeeze past the pair of us. I was just back from work, hungry
for my supper, and he was busy. Hadn't seen much of him for

a while. The garden took all his attention and, of course, he was responsible for the field of tobacco plants. I hadn't seen him to talk with for some time. Knew him, of course. Another one that went to the same school.'

Patrick made a note. So, the petrol station manager, the cigarette factory manager and the gardener all went to the same school. Not surprising, of course, once you took into account that Youghal was not a big place. Another matter came to him, another crime.

'There had been some trouble, hadn't there? Some trouble concerning the manager of the cigarette factory, something about a girl, that's right, isn't it? An accusation of rape, wasn't it?' suggested Patrick. 'Not your daughter, was it?'

'No, not my daughter,' said the man. Patrick waited. He had hoped to elicit some more information by that suggestion but no more was forthcoming. The garage man's lips were tightly shut, and he wore the look of a man who has no more to say. Interesting, but probably not important. This accusation of rape, or attempted rape, had probably divided the local community. Patrick turned back to the question of the petrol.

'What would a man want a can of petrol for? Would you have any idea? He didn't have a car, did he?'

'Might have wanted to burn some rubbish. You'd have to ask him.'

'You have not seen him since?'

'I have not seen him,' repeated the man. 'Delivered the can of petrol, took the money and that was that.'

There was a note of finality in the man's voice. Already he was on his feet. Patrick made no move to stop him. After all, burning rubbish was a possible reason for the purchase of some petrol. But why up here in the city? It would make more sense if he had bought it in Youghal. But then, on the other hand, he knew this man, knew that he sold petrol, and the petrol can would be an easy thing for a man with a horse and cart to take back with him to Youghal.

'Thank you for coming to tell us about it,' he said. He did not rise. It was possible that the man might have something else to add, but he didn't. He was the one who got up and with a quick nod in his direction, saying, 'I thought I would

come and explain,' he made his way to the door and Joe, after
a glance at Patrick, went and opened it politely.

'Anything new?' Joe had closed the door and waited until
the sound of footsteps on the corridor had died away.

'Well, we know where the petrol came from now,' said
Patrick. He grimaced slightly and added: 'To be honest, it's
not too significant if you were going to have to base the whole
case of murder upon it. Yes, the gardener probably did use
petrol to burn rubbish. There'll be a lot of leaves and dead
plants by the end of the month, you'll see fires everywhere in
the autumn months, I've often noticed them in those big gardens
in Montenotte and those places down by the river, near to
Blackrock Castle. Makes sense for a gardener in a big place
like Myrtle Lodge in Youghal to buy some petrol, to have it
ready for the autumn bonfires, and why not from an old school
friend. He could easily take it back on the horse and cart once
he had unloaded all that wet rubbish stuff for the privy.'

Joe nodded and said thoughtfully: 'I suppose the question
is, did he take a full can back or did he daub some onto the
wall between the shed and the privy before he removed it?'

'Easily done, wouldn't it be?' said Patrick. 'And even if I
go down to Youghal and demand to see the can, I can't say
anything if some of it is missing. The man wouldn't be so
stupid as not to throw a few spoonfuls of petrol on top of
some rubbish and to light a fire as quickly as possible when
he got back to Youghal.'

'Impossible for us to know how much and whether he had
plastered some on the wall between the shed and the privy
before he left,' agreed Joe. 'Remember he had sent the boys
down the town. That, in itself, looks a bit suspicious to me,
doesn't it to you?'

Patrick grimaced but said nothing. He would allow Joe to
develop his argument and give himself time to think about it
before voicing any difference or even any agreement.

'And, of course, he had a motive, the gardener did,' went
on Joe. 'This unpleasant man had raped his daughter – well,
so the pregnant daughter said – and no consequences. The
master of the house took no action, the girl's father, the gardener,
had just been told to keep his mouth shut, possibly told to shut

up or to clear out and, of course, you know, Patrick, jobs are not that easy to come by. Not so many big houses left these days, and certainly not enough houses with gardens big enough to need a new head gardener and money enough to pay for that sort of staff. And without a good reference he would not have even that remote chance of getting a new job. And so, he shut up. But that doesn't mean that he didn't plan to get revenge. I'd say that he is our prime suspect, at the moment, anyway.'

Patrick got to his feet. 'Type it all out, Joe, will you. We don't need to arrest the man, but I'd like to get that girl out of prison as soon as I can.'

SIX

This morning, the Reverend Mother was finding it difficult to concentrate on the work at hand. She was meant to be taking advantage of the school holidays and a quiet convent to make a dent in the endless correspondence that took up so much of her time. But she was distracted and couldn't help thinking about the events up at the cigarette factory the previous evening. She was remembering back to a month or so ago when she had first heard the words 'cigarette factory'. What if those girls had never been offered a job in the newly established cigarette factory? She had almost immediately been sorry to have been involved, but that had been for her own concerns, her dislike of wasting time socializing – she had never dreamt of harm coming to her girls, who had spent almost ten years in her care. That offer of employment had seemed so wonderful that she had been willing to forgo her usual dislike of social occasions. The girls, she thought, seemed to be happy and although six shillings a week was not much, it was enough to help some very hard-pressed families.

Moreover, she had not wanted to be involved in the publicity for the newly set-up cigarette factory. It had been a mistake, she had sometimes thought, to have invited her cousin, Robert Murphy, back into her study for a celebratory cup of tea after the surprise of his offer to employ her ten school-leavers to help in the making of cigarettes from tobacco grown from the original plants brought back in a ship from the New World four hundred years ago.

After such a generous offer of employment, she had been in such an exalted mood of excitement and pleasure that she had been tempted to agree to his invitation to attend a celebratory opening party held, not at his own dwelling, but in his friend and neighbour's more famous place, the former residence of Sir Walter Raleigh, in Youghal.

She should never have done it, she told herself. Her life was a very busy one and there was no time in it for idle social events. She had, unfortunately, become interested in his explanation that his own residence had housed Edmund Spenser during the time when he had been writing his famous work *The Faerie Queene* and that several of the picturesque scenes described in that work had been taken from views of landscapes to be seen from his house. But of far more importance to her relative was that Walter Raleigh's name was associated with the bringing of tobacco as well as potatoes to Ireland and that made him, he had assured his cousin, of far more importance than Edmund Spenser – two such important items to modern life in Ireland, potatoes, and tobacco – and both of them associated with the one man.

'A well-read woman like yourself will gain so much inspiration from seeing where Sir Walter Raleigh lived,' he assured her, adding, 'and I will make sure to show you the fields where my tobacco plants grow and that will be of great interest to your pupils, so much more interesting to the world than Spenser and his Fairy Queen,' he had said, betraying, she thought, a lamentable lack of knowledge of English literature, though she had to admit that he was probably right when he said that her pupils would be more interested in cigarettes.

Still, Lucy, her favourite cousin, and greatest friend, had also been invited and the thought of a long confidential conversation in the back seat of Lucy's luxurious car, with the sliding window between the ladies and the chauffeur carefully closed, had been very tempting and so the Reverend Mother abandoned her school to Sister Mary Immaculate and set out on one morning of thick fog on the thirty-mile journey to the seaside town of Youghal. Lucy's chauffeur was an experienced driver, and he negotiated the fog-filled streets in an expert manner and by the time that they reached Glanmire the mist had begun to clear and the Reverend Mother's conscience, which told her that she could have gone by train and not imposed a journey through the city streets upon her cousin's chauffeur, was relieved and so she turned back to the interesting conversation about this cousin of whom she knew almost nothing.

'Do you remember when once we calculated that we had

forty-five cousins,' she said to Lucy, with a smile of reminis-
cence. 'We started trying to draw a family tree, but we became
bored with it. There were just too many names and there was
nowhere to fit the marriages and the children who were arriving.
This Robert is a first cousin once removed, isn't he? A generation younger than we were. The son of Thomas, isn't that
correct? One of a pair of twins, if I remember rightly.'

'You do like to look back into the past, don't you,' said
Lucy in slightly exasperated tones, taking out an elegant
compact from her handbag and unfolding it so that she could
examine her perfect complexion, touch up her lipstick and pat
some more powder onto her cheekbones.

The Reverend Mother smiled affectionately. No one, she
thought, would take them for first cousins of virtually the
same age. Lucy had determined not to let age show upon her
exquisitely painted face or in her hair, which was delicately
tinted to the palest shade of gold. She didn't like the reminder
that she now belonged to the elderly generation and that
another two generations of the family were thrusting their
way up into the wealthy merchant class of Cork city. It was
time to change the conversation.

'Tell me about this Robert Murphy,' she said. 'Has he got
lots of money?'

'I doubt it,' said Lucy. 'Not now, I would imagine. Neither
he nor his brother inherited the gene for making money. He
calls himself an entrepreneur, keeps trying in different ways
to make money. Always on the verge of making a fortune.
Tried to get something out of us for this latest enterprise. My
Rupert wasn't at all keen, told him that he would think about
it. I suppose that he's still hoping. He's the optimistic type
– doesn't know my husband! He invited him to the grand
opening, but of course Rupert had no intention of going so I
said I would, especially when I heard you were invited –
anything to stop you going down there by train and then
walking up that hill.'

The Reverend Mother had another qualm of conscience. Her
ten former pupils had been bidden to attend this grand opening
party – had been given railway tickets for the return journey.
She understood that they were to put on a demonstration. 'I

should have gone with the girls,' she said aloud. 'It's probably the first time any of them have been on a train.'

'They'll have a nicer time on their own. And if I know girls, they would have driven you mad giggling the whole way,' said Lucy, brushing the subject aside and returning to the more interesting gossip about relatives. 'Yes,' she said, 'Robert came into quite a big sum of money when his wife died. You remember that he married well, some family who lived nearby, I think. Keating – that was the name. She had quite a fortune, Annette Keating, an only child and both parents killed in a road accident. Someone told me that the parents weren't too keen on Robert, were against the idea of a match, but once they were killed, well she was a determined little thing, and she went ahead with the marriage. She was still under age, of course, at the time, but she convinced her guardians that this was what she wanted and that her mind was completely made up. And so, they got married and, with her money, of course – he managed to persuade her guardians – he bought that place in Youghal, on what was Sir Walter Raleigh's land and that gorgeous Elizabethan house which was built around that time, and they lived there together for a few years, leading the life of the landed gentry. And, then, believe it or not, she, also, five or six years later, died in a road accident, just the same way and in the same place as her parents. A lot of talk about that! It seemed as though Heaven had wreaked justice upon an unnatural daughter who had gone against her parents' wishes, but there were some rumours that she committed suicide as she had not seemed happy for a long time,' finished Lucy.

'What utter nonsense,' said the Reverend Mother briskly. 'Probably driving too fast. That sort of thing goes in families. One copies the other.'

'You may be right. Her car went over the cliff just near to the house, that steep cliff leading down to the Blackwater Estuary. Poor thing. Quite young too.'

'Were there any children?'

'No, no children, I did hear that she was pregnant when the accident happened, but of course, I suppose, the baby died with her. The car – she was driving it herself – well, the car went out of control and went off the road and it just rolled over and over and was apparently badly smashed. Very sad.'

'Did he marry again?'

'There were a few rumours that he was looking for another rich wife. They say he wasn't too well off, but then, of course, the war began in 1914 and he volunteered immediately. Clever fellow. Was taken into the engineers and apparently did very well, became an expert, and when he came out of the army, once the war was over, he set up some sort of engineering business, making alarm clocks, I seem to remember. Wasn't a success. He was no businessman, poor fellow. One of these men who want to make a fortune by getting a clever idea, wants to be another Henry Ford, but just didn't have business ability. Has tried all sorts of things – wasting his money. If the cigarette factory makes a fortune, then he'll probably look for a second wife and father some children. At this moment what everyone remembers about him is that he is still living on the remains of his first wife's money, and he doesn't like that. Wants to be well known for his own cleverness in making a fortune. Men are odd like that – you wouldn't know, of course, but men are very proud, especially from that side of the family. You remember how their grandfather made a fortune from hides and skins, a very enterprising idea in a city where thousands of cows are slaughtered for meat and where the skins were available from the butchers for a very small sum, yes, he was a clever and enterprising man but what they remember for him, and continually bring up in conversation, was that he saved the Munster and Leinster Bank by leaving his quarter of a million pounds in it when it ran into trouble about twenty years ago – oh, and the fact that he bought his own ship about fifteen years ago to export his leather to Canada when insurance prices for sea journeys became sky-high during the world war. They put a flagstaff up on the terrace of his house by the river and used to hoist it every time his ship sailed up the river towards Cork harbour. Still there, I think. I'm sure you remember it, don't you? A very enterprising man, our relation, but none of his family, so far, seemed to have inherited his business sense.'

The Reverend Mother thought about this for a while. She

was not too interested in family history or fame, but she saw an opportunity for her pupils in this latest money-making endeavour.

'You know what, Lucy,' she said thoughtfully. 'If this relative of ours is determined to make money from his cigarette factory, which, providentially, he has housed so close to my school, well, I will have to make sure that I train up girls to work for him. These girls he has now, even if they prove satisfactory, are bound to get tired of it and move on to Liverpool once they have the fare for the ship journey, or else they will get married, or more likely just pregnant, so I'll have to make sure that I can supply a new set of girls for him whenever he needs them. I wonder how you train girls to be neat-fingered. And don't say shoplifting,' she added, and Lucy giggled.

'Wouldn't dream of it,' she said demurely. 'Well, you can talk to Robert about that, can you? Or else to that manager of his, Mr Timothy Dooley. Apparently, he was in the army with Robert, and I suppose Robert gave him the job because of that. What did you think of him, by the way? Didn't care too much for him, myself.'

The Reverend Mother said nothing. Gossip had a way of getting around and she had no wish to jeopardize her pupils' employment prospects by an indiscretion which might, thoughtlessly, be repeated. Lucy, she knew, would not pursue the matter so she occupied herself in shifting her position and placed her feet on top of the well-worn bag which she had rooted out from a cupboard on the landing outside her bedroom. The zip was slightly open, and she tucked in the piece of material that had escaped and closed the zip firmly. The bag, she thought, was like herself, getting old and tired.

'What on earth is in that bag of yours?' asked Lucy, looking down. 'You haven't brought your own bedclothes with you, in case they ask you to stay the night, have you?'

'Aprons,' said the Reverend Mother. 'A new set of aprons for the girls to wear for the photograph to appear in the *Cork Examiner*. You see, I went to see them and, well, they sit on the ground, in these very short skirts that are so fashionable these days, and they pick up pinches of the crumbs from the

dried leaves so I thought it would be more hygienic if they
wore aprons.' She looked blandly at her cousin and her cousin
looked knowingly back at her.

'I had wondered why the manager wanted girls instead
of boys,' said Lucy. 'He'd probably get better value out of
training boys than girls. Girls are a nuisance. My housekeeper
is always complaining about them. Giggling in corners and
forgetting instructions and then, sooner or later, one gets
pregnant and then another and she has to start all over again
to train a new set of girls. But, of course, if his manager is
one of those who likes little girls . . . especially if he can see
. . . well, you know . . .'

The Reverend Mother considered this. Lucy's words had
stirred up that vague sense of unease which had been with her
for the last few weeks. She had not liked that manager, Mr
Timothy Dooley, too much. The 1920s had brought in short
skirts which had seemed to grow shorter every year and it was
useless trying to make girls wear even their school uniform
with below-the-knee skirts. She had to be tactful with Sister
Mary Immaculate, who wanted to pin a flounce to the bottom
hem of any skirt which would not touch the floor when its
owner knelt at her command. The Reverend Mother had put
a stop to that rather degrading process. 'The girls in this school
kneel to their God and to no one else, Sister,' she had said
with heavy emphasis and then had walked away before Sister
Mary Immaculate could think of any appropriate argument.

With a feeling of shame, now, she dismissed the slightly
triumphant memory of how she had left the annoying woman
without any further argument to produce and turned her mind
back to the prospect of employment near to their homes for
young adolescent girls. She would have to nurture the link
between the school and factory; keep both her cousin and his
manager satisfied and make sure that her girls got first preference when the business expanded, but at the same time she
had not liked his manner with the girls and had been particularly worried about Maureen and had decided to have a quiet
word with the girl if she saw her during the next few weeks.
The child had a poor role model in her own mother. She would,
of course, have to be very tactful and not mention any names.

Nevertheless, she had not liked the way that the manager had smirked at the bare knees and legs when the girls were sitting on the floor, sorting the crumbled leaves of the tobacco plants. She heaved a sigh. Her life was, she often thought, an amalgam of compromises. Yes, she could not afford to do anything to anger those who were providing employment for her pupils at such a convenient distance from their homes. She could only hope that her suggestion to Robert that the girls could be supplied with aprons from the convent would not prove to be irritating or unreasonable. The wonderful Sister Bernadette had made ten calf-length, voluminous aprons from the outside sections of old sheets that had gone past the darning stage, and she had taken them around to the factory herself and persuaded Robert that it would look much more hygienic if the girls wore these while sorting out the material to be packed into the cigarettes. And now she had another set and Sister Bernadette had assured her that it would be no trouble to wash and iron them at the end of every week. But was that enough? These girls were young and had lived a life of stringent poverty from as far back as they could remember. Six shillings was a fortune to them! Even an extra penny or two on top of their weekly wage might persuade someone with Maureen's volatile nature to forget the careful teaching and warnings that she had received during her time in school.

'Don't sigh,' said Lucy. 'You're going to enjoy yourself today. Look, the sun is breaking through the clouds. I bet it will be a lovely day in Youghal. And think what it will be like for a historian like yourself to be able to say that you trod where Sir Walter Raleigh trod. I say, what would you bet that Robert has a puddle with an Elizabethan bejewelled cloak beside it?'

'All nicely staged for the photographer,' said the Reverend Mother, turning her mind with an effort from her charges and smiling at her cousin. 'I hope you have brought a crown, Lucy,' she said. 'You would make a wonderful Queen Elizabeth, you know – when she was in her prime, of course. You do have a regal look about you.'

'I hope you are not planning to get me to subscribe to your

latest scheme,' said Lucy. 'And don't you rely on Robert Murphy, either. Rupert says that he's famous for trying to get people to invest in his latest brainchild, but that he, personally, would never do so as none of the schemes seem to last too long but always end up losing money for those who invest in them. You know, of course,' she added, 'that Robert was nicknamed "Timmy" or "Danny" by his brothers from the Latin phrase, *"Timeo Danaos et dona ferentes"* – *"I fear the Greeks when they are bringing gifts."* That's about the only Latin I remember, so don't start talking to me in Latin,' she warned and added – 'I think I only remember that quotation because of poor old Robert. He always was laughed at by his brothers. Even when they were all grown up. Such an optimist, always coming up with some bright idea and trying to persuade his brothers to finance it. Don't laugh. If you're not careful, someone will apply it to you. I bet all the businessmen in Cork quail when they see your shadow on their doorstep. They know that they will be considerably out of pocket before you leave their office.'

'Nonsense,' said the Reverend Mother, but she had a moment of compunction. Perhaps it was hardly fair to do nothing but talk of money to her relatives and friends. 'Tell me about the house, Raleigh's house,' she said. 'You've seen it, haven't you? Has there been much done to it?'

'Well, we've been to a party there, Rupert and I, but it was very dull. They're very nice people and don't mind Robert cashing in on the Sir Walter Raleigh fame just because of his luck of finding some tobacco plants growing in his garden – the seed plants in from Raleigh's lands, of course, and must have been lurking unseen in the neighbourhood for generations. Nice people,' she repeated, 'but the party was a bore. Very poor food and that unpleasant fellow, his manager, Mr Timothy Dooley, brought in to give a talk and then hogging the limelight and insisting on giving speeches about how clever he is about growing tobacco and taking out his little notebook to read out meaningless figures. Nell, you remember Nell, Robert's youngest sister? Well, she was there, had been in school with my youngest, so Nell and I slipped out through a curtained door and had a good gossip. You'll like the place.

Not much changed since the days of Queen Elizabeth, so they say. Nice old windows. Mind you, I wouldn't go there in the winter. I bet that it's cold and damp. History is all very well but give me gas and electricity and keep your history for the shelves in the library,' said Lucy.

'What did Nell say about Robert's manager?' asked the Reverend Mother with interest. She remembered Nell as a sharp-tongued lady who spoke her mind. She drove a bright red Cadillac car around the city with a reckless professionalism that evoked both fury and secret admiration in her male critics. The Reverend Mother was interested in Nell's opinion.

'I seem to remember that it was something upon the lines of insufferable, stupid, slimy, gothic rapist,' said Lucy placidly. 'Nell never minces words, as you may remember.'

The Reverend Mother did not smile. 'Rapist', she echoed, her mind going to the ten young faces who had been placed in this man's power.

'Gothic rapist,' corrected Lucy. 'I don't suppose she meant much by it; she likes to shock, as you know. Probably just meant that he was a bit on the rough side with street girls, something like that.' She cast a quick glance at the screen between them and the chauffeur and inserted a long fingernail into the gap and then closed it more securely. 'Not Robert, you know. I've never heard anything bad about him. Just the manager, you know. There was some talk about how he was accused of raping the gardener's daughter. Made her pregnant and then said it was at the girl's invitation. Refused to marry her. Robert sacked him, but then relented. After all, it was one person's word against another – so he said – and, of course, this Timothy Dooley was very valuable to him. Went along with all of Robert's ideas and did his best to make them work.'

The Reverend Mother resolved to have a word with her cousin Robert. No accusations – she had no right to make any, but a strong hint that she was going to keep an eye on the girls who had so recently left her care. Robert, she thought, from her memory of him was a gentle character. Weak, but not vicious in any way, so far as she could remember.

'There was something about Nell getting married, some time ago, wasn't there?' she asked, deciding that it was best to change the subject before her cousin tried to extract a promise that her indiscretion would go no further. 'What happened about that?'

Lucy was only too happy to change the subject. 'Well, that was William Lynch. Everyone was sure that it would have been a match and a good one, too. Plenty of money on both sides, but it came to nothing. I don't know why, but William was going around the city, very sour, and saying to everyone – "*That one* will want a prince of the blood before she is satisfied."'

The Reverend Mother laughed an appreciation. She had rather liked the forthright Nell, whom she remembered well as a child, and resolved to have a private word with her as soon as they arrived at Youghal.

'You know,' said Lucy, 'it's a funny thing, but their father, Robert and Nell's father, was a great businessman and, of course, their great-grandfather – that hide and skin business in a meat market city like Cork was a stroke of genius. And their father went into the furs business. Made a fortune out of it, but not one of his boys inherited his ability. Edward went off to South Africa to grow tea but ended up just living on the income from the shares that his father had left him. Another of them went to Australia, sheep-farming, I think, but it was the same story, writes begging letters to relatives from time to time. Robert, for all his brains, someone told me that he is a mathematical genius, and he did well in the war, but he makes a mess of everything he tries since then. However, Nell, well, she was the only girl and so the only one of the family not to be involved in the business, but I'd say that she would have been the best businessman of the lot of them all, and my dear husband agrees with me. "Very sharp, very organized, good business-person – would do very well if she set up a business" – that's what my Rupert said about her, and she is not even a client of his – much to his relief, by the way – so many of our dear relations think that he should work for them for nothing since he was lucky enough to marry into the family – but not Nell. She's too independent.'

'Why doesn't she set up a business, then?' enquired the Reverend Mother.

'No capital,' said Lucy briefly. 'You need to have capital to set up a business. So Rupert says, anyway.'

The Reverend Mother thought about that for a while. She wondered whether she would make a good business-person and decided that she might. To her shame, the thought of how to make money often entered her mind while in church, and it took a determined effort to banish it. And yet money was essential to education. How the famed 'hedge schools' worked in Ireland she had no idea, but in her experience, young children were not interested in books unless they were attractive and highly illustrated – and that meant expensive. Could she go into partnership with her cousin Nell, she wondered. Provide some spare land – or even a building. A sudden idea crossed her mind. She had a beautifully built, spacious edifice in the convent garden. Would it, she wondered, be sacrilege to make some use of the church building which lay empty, mostly, after eight o'clock in the morning, for ninety per cent of the twenty-four hours of the day? With a sigh she pushed the query away and turned back to the question of this cousin, Nell.

'You'll have to introduce me, Lucy. I'm sure that she will have forgotten me. It's a long time since we met. I wonder could she teach me to drive,' she added idly, to reassure her cousin that she would not bring up any awkward subjects during the day's festivities. The slight twitch of the chauffeur's head at that statement made her wonder whether the screen between them was as soundproof as Lucy believed it to be. She said nothing, however, but changed the subject to exclaiming about the sunshine which had burst through the clouds as they neared the sea. It augured well for the festivities to be held in the historical precincts where Sir Walter Raleigh once trod.

SEVEN

The famous grounds belonging to Sir Walter Raleigh, outside the Viking town of Youghal, had been built on the hillside with magnificent views of the sea to the front of the house and to the rear a commanding sweep over the estuary of the River Blackwater, just as it reached the sea after a meandering hundred-mile journey through Cork, from where it rose in the Mullaghareirk Mountains in Kerry. The gardens were large, and it had a wide concrete expanse in front of the house where a row of cars was already parked. The Reverend Mother noted that her cousin's efficient chauffeur drove past the first gap and then carefully parked his owner's car at a slight distance from the house. She smiled to herself, noting that he had avoided parking beside a red Cadillac with numerous dents and scratches which was rather awkwardly, and certainly carelessly, left at an angle in front of one of the myrtle trees. There was, she thought, something rather familiar about that bright red colour and once she had availed herself of the chauffeur's proffered arm to dismount, she walked briskly in the direction of the battered car, whose owner was removing a handbag from the boot.

'I don't think that I would like a car as big as this if I were to have to drive it; one of those new Baby Fords would suit me better,' she observed to Lucy.

'Nonsense, Reverend Mother,' came a voice from the other side of the car, 'you might as well buy yourself a tricycle.'

The Reverend Mother thought resentfully that her wearing of religious habit and veil at large family gatherings instantly identified her and wished that there was an obligation upon everyone else to pin a name badge to their outfits. She had forty-five cousins – most possessing a wife or a husband and numerous children who were now adults but were, of course, also cousins and members of the family. The women, at least, wore an assortment of clothing varied as to individual taste and age which did occasionally but the men were uniformly dressed in suits, white shirts and ties, all bearing a family resemblance to each other. This should be Nell, but was she quite sure enough to greet her by name? Luckily Lucy, who attended more family gatherings than she, immediately came to the rescue.

'Cousin Nell, how well you are looking,' she said enthusiastically.

Lucy and I, thought the Reverend Mother, were probably a good twenty years older than most of their cousins. Both their fathers had been at the top end of a family of twenty boys and girls, many of whom had not married. It had taken many years later, when she and her cousin Lucy had been almost grown up, for another spurt of interest in matrimony. Nell, she seemed to remember, had only been in the nursery when she herself had left to join a convent of nuns. Probably quite a few years older than her brother, Robert. Perhaps her air of authority came from that age difference. She showed no hesitation in demolishing the Reverend Mother's joking suggestion.

'You're too old to learn,' she said decisively. 'Not to say that you couldn't be driving now if you had learned twenty years ago, you look quite *compos mentis*, but at your age you wouldn't be able to learn and then to keep all the numerous procedures in your head as you were driving. You'd probably be a danger on the road.'

The Reverend Mother thought fleetingly of explaining how many matters and how many pieces of information she kept in her head while managing a community and a large school, as well as being, at a moment's notice, quite fluent on the problems of the community in which she lived and possessing an understanding of how to extract as much money as possible for charitable causes from the wealthy who dominated the life of the city. Nevertheless, a sense of fairness made her say, 'I'm sure that you are right, Nell.'

That mollified Nell and she pointed to the damaged wing. 'Not too good, myself, these days, I'm afraid,' she said, 'not that it was all my fault – terrible ditherers and slow coaches on the roads these days! Some idiot who couldn't make up his mind as to whether he was going left or right . . .' And then, briskly changing the subject. 'What do you think of Robert's new enterprise? He has the devil's own luck, you know. Our uncle Patrick died recently and left him two thousand pounds. Two thousand pounds! – nice little sum, isn't it? Used it to build that factory of his. Built it in a flash using wood for the floor, the roof and the walls. Made with double wooden walls, stuffed with sheep's wool so that he doesn't have the expense of heating it for the workers. Didn't want to have fires because of all the dried leaves lying around. Not a bad idea. Robert has brains. But so have I,' concluded Nell bitterly. And then added: 'Men! Always feel that they have to bequeath their money to other men. He could have left me that two thousand. I know just what I would have done with it. But no, not a penny. Couldn't believe it when the solicitor read out the will. Why on earth should Robert get everything? You'd think Uncle Patrick could have remembered me!'

'I bet you had plenty to say about that,' said Lucy with an affectionate smile at her cousin and then added, 'Now you must excuse me, you two. I must go and say hallo to Cousin Sheila. Haven't seen her for ages.' Lucy with a quick handshake went off and the Reverend Mother was left with Nell, who, by the expression upon her face, was still brooding on the unfairness of the deceased Uncle Patrick.

'I'm sorry that you were disappointed,' she said politely. 'What were you going to do with the money?'

'I thought of financing a garage – there will be big money in that. Soon everybody will want a car. *"Buy your car here and we will teach you to drive and will keep it in good order for you."* That will be over the door. I know a man who wanted to buy a car for his son to celebrate the lad's twenty-first birthday and I gave him a piece of good advice. *"Buy him driving lessons at the same time."* Well, that was in 1916, more than ten years ago, but the fellow followed my advice. Engaged a chauffeur for a fortnight and the chauffeur and the lad drove all over Ireland, all around the coast, and played a game of golf at every links on the way, so he still boasts. But whatever it was about playing golf, young Willie learned to drive very well. It's a pleasure to see him reverse and turn a car in the middle of a narrow road. Goes a bit slowly for my taste, but there's no doubt that he knows how to drive. I tell him that if he runs out of law cases, he can always hire himself out as a chauffeur. But, of course, there's no money in being a chauffeur just now. Everyone is driving these days – buy a car, jump into it, go for a drive down the straight road and *Bob's your uncle!* But the fact is that there are terrible drivers on the road and lots of bad accidents. Look at my lovely car – an idiot who couldn't drive properly! So, that's what I will do with a sum of money when I get it.'

'When you get it?' The Reverend Mother raised her eyebrows. How did people get hold of a sum of money?

Nell shrugged her shoulders. There was an odd expression upon her face.

'Who knows! Bad hearts in our family! Robert made a will leaving me his money when he dies. He thought it was a joke as he is so much younger than I – in any case, I suppose he can cheat and change his will. Probably will if he gets married. But I am keeping an eye on him and that manager of his, Mr Timothy Dooley. I'll make sure that the factory is a success and who knows, I might be able to get a substantial loan from him if it turns into a thriving business. It should do well if they manage it properly. Everyone wants to smoke cigarettes these days. Cigars are just for old men. And, of course, now that women have taken up smoking, that has doubled the market. Wouldn't do it myself. Told Robert that. You'll poison your lungs with the smoke from that deadly weed – smoke in the lungs can kill someone: that's what I said to Robert before he started on this affair. Told him that I had heard that when I was in the Princess Royal's Volunteer Corps during the war. We were taught that. Why should one kind of smoke be better than another kind? Told him that he'd be better off with a pipe. I said it to Robert only the other day. "You know, Robert," I said to him, "people with pipes are forever cleaning out the gunge from the stem of their pipes with a pipe cleaner: now with these cigarettes, that gunge sticks onto your lungs and there are no little cleaners to scrape out lungs. You mark my words, people in the future will be calling those tobacco leaves of yours the *Deadly Weed*." That's what I said to him. Didn't listen to me, of course. Never did have much sense. "Sell the cigarettes if you want to, but don't smoke the stuff yourself! People die coughing because of getting smoke in their lungs," that's what I said to him, but of course he didn't take any notice of me. Men! Still, why should I bother. If he kills himself with smoke in the lungs, then I'll inherit his money.'

'I'm a bit like a mother hen,' Reverend Mother told Nell. 'I worry about my chicks. I should be so pleased that ten of my fourteen-year-olds have got a job which, if they can keep it, and can avoid pregnancy for a few years, will save them from dire poverty. You know, the death rate, in the slums of Cork, in the area around my convent, is twice as large as it is in other parts of the country. That's a figure that I can't get out of my head, and nothing that I try to achieve changes the numbers,' she added.

'Perhaps you should teach them birth-control.' Nell was certainly living up to her reputation. No other member of the family would have mentioned such a subject to the Reverend Mother. She decided not to argue, nor to put forward the position of her Church upon such a subject.

'Girls in full-time education, girls of well-off families, girls or young women with a well-paid job very seldom become pregnant outside marriage,' she said quietly. 'I pin my hopes to this fact, Nell. Nor do they rush into marriage when they are fourteen or fifteen years old.' She allowed her cousin to think about these statistics for a minute before going on.

'I'm not someone who tries to achieve the impossible,' she said. 'I'd like to dissuade my girls from becoming pregnant before they have the money to support a child, but if not, then I feel that proper housing must be provided for all. Why should the poor be treated worse than domestic animals? The cows in the fields, the hunting dogs in their kennels, have warmer and dryer conditions and better food than many of the children in my school. Why should families find themselves on the streets because they could not find the rent imposed by land-lords? And why should women with small children and babies be forced to live in damp, crumbling, rat-infested houses? And how can it be the fault of very young girls if they are seduced, or even raped, and pregnancy results?'

The Reverend Mother looked across at Nell grimly and was

glad to see her lost for words for the moment. The role that men, often men of respectable classes, played in the abundance of unwanted, ill-cared-for, half-starved children in the slums was, the Reverend Mother thought, brushed aside by those who felt that the poor should do something to help themselves. She noticed how a spark of interest came into her cousin's eyes, a look as though she had suddenly said to herself: *That reminds me.*

'That reminds me, Reverend Mother,' Nell said aloud. 'I wanted to have a word with you about these ten girls of yours. I would, if I were you, warn them to take care of themselves. That man Robert employs as a manager is a nasty character. Oddly, Robert, himself, was the one that told me that. Apparently, this Timothy Dooley raped a girl on the tobacco farm, the daughter of Robert's gardener. Robert fired him, but then, typical man, took him back as he was so useful. Made him pay something to the girl, but, of course, as you know yourself, the leopard does not change his spots. I thought that I should have a word with you, but I suppose that it's not much use. None of these girls will want to give up their job, will they?' She looked sympathetically at the Reverend Mother. 'And, of course, you have no jurisdiction over them, have you? Would it help to have a word with their mothers?'

'Thank you very much for confiding in me,' said the Reverend Mother in a stately fashion. 'And now tell me, if some rich donor were to present a car to the convent, what would be the best model to get? How much, for instance, would a car like yours cost?'

That, she thought was a good move. The yearning for a convent car was part of an elaborate joke which she played with her cousin and with Dr Scher, the convent doctor, and friend. She hadn't the slightest intention of ever allowing a donor to present a car to the convent and would demand hard cash in its stead. However, now it changed the subject neatly and while, with years of practice, she maintained, she hoped, a look of intelligent interest and kept her eyes upon her know-ledgeable cousin, she pondered what to do about the problem of this report of the manager of the cigarette factory. It had seemed such a wonderful chance for the girls that she had jumped at the opportunity without examining the working conditions.

She tried to tell herself that since the girls had reached school-leaving age that it was none of her business, but she knew that she could not evade her responsibility. The sudden idea that she might get that martinet, that overseer of short hemlines, Sister Mary Immaculate, to drop into the cigarette factory every few days, she dismissed as ineffectual and impossible to achieve. Sister Mary Immaculate would not scruple to have a word with the bishop's secretary about such an unorthodox use of the Reverend Mother's second in command being used to supervise girls who were no longer pupils of the school, and, in any case, few of the girls liked Sister Mary Immaculate and the ones who had left the jurisdiction of the school rules would ignore her lectures. A woman without tact, she might antagonize the manager to the degree that the girls would lose their jobs.

Perhaps, she thought, an informal conversation with her cousin Robert might work. Surely, he could employ an older woman to supervise the girls. It might be in his interest, also, she thought and would spare his manager for more valuable work. She milled around her busy brain some tactful phrases as she listened with an attentive face to the explanation of petrol consumption and maintenance of cars until the sight of a profusion of heads, appearing above the myrtle bushes, came straggling through the gate.

'Here they are,' she said proudly. 'Here are my girls.'

Followed by Nell, she made her way rapidly down the path, as anxious to see them as any mother hen, she thought. Railway tickets had been purchased for them, she had been told, but was slightly annoyed to see that the unpleasant manager, Mr Timothy Dooley, had accompanied them, and that Maureen was side by side with him chatting in an animated fashion as they made their way up the path towards her.

The Reverend Mother held out a hand to Nell. 'It was very interesting for me to have met you and I have really enjoyed our conversation and will profit from it, I hope,' she said with sincerity. And then, on an impulse, she said: 'Come and meet my past pupils.' She was not sure what had made her proffer that invitation, but she was, she hoped, open-minded enough to know that her cousin was probably wiser than she on more matters than the difference in running costs between a Baby Ford car and a Mercedes Benz. She continued to chat as they made their way up the avenue and allowed Nell to tell her the history of how Sir Walter Raleigh not only planted potatoes and tobacco in his Youghal estate but was also responsible for the abundant myrtle bushes. Pretty little bushes, thought the Reverend Mother admiring the profusion of white flowers and glossy dark green leaves, but resolutely refusing an offer from Nell of bribing one of the gardeners to give her a 'slip' to plant in the convent garden.

'I only grow potatoes in my garden,' she said firmly and then while Nell was still puzzling over that statement she said quickly, 'You used the word "rape" when speaking about Robert's manager, Mr Timothy Dooley . . .'

'Don't tell me that is a mortal sin to use a word like that, and that you will report me to the bishop,' said Nell flippantly.

'The deed is indeed a mortal sin, but the word may be necessary to describe the deed and as such is itself innocent. My patron saint, Thomas Aquinas, is quite clear on that issue,' said the Reverend Mother in her most pedantic manner. Nell, she thought, was playing for time. Were her words without substance, or did she have solid evidence? Absent-mindedly she crumpled one of the flowers from the myrtle bush and inhaled its strong lemon scent. It would she thought fleetingly be a nice plant to have in a tub beside a front door. Dr Scher, arriving home from hospital or morgue, would feel refreshed by the scent. She would, after all, she thought, beg a present of a small bush and perhaps even a tub from her cousin Robert.

'Yes,' she said in a low tone. 'Rape is a very serious, a mortal sin for whosoever commits it, but for the victim it can spell ruin. I feel that I still have a responsibility towards the girls whose parents will have relied on me to find them a suitable working place. If there is any substance behind the word that you mentioned, I would like to know the circumstances.'

There was a hesitation for what felt like a full minute, and then Nell spoke without her usual lightness of tone. 'I probably

should not have spoken of it, but since I did, I can see that
you have a serious reason to enquire. Perhaps I used the word
"rape" rather flippantly, but Robert was complaining about
having to get rid of a pregnant field worker and that he, as
well as the man responsible, had to fork out a sum of money
for her as she was "*crying rape*" – these were the words that
he used – and since she was accusing a very valuable man to
him, he had to give her something additional to keep her quiet.
I must say that I told him the girl may well have had truth on
her side, but he just shrugged his shoulders and said that it
was an easy accusation to make and a very difficult one to
disprove.'

'True,' said the Reverend Mother. She could see that Nell
had her eyes upon the group of ten girls, who, rather touch-
ingly, had, on seeing the Reverend Mother, reverted to school
discipline, and had formed into a neat crocodile, proceeding,
two by two, up the path towards them.

'Well,' said the Reverend Mother cordially, 'what grown-up
young ladies. And today you are going to have your picture
in the *Cork Examiner*, isn't that right?'

'That's right, Reverend Mother.' As usual it was Maureen
who spoke first, and she turned and pointed to a large tarpaulin
spread upon the gravelled surface in front of the Elizabethan
house where a couple of servants were arranging cushions,
set at mathematically exact distances from each other and
forming a perfect circle. 'We're all going to be sitting in a
circle there,' she said, 'and we'll be pretending to make
cigarettes.'

'That will make a lovely picture,' said the Reverend
Mother, eyeing the ivy-clothed stone walls and the steepled
roofs of the four-hundred-year-old house. Truly a spectacular
backdrop for these young denizens of the slums of the
inner city. 'By the way,' she added, 'that reminds me, Sister
Bernadette and the lay sisters have stitched another set of
new aprons especially so that you will look very smart for
the photograph. Here they are.' She handed the bag to
Maureen and took one out.

'Beautifully stitched, are they not,' she observed to her
cousin Nell. 'You wouldn't believe that they are made from

old sheets which have gone past the darning stage, would you? Sister Bernadette is very clever, isn't she, girls?'

'Yes, Reverend Mother,' they chorused obediently, but there was a marked lack of enthusiasm, and girl after girl eyed her neighbour uneasily and then turned their glance upon Maureen, the ringleader.

'The thing is, Reverend Mother,' said Maureen eventually after a minute's silence when the air seemed to be full of the silent words: *'Tell her!'* 'The thing is,' she repeated, 'Mr Dooley don't like us wearing them aprons. Says they get in the way.'

'Nonsense,' said the Reverend Mother, and without stopping to take a breath, went on, 'We'll show him. You will look great in these starched, snowy white aprons. Let's go and practise. Will you come, too, cousin?'

'Yes, of course!' There was an amused note in Nell's voice, but she proved very sensible, immediately rearranging the cushions so that now they formed a wide semicircle with the house as a backdrop and then seating the girls on the cushions, demonstrating how they were to bend their legs to one side and helping to arrange the aprons so that they covered their knees, and the surplus material was tucked out of sight.

'There that's just the way that we did it in Buckingham Palace when I was presented to Queen Mary – a long time ago now, when I was about eighteen years old, but I still remember it! We all sat just the way that you are sitting now, our legs tucked to one side and with our dresses covering our knees, that was very important. If you showed your knees you had to leave Buckingham Palace.'

The Reverend Mother bit back a smile as every one of the ten girls looked down and checked on the capacious apron which covered their knees. They were looking well, she thought. The extra money coming into their houses would mean better food.

'Well, isn't that lovely!'

Robert and the manager had arrived on the scene, followed by Eileen McSweeney and the *Examiner* photographer. The Reverend Mother smiled with affection at Eileen. A former pupil, Eileen had proven herself one of St Mary of the Isle's success stories. Brought up amongst the poverty of Barrack Street, but born with an energetic intellect, she had applied herself with determination during her studies and was now studying law. Today, though, Eileen was in her other role as reporter on the *Examiner*.

Robert seemed genuinely impressed by the picture made by the ten girls. The Reverend Mother watched the faces and decided to act, instantly.

'Sister Bernadette made those aprons especially for the girls, cousin,' she said. 'They do look well, don't they? Best linen and so well-laundered.'

'So hygienic!' enthused Nell, with an amused glance which the Reverend Mother ignored, but she repeated the 'so hygienic' catch-phrase with a nod of her head.

Robert, to her pleasure, agreed enthusiastically and called upon his manager to join in the praises. Not a word was said about the former batch of aprons and the Reverend Mother wondered what had happened to them. She noted approvingly that Eileen was making rapid notes and promised herself that she would have a word with her past pupil later on so that the story of the sets of aprons made from frayed bed sheets by Sister Bernadette and the other lay sisters would feature in the *Cork Examiner*. Hopefully that would ensure that the girls would be allowed to wear them on hygiene as well as appearance grounds.

'So, so hygienic,' said Nell aiming her comment between her brother and the *Cork Examiner* reporter. There was an undertone of a sneer in her voice, but Robert ignored her and so Nell moved over to instruct the *Cork Examiner* photographer in how to take a good photograph which would make the most of the historic building and the fresh-faced girls.

Eileen, noticed the Reverend Mother, gave a sharp glance from one woman to the other and then looked at the ten girls, demurely clad in their voluminous white aprons.

'Hygienic,' said Eileen aloud. 'I could use that word for cigarette smoking – I could emphasize that it is much cleaner and more tasteful than smoking pipes. How about that, Mr Murphy?'

'That's what I thought; fire purifies, makes you breathe in

clean purified air. And, of course, we make sure that the cigarettes are as pure and clean as possible,' said Robert, without a moment's hesitation, and Eileen obediently scribbled her well-practised shorthand as he pontificated upon his desire for perfect hygiene in the making of those cigarettes which would be placed in the mouths of all Cork citizens. Once the whole of the city began smoking his Raleigh's Cigarettes, then pneumonia, asthma, bronchitis and other chest problems would become a thing of the past, he said enthusiastically. Robert, thought the Reverend Mother, had taken quite a liking to Eileen and he answered all her questions with a lot of detail, eventually inviting her to come and see the field of tobacco weed which was ready to be harvested and then turned into cigarettes for Cork citizens to regain the health that their unhealthily foggy city had deprived them of. Nell uttered a sound that was halfway between a snort and a laugh, but she didn't reiterate her catchphrase of 'the Deadly Weed'. After a few minutes she just turned upon her heel and allowed him to pontificate to the readers of the *Cork Examiner* about the health benefits of cigarette-smoking for all who wanted good lungs.

The Reverend Mother was somewhat sceptical about this claim. Surely it couldn't be good for lungs to inhale smoke, but she put the matter aside. Six shillings a week and training in the life of work was an important offer for her girls and she would make sure to keep on friendly terms with Robert and to encourage his view that a group of girls who were already friends would make good employees to work, side by side, shoulder to shoulder in the confined area of his new factory. She might have a word with him about slightly increasing the wage after about six months, but in the meantime, she would do everything in her power to make this venture a success. When Eileen arrived back, she beckoned her and said bluntly, 'You will give it a good write-up, won't you? It will mean a lot to those girls to have steady employment to occupy their days.' Her eyes went thoughtfully to Maureen, who was giggling at some joke made by Timothy Dooley. That child, she thought irritably, could do with another year in school, time to grow up.

'Yes, of course, Reverend Mother,' said Eileen. 'And I plan

on doing something about Sister Bernadette and her use of worn-out sheets to make these lovely aprons, also. Will that be all right?'

'Sister Bernadette,' said the Reverend Mother sedately, 'is a great admirer of the *Cork Examiner* and is the first to receive it when the delivery boy arrives. In fact, she saves me a huge amount of time as she makes sure that I know any piece of news which would interest me and makes sure that I don't miss any items about the bishop or about a funeral that I should attend. To see her own name in the paper that she so respects will be immensely exciting for her. An invaluable woman and I would be very pleased if you could give her pleasure by your article. She never fails to bring me the *Cork Examiner*. I would be lost for news if it were not for her.'

Little did she think, then, that the next news, on the Cork Examiner, of the Cigarette Factory would be the story of a fire.

EIGHT

'Good morning, Reverend Mother,' said Inspector Cashman. 'I hope I am not interrupting your work.'

'Not at all,' said the Reverend Mother, feeling a twinge of conscience at how little work she had managed to achieve that morning so far. 'Come into my office, Patrick, I'm very glad to see you.'

'None of your girls were injured in any way, but . . .' he said rapidly as she unlocked the door.

She ushered him in and found him a seat in front of the fire before picking up upon his last word.

'But . . .' she repeated, taking the chair opposite to him. He had, she saw, a troubled expression on his face, and she gave him time. Patrick, even when he was a six-year-old boy in her infants' department, had never liked to be rushed. Of course, now, he was an inspector and would possibly inherit the position of superintendent when the present holder retired, but he had kept that cautious approach. Though, she often thought, the well-groomed man opposite bore little resemblance to the ragged, barefoot boy that she remembered from almost twenty years ago.

'Tell me what happened, Patrick,' she said and waited patiently while he took out a notebook and opened it at a page marked with a slip of paper.

'There was a fire at the cigarette factory on St Mary's Isle. It happened last night,' he said and looked across at her.

'Sister Bernadette told me. I did not know,' she said. 'We had a heavy fog and mist here last night and this morning.'

'It was not a bad fire. It appears that it started after the day's work finished and the girls were dismissed,' he said, and she noted how he checked his words from the notebook that he held open. 'As you say, Reverend Mother, it was a night of thick, heavy mist and there was very poor visibility. Some nearby residents thought that they smelled smoke, but you

know what it is like, these last few days, especially, Reverend
Mother. The tide was very low every day of this week and the
river smells very badly at low tide in this sort of weather. I'm
not sure whether the smell of smoke would be strong enough
to drown out the smell of the river. I'd say that having read
about a fire in the *Cork Examiner*, they convinced themselves
that they had smelled smoke.'

The Reverend Mother nodded. The river had, indeed, been
bad during the last week of very low tides and mists, but no
rain. Stagnant, sewage-filled water had not been swept down-
stream but had festered between the bridges and had been
particularly noisome in the sluggish curve around St Mary's
Isle.

'So smoke, lots of smoke, but no flames, is that what
happened, Patrick?' she said quietly.

He nodded.

He was finding this difficult; she could see that, but she
could not help him. What had happened? *None of your girls
have been injured,* he had said.

'At six o'clock, as usual, work finished,' he said, taking
refuge in a scrutiny of another notebook. 'Apparently it was
not the custom to sweep the powdered tobacco leaves and
stems from the floor as a certain amount would be lost in the
process – every spoonful was valuable, according to what I
was told, and so a very fine dust sheet was draped over the
top of them. That was after the girls, all but one, went home.
And not the manager, Mr Timothy Dooley, of course. He was
the one who locked up and made sure that everything was in
its place.'

'All but one,' she repeated.

He nodded. 'Yes, he needed one girl to help him lay the
dust sheet and make sure that the baskets of cigarettes were
stored on the shelves, and everything made ready for a prompt
start at eight o'clock on the following morning.'

'And he chose one, and having chosen one, she was the one
that helped him every evening.' The Reverend Mother was
beginning to understand. She felt a wave of anger. It was as she
had begun to suspect. This manager had abused his position
with a vulnerable girl who was not much more than a child.

Patrick nodded, looked at his notebook again. 'Her name was, is, Maureen, Maureen McCarthy,' he said.

'I see,' said the Reverend Mother. And she did, indeed, see. She had noted the use of the word 'was' and of his correction. He was reassuring her that Maureen was alive. Patrick was always meticulously careful. She felt her way to the next question.

'The one casualty . . .' Her voice, she knew, held a query, but it would be up to Patrick to tell the story in his own step-by-step fashion.

'The Fire Brigade put out the fire very quickly once they arrived upon the scene – it was, according to one of the officers, more smoke than flame and so they doused it and then when the smoke subsided a little, they put on masks and went in. They found one dead body, a man's body, seated on a chair by the table at the top of the room, his head was slumped over the table and there was a bottle of Paddy whiskey, half empty, on the table and,' here Patrick hesitated and referred once more to his notebook and then, without looking at the Reverend Mother, he said, quite rapidly, 'and two large, pint-sized mugs.'

'Two,' echoed the Reverend Mother. She knew little about whiskey but guessed that a pint-sized mugful of whiskey would be enough to inebriate a man. But why two?

'He drank too much, fell asleep and then was asphyxiated by the smoke, is that what happened, Patrick?' she continued rapidly, but the word 'two' still hung in the air between them and was not something that she could ignore. She had to know the truth.

'Someone was with him, drinking with him, but that person perhaps had less to drink and so was sober enough to escape once the smoke began to pour in . . .' She continued and then paused. He said nothing but he did not contradict her. She forced herself to continue, 'but that person,' she said, 'did not give the alarm, is that correct, Patrick?'

He nodded. There was, she thought, a very worried – almost a guilty – expression upon his face. Patrick had something to impart, something that he was finding it difficult to communicate to her. She guessed what it was but waited. It was for him to inform her.

'I interviewed all of the girls this morning, all ten of them,'
he said. 'The superintendent suggested that we meet them on
their way into work and Joe told them not to say a word to
each other or they would end up in gaol. Terrified them, so
he said.' Patrick looked apologetically at the Reverend Mother
before adding: 'We had to make sure that they didn't agree
on a story beforehand, so we met them early in the morning
and when we got them to the barracks, the constables lined
them up outside and forbade them to speak to each other. Joe
interviewed them inside the timber shed – the window and
door had been opened earlier and it was fit for the purpose,'
said Patrick, looking up from his notes and across at the
Reverend Mother. She gave a reassuring nod. He was, she
knew, meticulously careful to do the correct thing and she was
sure that he had been satisfied the room was safe and freed
from smoke. 'As soon as each was interviewed, he sent them
home, telling them that they were not to speak a word to the
other girls unless they wanted to end up in gaol. Of course,
he said, they probably met up further down the road but at
least that was only after they had been interviewed. They are
all over fourteen, but they are young and so we did everything
very carefully.'

The Reverend Mother bowed her head. She understood his
need to be meticulous and she appreciated that he was telling
her everything to demonstrate that he had been fair to all,
but she did wish that he would get to the point. Something
was going to emerge from these ten statements; she knew
that.

'Joe had asked them to tell him everything that had happened
during that afternoon, Joe and I talked it over while the
constable stayed with the girls. We did everything very carefully,' he repeated.

'I'm sure,' said the Reverend Mother. 'And did you find
that the statements told the same story?' she asked.

He nodded with a slight air of thankfulness. She had allowed
him to progress to the salient point.

'When I read them through, I was thankful that we had
taken such care to make sure that they could not communicate
with each other before being interviewed. You see,' said

Patrick with a slight grimace, 'they were so remarkably similar.'

The Reverend Mother bowed her head but suppressed the smile which was twitching at her lips. Patrick had been an only child and rather a solitary boy during his youth and young manhood. Joe had been one of a large family of boys. Their knowledge of girls of that age was probably minimal. She, herself, had immediately guessed that the ten girls got together as soon as they heard the news on the night before and had agreed upon a story. Patrick, she knew by the uncomfortable look upon his face, had something else to tell her and so she decided to help him.

'Would you like to tell me what was said, Patrick?' She kept her voice neutral. It was up to him whether he confided in her or not. Strictly speaking, she had no rights in this case. The ten girls were no longer pupils of hers, no longer under her care.

Patrick selected one sheet of paper, compared it with another and then another, meticulously reading each one and then replacing it. Then he spoke:

'The girls finished their work at six o'clock in the evening. Nine of them went to get their coats and went outside. They walked to the gate and waited there for the tenth girl – Maureen McCarthy, who had stayed behind to help the manager, Mr Timothy Dooley, to cover over the tobacco leaves. When Maureen arrived, a few minutes later . . .' Patrick's eyelids flickered momentarily but then his head bent over the sheets of paper again: '. . . a few minutes later,' he repeated, 'they walked home. No one saw or smelled any smoke, and they were sure that there had been nothing of the sort when they left the factory. They all stayed together until they reached their homes on Barrack Street.'

'But . . .'

'But our witness saw the girl leave at eight o'clock when the bell went on the Protestant Cathedral – a good two hours after her friends.'

'Although her friends said she left at the same time, or within minutes of the time when they left, so . . .' The Reverend Mother allowed her statement to hang unfinished.

'That's right, Reverend Mother. But . . .'

'But there was a half-emptied bottle of Paddy whiskey and two mugs upon the table,' stated the Reverend Mother.

'That is correct,' said Patrick. 'A man may perhaps drink half a bottle of whiskey by himself, or it may have been left over since another time, but a solitary drinker has no need of two mugs.'

The Reverend Mother thought about this for a moment. Her mind went to the recent hospitality at Raleigh's house in Youghal. Surely there had been jugs of water and bottles of soda as well as bottles of whiskey upon the trays.

'Perhaps the second mug was for water,' she suggested.

'Possibly,' he said, but the tone of his voice told her that he felt this was quite unlikely. A mug, she guessed, would not be convenient for pouring the correct amount of water to dilute the whiskey. He leafed through the sheets of paper and selected one.

'This is Maureen McCarthy's evidence,' he said. 'According to this, she stayed to help the manager, Mr Timothy Dooley, lay the dust sheet over the crushed tobacco leaves, then she got her coat and joined the other girls at the gate, and they walked home together.'

'So, all ten statements fit neatly together,' said the Reverend Mother. 'But I think that you have something else to show me.' Her eyes went to another couple of sheets of paper, neatly clipped together and covered, on both sides, with neat handwriting. Patrick's eyes followed hers.

'Yes,' he said. 'This is the evidence taken down by Joe and countersigned by our young constable, Billy Hayes. It's the statement made by our witness, a Mrs Maloney, who lives near to the factory and can see everything from her front window. She has made her mark, here.'

'I know Mrs Maloney,' said the Reverend Mother, rather grimly. 'You should recruit her. She would make a very good addition to your team. She has strong views on law and order.'

Patrick looked rather taken aback, so she added quickly, 'Don't mind me. Tell me what Mrs Maloney said.'

'I'll summarize,' said Patrick, with a hasty glance at the pages. 'It appears that Mrs Maloney keeps a keen eye on the "goings-on" at that cigarette factory. According to her, ten of them go in, together, every morning, but when six o'clock comes, only nine girls come out and they go home to their mammies like good children, but the red-headed one doesn't come out for another hour or two.'

'Every day,' queried the Reverend Mother grimly. Mrs Maloney, she thought, was a gossip and a malicious woman, but her information was, as far as one could tell, usually quite accurate.

'Every day,' confirmed Patrick with a quick glance at both sides of the sheet of paper in his hand.

'And yesterday?'

'Yesterday, also,' said Patrick. He read aloud from his notes: 'Nine of the girls went home at six o'clock, just when the Angelus bell was ringing at six o'clock – nine of them, but not the red-headed one.'

And then when the Reverend Mother said nothing, he added: 'Of course, it is one voice against ten.'

The Reverend Mother sighed. 'You know, Patrick, my patron saint, Thomas Aquinas, said many a wise thing, but one of my favourites is: *Three things are necessary for the salvation of man: to know what he ought to believe; to know what he ought to desire; and to know what he ought to do.*" I regret to say that I go by that statement, and I add another one to it. I know *what* I ought to believe, but I also know *who* to believe. God gives us brains to seek the truth. I understand your need to be careful, but I suspect that you, like myself, have sometimes to make difficult decisions based upon your experience of people, of their true motivation and their trustworthiness – so, of course, you will have to balance the probabilities. What exactly were Mrs Maloney's words, Patrick?'

Once again, he picked up the sheet of paper though, she guessed, probably the words were seared into his brain. Nevertheless, he read aloud in a toneless voice: '"I see 'ed the red-headed one come out about a couple of hours later, at the same time as every night. The bells from the Protestant Cathedral was ringing, that's when she goes home, the bold hussy . . ." that's what she said.'

'That would have been for their evensong, Reverend Mother,' said Patrick, looking up from the page that he was holding. 'I checked with Joe since he is a Protestant and knows all about evensong,' he added before returning to the page and scanning down through it, his lips moving as he carefully read it, word by word.

'Any sign of smoke?' asked the Reverend Mother, thinking how sometimes Cork people seemed to have a language of their own. An English person would translate the word 'bold' as meaning courageous, but to any Cork person it would immediately sum up, even without the accompanying 'hussy', Maureen's lack of moral fibre.

'Mrs Maloney said that she thought she smelled something, but I'm not too sure about that. She might have, but she might have just made it up. The river has been smelling very bad this week, Reverend Mother. I'm not sure that a whiff of smoke would strike anyone, especially at that time of the day when people would be cooking, and the public houses would be lighting their fires.'

The Reverend Mother bowed her head. Sixty years of residence in close proximity to the very polluted River Lee had, she guessed, almost immured her against various odours. And, of course, old age had diminished her once keen sense of smell. Yes, she supposed that he was right. The river did smell even worse than usual when the rain turned to fog and mist and when the water became more sluggish. Nevertheless, many years of contact with Mrs Maloney would ensure, if she were a betting woman, that she would put her money on the veracity of that piece of information from the parish gossip.

'So, Mrs Maloney said that Maureen McCarthy stayed as late as that every evening?'

Patrick nodded. 'I did ask her about that. And her answer was that the girl stayed longer than she should every evening – she was rather scornful about the excuse that she was helping with covering over the dried leaves and putting away the finished cigarettes – said she could have done hundreds of such jobs in the time that she stayed behind. I'm afraid that she implied that the girl had a relationship with the manager. And she said that she saw the manager, Mr Timothy Dooley,

come out a while after the girl had left every night . . .' He
went back to his page of evidence and read aloud: '"Many a
night, I see'ed him throw out an empty whiskey bottle – he'd
been filling her full of whiskey so that he could have his way
with her".' Patrick stopped and scribbled something into his
notebook.

'Just wondered how she knew it was a whiskey bottle,' he
said in explanation. 'I'd better get the constable to check on
that. If she's telling the truth, and if he does it every night,
there should be quite a few bottles to be found in the under-
growth. But I don't know how that old woman could have
told what kind of bottle it was from a distance. She didn't
seem to see too well when I was talking to her. She was
peering up at me.'

Probably went out after the manager had gone home and
put it to her mouth to get the last drops, thought the Reverend
Mother, but it was not for her to interfere in the gathering of
evidence. Aloud, she said. 'Would Mrs Maloney be considered
a good witness?'

Patrick gave that question his usual careful attention. 'I
think so,' he said. 'I can imagine her going down well in court.
She puts in all the details, like the reference to the Angelus
bell and to the Protestant evensong. Yes, I think a jury would
believe her evidence, rather than the girls' evidence, and
certainly a judge would take Mrs Maloney's evidence very
seriously.'

She said nothing. She agreed with him. Mrs Maloney was
a nuisance, bringing evidence about children stealing from
shops and from delivery carts to the Reverend Mother on the
grounds that the parents of the culprits would not take any
action, but nuisance was one thing, accuracy was another and
the Reverend Mother did her the justice to believe that ninety-
nine times out of a hundred she was correct in her
accusations.

'But the nine other girls said that, on that evening, Maureen
left the same time as they did. That they had waited for her
at the gate. They all told exactly the same story, in almost
exactly the same words.' Patrick sounded puzzled and worried.

'I see,' said the Reverend Mother. She said no more, but

her heart sank. *Exactly the same story, in almost exactly the same words* sounded to her like a faked story. She had heard plenty of these word-perfect stories during her long years of running a school. Most of them, she had to admit, from this particular age group of girls, who were expert in getting together in a little cluster and agreeing on a narrative. The younger children never displayed the same ingenuity and most depended upon saying: 'No, I never!'

'The superintendent insisted that the girl be arrested,' said Patrick. He coloured a little as though conscious that these words sounded like a weak excuse and then added hurriedly, 'He was furious with her as she spat in his face. But, in any case, we had to get her away from the other girls, Reverend Mother. The superintendent felt that she couldn't be left at liberty when there was a danger of them agreeing on a false story. We must find out the truth. Whoever started the fire, the girl ran out when smoke was pouring from the building, if Mrs Maloney's evidence is correct. She may have had nothing to do with lighting the fire, but she did not raise the alarm . . .'

'And a life was lost which perhaps could have been saved,' said the Reverend Mother.

'On the other hand,' said Patrick earnestly, 'this girl is only fourteen years old. Not much more than a child. Children do tell lies. Children do fear to be blamed for things. I remember when I was a boy that I saw someone throw a stone through a shop window and I ran away as fast as I could just in case I should be blamed for it. Would her mother be any good at talking to her?'

'Unlikely,' said the Reverend Mother bleakly. 'My impression is that she's thoroughly sick of the girl and anxious to be rid of her. In any case, I've heard a rumour that the mother has left her younger children in the care of their aunt. Possibly for just a short time, but I am worried about the situation.' She brooded on this for a moment and then said earnestly: 'I can rely on you, Patrick, to let me know if I can be of any assistance. These girls were in my care so very recently. I still feel responsible for them, especially as it was through my influence that they got work at that cigarette factory.'

Patrick hesitated for a moment and then said: 'Would you be able to visit her, Reverend Mother, talk to her, persuade her to answer questions and to tell the truth?'

She looked at him rather bleakly, he thought, but after a moment she said: 'I shall do my best to obtain permission from the bishop, Patrick, but somehow, I don't think the bishop would be happy about me visiting a prison. I shall try, but if you don't hear from me, well, you can take it that I have not been successful. You may be able to remember that I did seek permission, a few years ago, to visit a woman who had ten children in my school, but that he was shocked at the very idea.'

And with that she rose to her feet and walked to the front door with him. He could see that she thought that it would be of little use to appeal to the bishop to allow her to visit the gaol and he was sorry that he had mentioned the possibility as it would cause her pain.

'Don't worry,' he said as he shook hands on the doorstep. 'I'll think of something, or someone who might be able to talk sense to her.'

NINE

The previous evening, Eileen, at home in front of her typewriter, had heard the news of the fire almost as soon as Patrick. Their next-door neighbour was a night street cleaner and rapped on their door on his way home from work. Her mother had gone to the door and then returned. She had such a look of shock upon her face that Eileen was alarmed.

'A fire at that new place, that wooden building down on St Mary's Isle. That's where all those girls from up the road here, that's the place where they all work. You know all about it, Eileen. You went down there to Youghal to interview the man that owns it. You had that article published. Don't you remember?'

Eileen didn't wait. Quickly she had grabbed her jacket and was through the door and reviving the ancient engine on her motorbike. Five minutes later she had arrived at St Mary's Isle to find that Mrs Maloney, the parish gossip, had bad news for her.

'You're too late, Eileen,' she said. 'One of the real reporters has been here and gone. I told him the whole story. They found the man that is the manager, you know. Burned to death! It will all be in the paper this morning. Photos and all! You should get yourself a telephone, girlee, and I'd let you know bits of news from time to time!' And the annoying woman chuckled with amusement at the idea of someone from Barrack Street having a private phone installed in their own house.

And there it was already in the newspapers. Each shop that she passed now this morning on her way down to the university library displayed dramatic headlines. But then she had to wait at the junction to south main bridge and she was able to read, scrawled on a large sheet of white paper: 'ONE ARREST'

Nothing that she could do now, she would soon find out the truth, but for now she had to get into the university as quickly as possible because the library would only stay open until ten o'clock, due to the renovations and repairs during the summer holidays.

Eileen hated the summer holidays. The university, she felt, had excessively long breaks from lectures. She was impatient to finish her studies and to find a proper job. A four-month holiday from the end of May until the end of September was, she felt, a ridiculous waste of time. Most students, she knew, enjoyed the long holidays. Many went abroad for these months, but others just lounged on the sandy beaches to the east and to the west of Cork city. She had no car, and no opportunity to borrow a car from an affluent parent – train tram and bus fares were all too expensive, and her motorbike was on its last legs, and she needed to be within easy reach of a garage as it frequently broke down. She reserved the money from her university scholarship to pay her fees, to help her mother and to buy books. Books were immensely expensive, but the librarian at the university library was very kind to her and gave her long loans on books which otherwise she would have had to buy. She was a friendly woman, knew all about Eileen, knew that she supplemented her scholarship with work for the *Cork Examiner* and always passed on any snippets of news which came her way, even sometimes shared a sandwich and some biscuits during the long summer morning hours when Eileen was often the only student in the library.

'Early bird as usual; you'll have the place to yourself this morning,' she said as she unlocked the door and then when Eileen had helped her with slotting the bolts of the heavy doors into their holes in the stone floor, she said: 'Did you hear about the fire last night, over on St Mary's Isle?'

'No,' lied Eileen. The librarian was a lonely woman who read three newspapers from cover to cover every day and then used titbits of news to give her an excuse to engage in conversation. She schooled her face to show amazement, horror or any other reaction that should be required.

'Not much of a fire, apparently. I got the news from the postman,' said Mrs Finnegan, placing a bunch of letters upon her desk and rapidly sorting them into neat piles. 'It was that new factory, the cigarette factory. More smoke than fire, according to the postman, but he did say that the police were there so it could be arson.' The librarian shrugged her shoulders before visibly turning to more important matters.

'I'm afraid that it won't be much good you trying to work here this morning, Eileen, as the men are coming to treat that patch of woodworm over there near the German literature shelf. You know what workmen are like! Nothing but talk and if I shish them, they whisper so loudly that it's even more distracting. I'm going to take myself off to the upper regions of the Aula Maxima and check English literature books there until they are finished. I'll be up and down ladders all the morning, but it's better than sitting at my desk and trying to work with all the distractions.'

'That's all right, Mrs Finnegan. If I could just take away Book Two of *Blackstone's Commentaries on the Laws of England* – that should keep me going. I'll be very careful with it,' she added, reminding herself, as always, not to take advantage of Mrs Finnegan's good nature. Strictly speaking these valuable old books should not have been removed from the library and she had spent precious money on buying a brand-new attaché case, padded, and lined with silk, to demonstrate that she would take the utmost care of the precious volumes.

'I know you will, Eileen,' said Mrs Finnegan with a harassed look at the van which sped around the inner quadrangle and drew up outside the Aula Maxima. 'It will be our secret,' she added in warning tones as she rapidly located the volume and handed it over.

Eileen arranged the book carefully into the small attaché case and slid away from the library, pleased that she had left her motorbike at the outer entrance to the porter's lodge. Mrs Finnegan, a woman who arrived early and left late, had never actually seen the motorbike and Eileen hoped that she would never find out that her precious volumes rode pillion through the streets of Cork. She would, she planned, bring the book home to her mother's cottage on Barrack Street and leave it there, safely ensconced inside the attaché case.

Eileen was never one to miss an opportunity. Study could be done at any hour of the day or the night, but there might be spare money to be earned by writing about this fire on St Mary's Isle. She would pop into the police station and have a word with Inspector Patrick Cashman. After all, they had been close neighbours as children, and she hoped that he would give her first preference if he were to talk to the newspapers.

She passed the police station on her way to the steep hill of Barrack Street that led to her home, wondering for the millionth time why it was called a 'street' rather than 'hill' since it was so extremely steep. Very busy there at the Garda Síochána, she noted. Several strange cars, three with the Cork IF registration number and one, a splendid Mercedes Benz, bore the IK Dublin number plate. The smallest of the three Cork cars was the Cork Police Barracks' Baby Ford, the second car, a Vauxhall, was, she thought, belonging to the Lord Mayor, and the battered Hillman, she knew, to her annoyance, was belonging to a reporter at the *Cork Examiner*. Never mind, she told herself as her motorbike choked and spluttered on its way up the steep hill, never mind, she would often find an angle to a story which the salaried reporters missed.

Nevertheless, after she deposited the precious book in her mother's cabin and was on the way to the *Cork Examiner* office, she switched off her engine when she was a few minutes away from the barracks and allowed her motor bicycle to freewheel down the remaining stretch of hilly Barrack Street until she reached the police barracks and silently steered into the car park. She parked unobtrusively by a blank, windowless wall and slipped off the saddle, took into her hand her attaché case, and had a quick look around.

The window to the superintendent's office was quite near and there was a buzz of voices coming from it. Inspector Patrick Cashman would undoubtedly be in there, so now was not the moment to ask to see him. Ducking down so that she might not be seen through the window she went on until she reached the corner of the building. No one to be seen and so she continued until she reached a rather dirty window at the back of the barracks. There was a telephone ringing when she arrived, but it stopped almost immediately, and a voice could be heard. Good, she thought, Joe is in his room. She

stood there, very quietly. Joe's mother had hung a pair of
elaborate net curtains upon her son's window on the day
following his promotion to the status of sergeant and to the
possession of a room of his own and Eileen, who had been
amused by their gentility in the past and had not hesitated to
tease Joe about them, now silently cursed the proud mother.
She could see nothing through their elaborate embroidery but
after a few minutes of intense listening she decided that she
could no longer hear a voice from within and had to take a
chance that Joe had replaced the receiver. Gently, she scratched
the glass with one fingernail, achieving quite a loud squeak,
loud enough, she hoped, to alert a solitary man to her presence, but not enough to disturb any conversation that might
be going on.

And it worked. She heard the scrape of a chair and then
heavy footsteps and then the curtain was jerked back, and
Joe's face appeared. Eileen joined her two hands together in
a praying position and looked as imploringly as she could
manage in a dumbshow.

He grinned. Put one finger to his lips and jerked a signal
towards the back of the building. Quietly she stole around and
waited until he came from the opposite side.

'Well, what brings you to honour our humble barracks,
young Eileen,' he said pleasantly.

'Actually, I'm almost the very same age as you are,' pointed
out Eileen. 'And I'll tell you that I was the one who bought
you a birthday card last week so that Patrick could present it.'

'And the bottle of whiskey?' queried Joe.

'No,' said Eileen. 'Patrick bought that himself. He didn't
mind buying whiskey, but he thought that he would look a
fool if he bought a birthday card. I bought two, that one
with a racing car that he could give to you and a very girly-
looking and pretty card so that he could give that one to me
on my birthday. Don't forget to remind him. It's tomorrow
– the thirtieth of July. And you'd better buy a bunch of
flowers, too, for me. He'd die of embarrassment if he had
to do that.'

'Is that why you've got me out of my office? And the day
that is in it!'

'Busy . . .' queried Eileen with a lift of an eyebrow. 'Big important fire?'

'More smoke than fire,' said Joe. 'But a man died of smoke inhalation.'

'Man . . . very important man . . .'

'Not really,' said Joe, and then he nodded his head towards the car park. 'Ah, you mean all the visitors. Nothing to do with the fire. We've been expecting that fellow from Dublin and of course since he is the big chief, the Commissioner, if you please, so the Lord Mayor turned up to do his "Welcome to Cork!" act.'

'The Commissioner, the Commissioner of the Police,' Eileen was alert. 'Is that why Dan O'Mahoney from the *Cork Examiner* is here?' she asked.

'Got it in one,' said Joe. 'Now ask me why the Commissioner of the Police has come all the way down from Dublin with his chauffeur and his sidekicks?'

'The fire, but why? How?' Eileen gave a puzzled frown.

'I thought that you were supposed to have brains,' said Joe scornfully. 'Don't you know any geography? Long way from Dublin to Cork. Why come for a little tinpot fire? Anyway, how would he know about what was happening in the middle of the night down here? No, stupid. Our super-intendent is retiring this September . . . What does that suggest to your great brain?'

Eileen shrugged. 'A going-away present?'

'A bit premature, wouldn't it be? Might make the man feel that they were pushing him out before his time was up. Think again. You'll kick yourself if you don't guess.'

'They came to have a look at Patrick, is that it?' said Eileen slowly. An icy feeling of apprehension filled her as he nodded. She hoped desperately that everything would go well. Patrick, she knew, was a worrier. He would not be at his best if he felt that he was under inspection.

'How is Patrick feeling, Joe?' she asked.

'Very tense. Well, you know him. And the superintendent, our superintendent, has jockeyed him into something that he didn't want to do. One of those girls from the cigarette factory has been arrested and locked up in the women's gaol.'

'Arrested? A girl! Charged with what?'

'Assault and battery for now – between us, she spat in the face of the superintendent – but really on suspicion of murder. The old lady who lives nearby says that she started the fire and then ran away. So now she has been arrested. And she is only fourteen years old. Just a kid. Probably scared out of her wits under the cheeky face! Patrick is in a terrible state about it, but he had to obey orders. Went up to get the mother, but she wasn't there. Gone off with a sailor, apparently, so said her sister who is looking after the kids. She didn't think that Maureen's mother would be back for a few days or a week if she struck it lucky – so the woman said.'

'That's dreadful. Can't Patrick do anything?'

'What can he do?' said Joe. 'He's got his boss man and the boss man's boss man from Dublin sitting on him. Our superintendent has already informed the *Cork Examiner* man that someone is "helping the Gardai with their inquiries". That's the latest way of saying that someone has been arrested for a crime, but, sure you know that, an experienced reporter like yourself. You can go and join your friend, the reporter, if you like. He hasn't been allowed in with the bigwigs. Our young constable is filling him in on the details about the fire and the factory and all that sort of thing. I left it to him because then Patrick can always disown everything if the superintendent ever lets him out of that room. Tea, coffee, and chocolate biscuits have gone in. Don't you wish you were there? Whiskey *galore*, of course. You'd enjoy yourself.'

'Don't be stupid,' snapped Eileen. 'Can I go and see the girl? Can you give me authorization?'

'No,' said Joe bluntly. 'Not a chance. This could be murder. A serious crime. The girl is over fourteen. Her mother, or rather the aunt, could see her, I suppose, but not you. And we don't turn journalists loose on people accused of crime. You'll have to pick up your news somewhere else.'

Eileen got to her feet. 'Well, I can see that I'm wasting my time with you; I'll come back when there is someone with a bit more authority to be seen,' she snapped and walked out quickly. She was deeply upset about that girl – fourteen was very young, though she knew that nowadays no one under sixteen could be hanged, it still meant a long prison sentence, perhaps a life sentence, if the girl were convicted. Eileen wheeled her bike out onto the road and went down towards the river and over to St Mary's Isle.

The Reverend Mother was standing at the gate of her school, patting the hand of a woman enveloped in a torn and stained shawl. Without hesitation, Eileen kicked the accelerator and passed the convent without a second glance. The woman was weeping, and she could guess the reason for the visit to the Reverend Mother. A child had died. Or an eviction had taken place. There was little that the Reverend Mother could do in either case, little except give comfort and make some practical suggestions, but Eileen knew better than to interrupt. She parked her bike in front of a shop, went inside and purchased herself a chocolate bar and then went out again. The woman, not now weeping, but with a dull expression of misery, had crossed the road and the Reverend Mother was standing by the gate, watching her go past. Eileen pushed her bike back to the convent so as not to disturb the thoughts of either and was pleased to see how the Reverend Mother's face brightened at the sight of her former pupil.

'You've come about Maureen McCarthy,' she stated, and Eileen smiled.

'You have a hot line to the man up in Heaven,' she teased and was glad to see that the Reverend Mother returned her smile. 'I won't keep you,' she went on. 'Just wanted to know whether there is any chance that you, yourself, could visit Maureen and get the truth out of her. She's turned stubborn – refuses to say anything, assaulted the superintendent, apparently. Terrified, probably. I've asked but been turned down. Her mother is . . . well, away, but I suppose you know that, also.'

'Yes,' said the Reverend Mother sadly. 'Yes, I do know, but, I'm afraid, Eileen, that I can't visit the child. I need permission in matters where I leave the convent to visit any building for any purpose except a visit to a relative. Though I do, without troubling to ask for permission, pop in to see Dr Scher from time to time, but that could be explained as part of my duties in caring for elderly and sick members of our community, but certainly to visit a prison, I have to seek permission from a higher authority – nuns, you know, take a vow of obedience,' she added, and Eileen could tell that she was picking her words carefully. As to a higher authority over the Reverend Mother who always seemed to rule the roost, Eileen guessed that it had to be the bishop. Old as the hills and very set in his ways was the verdict of most of her university and journalist friends on his lordship the Catholic Bishop of Cork. In the meantime, a fourteen-year-old girl was locked up in a gaol cell with no one to comfort her, or, more importantly, sort out her story.

'I was thinking as I came along here that I might go to see her, have a chat with her, give her some advice, I might pretend to be her older sister, but, of course, Patrick is so starchy that he would never go along with something like that – and, of course, he knows quite well that I am no relative,' she said and added, 'That's the trouble about living in a place like Cork. Everyone knows everyone else's business and as for relations, "*well, I know him: seed, breed and generation,*" isn't that what everyone says when a name is mentioned? I haven't a hope of persuading Patrick and Joe has to do what Patrick says.' She sighed heavily. Joe, she thought, might have been talked around. There would have been little fear of the super-intendent knowing the ins and outs of relationships in the teeming streets of the Cork slums, but Patrick was scrupulously truthful and honest. So, what could be done? She bit her lip and looked at the Reverend Mother who was watching a bright red Cadillac sweep up the narrow street, scattering, to left and right, horse and carts, the odd van and many messenger boys with overladen bicycles.

'Leave it with me,' said the Reverend Mother hurriedly to Eileen. 'I might be able to do something. I have an idea.'

Reluctantly, Eileen mounted her bike. After a moment's thought, she turned and went, not in the direction of the *Cork Examiner* – another reporter was covering the story of the fire and death in the cigarette factory, not back to her mother's house where she could study the law book on her course that she had borrowed only an hour ago, but back towards the university.

She knew what she was going to do. Lots of the professors at the university were fuddy-duddies, but there was a new law lecturer in criminal law, Tom Jenkins, who came from a place named Ashford in Kent in England, and he was a different matter entirely. He seemed to have a burning interest in the subject and Eileen had found him always interested in discussing legal matters. 'You should specialize in law regarding children,' he told her, once. 'No money in it, of course, but you'd do a bit of good in the world and that seems to be what you want to do.'

She had shrugged off his suggestion – money was important to her. She had her mother, prematurely aged by scrubbing floors almost every day of her life since her daughter was born and since the father of her baby had deserted her. Eileen had to be the breadwinner now. Her mother suffered from all the diseases that the fog-filled city made so common – asthma, arthritis and skin problems. She would, she thought, follow the suggestion of her boss that she go in for estate law. There was, he told her, good money in that.

Nevertheless, Professor Jenkins was an enthusiast for law reform and an enthusiast is always easy to guide into a discussion and so she rode her bike back up to the university and parked it outside the window of the gatekeeper's room – gave him a thumbs up – she really, she thought, should bring him a present one day as he guarded her bike for her and was a good friend.

And then she went down the stone-paved corridor and knocked on the door marked Professor Jenkins, Criminal Law.

'Come in!' The clipped English accent always sounded a bit forbidding. Eileen wondered for a second or two whether she should be disturbing a busy professor about a matter which could not possibly concern him, but then she thought of Maureen, muttered to herself: 'For Christ's sake! Fourteen years old and thrown into prison!' and she opened the door with a flourish and went straight in.

'Ah, Miss . . .' Didn't even remember her name, she thought. Nevertheless, she gathered her courage and went across the floor and stood with her hand upon the empty chair in front of his desk.

'Nothing to do with the syllabus or with a holiday essay or anything like that,' she said rapidly and saw him lay down his pen and look at her with an air of surprise. She tilted her chin and looked him straight in the eye.

'Ah, I think I remember you now,' he said, though he still could not recollect her name, she thought, and she bit her lip to choke back a quick response. The Reverend Mother, she thought fleetingly, knew not only the name of every child in her large school, but knew all about their families, about the circumstances in which they lived and was always the first refuge for their mothers when disaster struck.

'I need some information,' she said briskly. 'What's the law about imprisoning a girl of fourteen years and accusing her of murder because her employer was burned to death in the factory where she worked?'

Without waiting for an invitation, she picked up a chair from the row that had been neatly lined up beneath the window, brought it over to the desk, sat upon it, placed her elbows upon the table, cupped her chin within her hands and waited for his response.

'I think I know what you are talking about,' he said slowly. 'I heard some newspaper boys crying "Fire! One casualty!" when I was driving into work.' He looked at her in a puzzled fashion and said: 'What's it to do with you? Do you know that girl?'

She ignored that question. It was, she thought, unworthy of a professor of law.

'What's the law about slapping a fourteen-year-old child into gaol and accusing them of murder?' she asked abruptly.

He looked interested, leaned back in his chair, and eyed her with a half-smile.

'You know,' he said in a conversational tone, 'when I told someone that I was applying for a post in Cork city in southern Ireland, they stared at me. "What on earth do you know about Irish law?" That was the response from all my friends.'

'And what did you say to them?' Despite her annoyance and despite her desperate need to seek help for that unfortunate girl, she did like this sort of conversation.

'What do you think?' He parried the question, still with that half-smile.

She thought for a moment. 'You said that it is just the same in anything that regards the majority of the people in Britain. You probably should have added: *"Despite all the hopes, all the aspirations of those like Pádraig Pearse who gave his life for Ireland, except for a few changes that benefited farmers, things have just trotted on in the very same way as they were going twenty years ago."* You know, Professor,' she said, warming to her subject, 'Pádraig Pearse wrote about *"cherishing all children equally . . ."* now you tell me whether a fourteen-year-old daughter of a university professor, or of a solicitor, who ran away from a fire in the building where she worked, would this offspring of a professional person be held responsible for the death of the man who remained behind?'

'She knew that another person, a man, was in the building? And she did not give the alarm, made no effort to seek help?'

Eileen shrugged. 'I presume she did and no, I don't think she gave the alarm, just ran away. That must be the grounds for the arrest. I've seen the place. Very small. Just one room. I've seen how they work, also. The girls sit on the ground, on a tarpaulin which is heaped with dried and crushed leaves of the tobacco plant. They rub the stuff between their fingers and squeeze it into small tubes to make the cigarettes. I'd imagine that when they go home in the evening that the crumbs and dust on the tarpaulin are covered over with another tarpaulin or sheet. But the stuff would be bone dry and if a spark fell, then the whole place might go up in flames. I know nothing about it, Professor, I am just concerned with the legal point of whether the police were correct in putting a fourteen-year-old into prison.'

'I can answer that one straight away,' he said. 'Yes, under British law, and that makes it ninety-nine point nine, nine, nine per cent sure that it is also "yes" under Irish law. A bit harsh, yes, but certainly the police did not err.' He paused for a moment and looked at her curiously.

'You know this girl?' he asked again with a note of concern in his voice.

She nodded. 'We were born and brought up in the same slum district,' she said defiantly.

'I see.' He looked at her speculatively. 'Did you go to see her? Get her story?'

'The police wouldn't allow me. They are being very careful at the moment as the big white chief, the Commissioner from Dublin, is down inspecting the Cork Barracks. I had a quick word with the sergeant, but that was all. Only her mother or the aunt who is in *loco parentis* would be allowed to go in and see her, that's what he said. And her mother has gone off with a sailor and her aunt is looking after about ten children. Unless I pretend to be her mother, but the police won't wash that – they know me too well.'

'I see. In any case you're a bit young to pass as her mother. You're studying law, though. Surely you know that the girl could see her solicitor.'

Eileen smiled at that. 'I don't think that the people who live on Barrack Street go in for having a solicitor,' she said.

He shrugged his shoulders. 'Obviously not, but some benevolent person might be induced to devote some of his professional time to a charitable cause.'

Eileen caught her breath for a moment, was he going to offer? He read her expression and hastily said, 'Not me, I'm afraid.'

No, of course, she said to herself. He'd be too ambitious, too worried about getting a bad name. For a moment, she wondered about trying to pretend to be a solicitor, herself – after all she was on the way and she was an apprentice, but then she shook her head. 'It's no good me trying to pretend that I am a solicitor,' she said. 'Inspector Cashman, who is in charge of the case, has known me since I was a small child. He knows that I am not yet qualified. So does everyone else at the police barracks. I'm only an apprentice. The inspector is a very honourable man; he would never lie.'

'Would your leader, the solicitor that you are apprenticed to, would he undertake this as a charitable work? Who are you apprenticed to?'

'Mr Rupert Murphy,' said Eileen, and when she saw his eyes widen, she added hastily, 'He only took me on because his wife is the cousin of the Reverend Mother of the school where I did my Leaving Certificate. He took me on as a favour to her. I wouldn't dream of asking him to do this.'

'Probably the busiest and richest solicitor in Cork city, in any case,' commented the professor. 'Well, the best thing that you can do is find some evidence. Give the police something to do, some other possibilities to investigate, but as to the legal point that you brought up, I can assure you that the police are within their rights. Now . . .'

Eileen rose to her feet. She had got what she had come for, though for a few moments she had hoped for more. Nevertheless, there was no reason why he should have done more. She thanked him sedately and went back out to collect her bike.

Hopefully the Commissioner from Dublin would have returned to his own city by the next morning, and she could cross-examine Patrick and find out what really happened and what might have set the place on fire.

In the meantime, she thought, she should do some shopping for supper – go back to her own house and study the book that she had taken out of the library. The sooner she could qualify as a solicitor, the sooner she might be able to help the poor and the defenceless of Cork city. And as soon as the bigwigs from Dublin had left the Guards Barracks, she would do her best to talk Patrick around and get into the gaol and see that girl by some device or other. Message from the Reverend Mother, perhaps. Some sort of holy emblem like rosary beads or something. The Reverend Mother, though forbidden by the bishop to visit that gaol, could surely commission a respectable university student to carry a rosary to a past pupil who was, unfortunately, incarcerated in a prison cell. She would go and see her immediately and see what could be worked out, thought Eileen as she made a return journey down the Barrack Street and headed down towards St Mary's Isle.

TEN

In the meantime, the Reverend Mother had been entertaining her unexpected visitor. She had lived in the neighbourhood since she was eighteen years old, and had never, herself, felt unsafe, but one glance at the shining ostentatiousness of her visitor's red Cadillac car made her hastily open the convent gate. This street was not a safe environment for a car that was probably worth as much as the convent building itself.

Her cousin, Nell, steered the car into the playground just as, to the Reverend Mother's delight, a group of her infant class children who had been lingering outside in the street, unsure of what to do with themselves during the holidays and wanting to escape their chaotic, busy homes, stood gaping by the gates of the school. They stood aghast, staring wide-eyed at the shining perfection of the splendid car and the Reverend Mother wondered how she would keep them away from it. Her cousin Nell also cast rather a dubious glance at them as she dismounted from her seat, but then straightened her spine.

'Great! Super! Just what I wanted,' she said in the 'posh' accent expensively acquired during ten years at a distinguished boarding school in England – an accent which set her apart from the ordinary Cork inhabitants. 'I need some messengers to bring these boxes into the hallway,' she continued. 'And I brought some sweets for people who can do it without dropping anything.'

The Reverend Mother warmed towards her. That was unusually sensitive to arrive bearing sweets – a big jar of them, too, which her cousin hastily handed over to her. 'Won't do them any harm, Reverend Mother, just toffees, spend my life eating toffees and have still got most of my teeth. Ah, good, someone is organizing them. I'm no good with children, never manage to press the right button.'

'Sweets are a good first step, aren't they, Sister?' asked the

Reverend Mother with a smile at the children's teacher. Nevertheless, she kept a hold on the jar until everyone was standing politely in a neat row and then she handed the sweets to Sister Mary Angela with a loudly spoken injunction to only give the sweets to boys and girls who had been very good and had not touched their visitor's car. Despite the injunction there would be, she guessed, several dozens of sticky finger-marks on the shining paint before her visitor removed the car. It can be washed, she told herself, and judging by the shining perfection of the paint, it was often washed in this city where the damp air and the rain were laden with smuts, decomposed lumps of decay and particles of grime. The scrapes, bumps and scratches that she had seen down in Youghal had been expertly removed and the car was a piece of shining perfection.

'Your car is looking lovely,' she said admiringly.

'You're the second person to admire it today,' said Nell. 'I met the Lord Mayor himself on the quays and he stopped to admire it, too. Not a bad fellow, old Jimmy. Knows a good car when he sees it. I told him that it was time that his own car had a wash, but he just laughed and said that even with twenty washes it would never look like my Cadillac. Now let me open the boot and please come and see what I've brought you, Reverend Mother,' said Nell, casting an approving glance at the over-awed children. 'You might need someone bigger to carry some of these things,' she added as she looked at the size of the children. 'Perhaps some older children. Some of these boxes are very heavy. They are filled with books – children's books – don't know why I've left them hanging around the house for so long – you'll make good use of them.'

The Reverend Mother beckoned to a lay sister who was engaged in the everlasting task of cleaning the windows of the convent and was pleased to see that the arrival of Sister Bernadette who did love these charitable members of the Reverend Mother's family and friends and could be relied upon to 'ooh' and 'ah' at the goods which were donated.

The boot of the splendid car was filled with boxes and bags and Sister Bernadette, after one glance, summoned another couple of helpers from her own kitchen staff who were all loudly thanked and praised by Nell. The Reverend Mother looked upon her cousin with approval. Nell was known for her sharp manners all over the city of Cork, but she was probably politer to these humble lay sisters than she was to the Lord Mayor of Cork.

After a few minutes, Nell, in her impatient fashion, left the boxes to Sister Bernadette and her helpers and abruptly asked: 'Anywhere we can go?'

'Come into my study,' said the Reverend Mother and added, loudly enough for Sister Bernadette to hear, 'Would you like a cup of tea? Some refreshments?'

'Nothing, nothing at all,' said Nell decisively and even more loudly. 'Just finished my breakfast. You've all been up since dawn, I suppose, but I couldn't fit another crumb. Yes, let's go into your study. I want to have a few words with you.'

One of Sister Bernadette's helpers rushed to open, first the front door and then the door to the Reverend Mother's study, giving, out of habit, a quick knock on the door of the empty room and the Reverend Mother ushered her visitor inside.

'Got something else for you,' said Nell gruffily. She plunged a hand into her handbag and took out an envelope, stamped with the name of the Munster and Leinster Bank, Cork. On the outside of the envelope was printed in the neat script of a bank clerk, '£100.'

The Reverend Mother opened it quickly and then widened her eyes. She had expected to find a cheque for one hundred pounds made payable to the convent – a cheque which she would have to record as a charitable donation and place into the convent bank account. And, of course, anything spent from that donation would have to be strictly accounted for to the bishop's secretary – and probably the bishop himself would take an interest in such a substantial sum.

But, no. Inside the envelope were small bundles of five-pound and one-pound notes, held together with rubber bands, easily spent and could be totally unaccounted for. Her eyes met Nell's and she saw a mischievous smile on her cousin's face.

'Thought they might be of more use to you in small notes. Changing money at the bank is such a damn nuisance. You're bound to want to buy some bits and pieces from time to time without having to explain why you want it.'

'I feel like a child on Christmas morning,' said the Reverend Mother. She produced a bunch of keys and locked the money into the bottom drawer of her desk. This drawer was the only one without a label and it was the one which held most of her secrets. A gift like this should be encouraged and paid for with a bit of gossip and so she said in her most confidential tones: 'You're quite right. When I am making out my half-yearly accounts, there are, I have to admit, some items with which I don't like to shock the bishop's secretary – such as rat poison, for instance. I buy rat poison in quantities that would cause a lot of unwelcome questioning and perhaps have questions asked about Sister Bernadette's meticulous housekeeping.'

'What on earth do you want rat poison for?' Nell was, as she had expected, amused, and interested and so the Reverend Mother indulged her.

'Well, you see,' said the Reverend Mother, beginning to enjoy herself, 'I get Sister Bernadette to collect as many empty tins with good strong lids as she can – biscuit tins are the best. I put poison inside the tin, but before that I get one of Sister Bernadette's delivery men to bore holes in them – rat-sized holes – and I seal the lids with a strong glue that I get from that same kind man. And then I give the sealed tin boxes to the mothers of children who arrive in school with rat bites. The rats climb into the children's beds at night, you see, especially in the poorest of the houses where every crumb of food has been eaten up. This city, the flat of the city,' said the Reverend Mother calmly, 'is overrun with rats. You wouldn't know that as you live in Blackrock, and your friends live in Montenotte or Bishopstown and if they have business premises or offices in the city, like your garage man, for instance, then they just engage a couple of rat-catchers who diminish the numbers and leave some discreetly hidden lumps of rat poison in attics or basements or even, I regret to say, disguised with some tasty food outside their houses and back yards – where children often eat the food and then die a terrible death.'

She stopped for a moment, remembered the time when a

child ran, vomiting, through the school gates and died in the
school playground in the company of his appalled friends. She
had phoned instantly for Dr Scher, but it was all over before
he could arrive. Hastily she brushed the memory aside. It was
more important to care for the living than to mourn the dead.
She had long since trained herself to this.

'The bishop's secretary graciously funds four visits a year
from rat-catchers to this convent as we are so near to the river
here,' she said and added, 'the sealed tin box poison is purely
my own idea. The mothers in my school are not good at
keeping their children safe as they are either out at work, or
else are so worn down and exhausted by the struggle for life
that they ignore their children most of the time. Of course,'
she finished, 'the boxes smell of dead rats after a while, but
they can be thrown out and another asked for. I do quite a
trade in rat poison,' finished the Reverend Mother placidly.
'And, I must confess, that I have a secret rat-poison fund.'

'I'd love to tell this story at a dinner party!' Nell had an
amused smile upon her face and the Reverend Mother thought
about the matter for a few moments until her cousin said
hastily: 'But I won't betray you! Don't worry. You look
worried. You know that I wouldn't risk this story getting to
the bishop's ears.'

'I'm not sure that I care much,' said the Reverend Mother
slowly. 'Perhaps it is time that the wealthy and important
citizens of Cork knew what was going on in the slums. But
could I ask a *quid pro quo*?'

'Certainly! A story like this is worth something. Another
envelope filled with five-pound notes, what about that? I'm
sure that my bank balance would stand it.'

The Reverend Mother had a slight struggle with herself, but
there were more important matters than money. 'No,' she said
slowly. 'I have a favour to ask. Would you consider it very
indelicate of me if I were to ask you to visit the prison? There's
a child there, in a prison cell, a girl aged barely fourteen, who
is under suspicion of murder – the murder of your brother's
employee, the manager, Mr Timothy Dooley, of the cigarette
factory. Her mother is . . . away . . . well, let me be honest
. . . her mother, I've heard, is absent on a drinking spree with

a sailor from one of the ships on the quays. I made the mistake of asking the bishop's permission to visit my former pupil, but he has prohibited any contact. I took vows and I live my life, very satisfactorily, within their bounds. I owe obedience to the bishop, and I cannot break that rule. You are a person of repute in the city. You are a friend of the Lord Mayor who, apparently, is now in the police barracks greeting the Police Commissioner from Dublin . . .'

She stopped. Nell was on her feet. 'Leave it to me,' she said in a business-like manner. 'Come and keep these children out of the way, will you? I need to get out without worrying whether any of them are under my wheels. I'd better be fast if I hope to catch the Lord Mayor at the police station. Luckily, he is a great talker. The poor child. I'll make sure that she has justice,' she said as she pulled the door open. 'That manager, Mr Timothy Dooley! I knew that he would try it on with one of the girls,' she hissed as she hurried down the corridor.

And then she stopped and said in the Reverend Mother's ear, 'I hope she is not pregnant. Still, if she murdered him, it sounds as though she has enough gumption to kick and scream if he tried to rape her. Let's hope for the best, shall we? I'll get her out of there if I possibly can, but if I can't, I'll at least get her talking, get a solicitor to stand up for her in court if the worst comes to the worst. Don't worry about her. What's her name, by the way?'

'Maureen McCarthy,' said the Reverend Mother in a low voice. She hoped that the entire kitchen staff and possibly some of the girls were not listening in to this conversation. Still, she consoled herself with the thought that Maureen was not shy and this talkative lively cousin of hers might be just the person to put her former pupil at ease. In the meantime, all that she could do was to line up all the children and make sure that none impeded the bright red Cadillac on its rapid progress on to the street.

'Where's she going, Reverend Mother?' shouted Paddy McMahon.

'Going for the police! I bet she's going for the police! Isn't that right, Reverend Mother?' said his friend Jimmy Fitzpatrick.

'Going for the police!' The excitement spread through the children as the Reverend Mother listened with amusement.

'She's got a gun in the back of her car!

'And the bullets are in that big box under the back window. I *see'd* it.'

'Naw – that's an umbrella!'

'It's a gun. I *see'd* it, too.'

'She's after the robbers. She'll shout: "Hands up!" Like in that gangster film, *Dressed to Kill*. D'you remember it, Paddy?'

'She's driving at a hundred miles an hour just like Ritzy Logan!'

Dr Scher had told her that Paddy and Jimmy were regular cinema-goers as they had found out that six jam jars was the equivalent to two cinema tickets, so they spent most of their time after school collecting clean jam jars from the well-off Georgian houses on South Terrace where he lived. His own housekeeper always reserved her jam jars for them. Dr Scher had sworn her to silence as the two boys had not wanted any other children to know about the trade and, in any case, Dr Scher didn't want any more of them to come pestering his housekeeper. The Reverend Mother had been amused by the story. If this was an example of how their imagination had been triggered by these films, she rather approved of the cinema owner's initiative. It might, she thought optimistically, lead these children to books and to reading for pleasure.

In the meantime, she ushered them out of the school playground and back towards home, encouraging them to see if they could help their downtrodden mothers with any household chores. She herself decided to take a short walk down to southernmost stretch of St Mary's Isle. She had the utmost confidence in Patrick, but Mrs Maloney would have old-fashioned views on what could be said to men.

Mrs Maloney was delighted to see the Reverend Mother and quite happy to accept her refusal of a cup of tea and to accompany her on a walk between the wooden shed and the gate where the girls had supposedly waited for Maureen on that eventful night.

'All nonsense, of course,' she said scornfully. 'Men! Don't tell me that they are policemen, Reverend Mother. They're still men and my experience of men is that they haven't a brain between them. They will believe anything until the truth jumps up and bites them. That's my opinion, Reverend Mother. These lassies, strumpets, I'd call them if it wasn't for respect for your holy habit, well, they'd tell lies to everyone, would even try it on me, if you believe that, Reverend Mother, but give them a man and they'll tell so many lies that you'd hardly credit it.'

'I thought you might tell me what was going on,' said the Reverend Mother, picking a stray dandelion wisp from her black habit. 'You know how it is . . .' She gave a vague pointless gesture and waited.

Not in vain. It was, she thought, like opening a sluice gate.

Not a nice man – not a nice man, at all. Mrs Maloney was quite definite about that. No morals, at all. Got girls pregnant, and then abandoned them – didn't care what happened to them – didn't care what happened to the *babbies* neither. They could starve. And as for lies! Well, that man could tell lies to beat the band. The Reverend Mother, said Mrs Maloney, would be shocked to the core if she *heared* the lies that man would come out with – trying to ruin the character of decent, honest women. His mother, if he ever had a mother, would die of shame if she heard the lies he had told.

The Reverend Mother listened with interest. From the references to 'decent' 'honest' women, she deduced that the late manager, Mr Dooley, had perhaps been spreading rumours about Mrs Maloney. She found that interesting. Mrs Maloney, she had always assumed, from the frequency of her complaints about the citizens and the children of the city, was, herself, the very pink of perfection. She wondered what story the late, but unlamented Mr Dooley, had been spreading about Mrs Maloney, but was more alarmed to hear about the abuse of young girls. She wished that she had had a talk with Mrs Maloney earlier and perhaps then she could have had a word with her cousin about his suitability. That gave her an idea and she waited for a gap when Mrs Maloney stopped from sheer lack of breath and then inserted her remark.

'I'm surprised,' she said, 'that the manager of the cigarette factory got away with telling lies about people. There's a law about that, you know. If anyone told lies about me, I would get a solicitor to take them to court and they would be fined – have to pay me a substantial sum and might even be put into prison. Or was it just children and poor people that he told lies about? People who couldn't afford a solicitor?'

That interested Mrs Maloney, but after a minute she shook her head. 'You being a nun, you wouldn't understand. He'd tell such lies about you. What if the police would believe them lies? Wicked man!'

And with that, Mrs Maloney, in the first time of their acquaintance, thought the Reverend Mother, voluntarily and abruptly finished the conversation, and plunged back into her own house, shutting her front door with a determined slam.

Interesting, thought the Reverend Mother, as she turned to walk back to the convent. She nodded, smiled and exchanged a few words with a couple of women with babies tucked beneath shawls but her thoughts were still busy as she walked on. It did sound very like blackmail. And yet, Mrs Maloney was, to the best of her knowledge, an upright citizen with a huge respect for the law. What had the manager of the cigarette factory been up to during the few short weeks that he had spent in St Mary's Isle? And had he left a trail of hatred and apprehension behind him in the nearby seaside town of Youghal?

ELEVEN

Patrick was beginning to develop a headache. The superintendent kept his room very warm, and the window was tightly closed against the foul air of the city. He had been handed a glass of whiskey and was now sorry that he had, nervously, swallowed it down in one gulp. This, he knew, was an important occasion for him. In another few months the superintendent would retire, and he had a burning hope that he might be chosen to succeed him. He should, he knew, take an active part in the conversation, say something memorable, something astute, blending wit with intelligence, if possible, but words had deserted him, and he was painfully conscious that ten minutes by the superintendent's clock had gone by without any contribution from him while the Cork Lord Mayor and the Commissioner from Dublin, the top policeman in the country, and his own boss, the Superintendent of Cork Police, exchanged anecdotes about city policing.

He was relieved when there was a knock on the door. Tommy, he thought, judging by the characteristic triple tap upon the door panel. Hopefully a summons for him – a riot on the quays, or even a case of shoplifting in one of the posh Patrick Street stores where the owner was rich enough and important enough to demand the presence of Inspector Cashman himself. The visitor didn't stop talking, but the superintendent jerked his head and thankfully Patrick went to the door.

Tommy wore his most officious demeanour. 'A lady here to see the Lord Mayor,' he said in a loud whisper, guaranteed to penetrate to every ear in the room. 'She's got a bright red Cadillac car,' he added.

What's her name, you fool? Patrick mimed the writing of a quick note upon his hand, but Tommy was not taking a hint, just smiling smugly across the room at the Lord Mayor.

And, of course, he was right. The Lord Mayor, who had

reached the end of his anecdotes about civil crime, immediately got to his feet.

'It will be Miss Nell, Miss Nell Murphy,' he said with a self-important manner. 'Probably wants to find out what happened to her brother's cigarette factory. He probably sent her. I met her this morning. Exchanged a word when we were both stuck in one of those awful morning traffic jams.' He looked at the superintendent, who looked at his boss from Dublin, but the Lord Mayor was having none of this.

'Tell Miss Nell to come in,' he said to Tommy, and Tommy, always one to recognize who was the most important person in the room, disappeared without a second glance at his own boss. Patrick felt better. This Miss Nell might have come to see about the factory fire, or she might have come about something quite different. Whatever it was, it would give him an opportunity to show that he could take immediate action. He got to his feet and walked towards the door. He remembered the woman and the car that she drove. Narrowly missed being taken to court on a few occasions – probably greased the constable's palm, he thought grimly. Nevertheless, she was sister to the owner of the cigarette factory, and it was up to him to see what brought her to the police station. He would, he planned, take her into his own room on some pretext, and that would get him out of this over-warm, over-chummy atmosphere while showing some authority and enterprise.

She foiled his effort, though. Was ready with a spot of drama. Rushed down the corridor, ahead of Tommy, swung open the door before he could reach it and bounced into the room.

'Oh, thank goodness you are still here,' she said to the Lord Mayor. 'Have you heard? I've been with the Reverend Mother, and she told me that the person who has been arrested for the death of the cigarette factory manager, Mr Timothy Dooley, is a mere child! A mere child, my Lord Mayor! We can't have this in our city, can we?' she appealed to his lordship. 'We don't put little girls in prison, here in Cork, do we, my Lord Mayor? The Reverend Mother is very upset about the matter. A child just out of school! How can she be held guilty of murder? I appeal to you.'

The Reverend Mother must have worked upon her, thought

Patrick. Or else she was incredibly naive. Children were put in prison every week, most of them for a short time, he tried to ensure, but there was nothing in the laws of Ireland that stopped this happening. Nevertheless, he jumped at the opportunity which she afforded.

'I'll see to this matter, sir, shall I?' he said to his own superintendent, but with an eye to the man from Dublin.

Both, he noticed, had instinctively and immediately looked at the table still laden with whiskey and beer, backed up with a large plateful of strawberry tarts, topped with cream, and some more robust cheese sandwiches.

'Carry on, Inspector,' said the Cork Superintendent, while the Dublin Commissioner nodded approval and glanced at the half-full bottle of whiskey.

'The inspector will sort matters out for you, Miss Nell,' said the Lord Mayor, suppressing a hiccup and taking a quick swig from his whiskey glass. 'Very efficient man, Inspector Cashman,' he said graciously. 'You can have complete confidence in him, my dear. You'll sort the matter out, Inspector, won't you?'

'Certainly, sir.' Patrick was on his feet, hoping desperately that this Miss Nell would forget the time when he had flagged her down on the Straight Road, and had told her that she was driving far too fast. To his relief, though, she smiled at him in a friendly fashion and waved a quick goodbye to the Lord Mayor.

'Come with me,' said Patrick, trying desperately to remember her name. She might be Miss Murphy, but then, again, she might be married; the Lord Mayor might be in the habit of calling her Miss Nell since her youth. He tried to compensate for the lack of a formal address by smiling in a friendly fashion and to his relief she smiled back and as soon as the door shut, she said: 'The Reverend Mother is my cousin, well, my father's cousin, and she speaks very highly of you.'

She said no more while they walked together down the long corridor and spoke only to decline Tommy's offer of refreshments but once the door was safely closed behind them, she came to the point instantly.

'The Reverend Mother is very worried about that child being

in prison and no one to be able to visit and to advise her. Apparently, the mother is absent – on a drinking spree with a sailor, – fun for all, I suppose, but not good for that poor child,' she said briskly, while Patrick did his best not to blush with embarrassment at this plain speaking from a well-dressed lady.

'Obviously the Reverend Mother does not want to interfere with the process of the law,' she added, 'but just to make sure that the girl is treated as, perhaps, your own daughter would be.' She had a slightly mischievous air as she spoke and Patrick, to his annoyance, felt a warm blush heat his face.

'But, of course, you are far too young to have a daughter, aren't you? How marvellous to be an inspector at your young age! You were a pupil of the Reverend Mother – not so long ago, isn't that right, Inspector? So she told me. She is very proud of you and knew that you would understand her concern for the child. She really does have a very high opinion of you, you know.'

She had a teasing note in her voice and Patrick relaxed. She had come from the Reverend Mother and the Reverend Mother was relying upon her to help young Maureen McCarthy. He despised himself for not challenging the superintendent about that arrest, but at the time to say nothing seemed to be the only thing to do.

'The superintendent felt that the evidence was very strong and that there might be a fear that the girl would disappear, just like her aunt. He felt that it was imperative to have her under lock and key until we could establish the basic facts,' he said aloud, suppressing all thoughts of Maureen spitting in the superintendent's face.

To his relief she nodded in an understanding manner.

'You were probably right. No point in making a fuss and putting that man's back up – he's your boss, isn't he? Not too bright, from all that I have heard. Left over from the old regime. Now let's put our heads together. What actually happened?'

Patrick told her all – related the evidence of the close neighbour and that of the girls. He was surprised how patiently she listened to everything. He had had an impression of her as an impatient sort of person who flew around the city, driving that bright red Cadillac at a ridiculous speed. But now she listened carefully, nodding from time to time, to his account of the other evidence, to the arrangement that Joe and his constable had made to ensure that each girl's evidence was unaffected by what had been said before, though she smiled a little at that and said: 'You don't know girls, Inspector, the Reverend Mother and I could guess, straight away, that the little monkeys would get together beforehand and agree on a story. Still, I mustn't interrupt. Go on with your account, Inspector.'

Patrick blinked. He had great confidence in the Reverend Mother's astuteness and if she thought that the girls had the foresight to agree upon a story before the police had had a chance to interview them – well, the Reverend Mother knew more about girls than either he or even Joe could possibly know. He picked up the thread of his narrative and had hardly finished the last words when she was upon her feet, marching up and down his room.

'Well, some other suspect will have to be found, isn't that right, Inspector?' she said decisively. 'An unpleasant man like that must have lots of enemies.'

Patrick nodded, but without replying he lifted the telephone receiver and dialled Joe's number.

'Joe, could you bring in the statement made by Maureen McCarthy and those made by the other girls, also, please. I have Miss Murphy here in my office and the Reverend Mother has asked her to look into the question of Maureen McCarthy, aged fourteen,' he said in his most formal of voices.

Joe, he knew, would not remind Inspector Cashman that he had copies of the statements in his own desk. Joe was quick-thinking and discreet and would immediately guess that Patrick wanted a witness while giving information to a talkative lady like Miss Murphy. In the meantime, Patrick passed the time by leafing through his notebook and hoping that his expression would deter the lady from talking until Joe came in.

He didn't have long to wait. A perfunctory tap on the door and Joe was inside, managing to greet Miss Murphy with a respectful bow of the head, arrange the sheets in a fancy, overlapping line in front of Patrick and then seat himself on a chair in the background, notebook at the ready and indelible pencil in hand.

'Very businesslike,' said Miss Murphy with an approving nod. 'Now, just so as I understand matters, the girl, Maureen McCarthy, denied that she had started the fire, but admitted that she had stayed behind after the others left.'

Patrick picked up the piece of paper in front of him and read aloud. '*We was quicker than usual and when I went out the girls were still waiting for me, and we all went home together.*' Patrick picked up another piece of paper and read it and then put it down. 'When asked what the manager, Mr Timothy Dooley, was doing when she left, she said that he was getting out his whiskey bottle as usual,' he said. 'We asked about the two mugs on the table, and she seemed puzzled. Her reply was that she hadn't noticed the two mugs, so she said. Hadn't seen a sign of fire and hadn't used the outhouse "*convenience*" before she went. Tried not to use it unless she had to because it "*stank, and it never got enough earth or sawdust thrown in on top of it.*" These were her words, Miss Murphy. The "*convenience*" was an outdoor lavatory built for the girls' privacy, I understand that the Reverend Mother requested that of the owner,' he added, with an effort not to appear embarrassed.

'And the other nine girls backed up her statement about there being no sign of smoke or fire when they left, is that right?' Miss Nell Murphy had listened very carefully and without interrupting, and Patrick had begun to relax and think that he could handle her interference.

'They went before she did – normally a couple of hours, according to our witness, but Maureen McCarthy said that she left early that night, at almost the same time as her friends – at six o'clock,' said Patrick.

'And the fire was discovered at eight o'clock, that's right, isn't it? So I can't see why Maureen McCarthy is under suspicion if her friends back up her statement that she left, with them, at six o'clock.'

Patrick began to feel that this was like being harangued by a lawyer in court – except that he had never had a female lawyer do that before.

'They might not be considered very good witnesses, because of their age and their friendship with the accused,' he explained. 'Whereas Mrs Maloney, as an elderly lady who has never been in trouble with the police and who could have no possible reason to lie, would by judge and jury be considered to be a good witness.'

'I bet that she is a sour old cat,' said Miss Murphy and Patrick wondered what he should say in reply to this statement. Joe, he noticed, was picking some minute speck from the cuff of his trouser leg and was of no help, so he decided to ignore the comment. The sooner he got rid of this woman, the better. The Lord Mayor had announced to her, 'the Inspector will sort matters out for you' and his own superintendent had told him 'Carry on' and so he would. The Reverend Mother had sent her for a purpose, and it had been a good idea. Quickly he addressed Joe.

'Would you escort Miss Murphy to the prison, Sergeant? Since we were not able to get her mother or even her aunt, the Reverend Mother thinks it would be good to have a lady to visit her and it might be a good idea to bring Eileen as well if you can get hold of her.'

'Good idea, sir,' said Joe and got to his feet instantly. 'Come with me, Miss Murphy. You won't mind if we go in the police jalopy, will you. A bit of a comedown from your posh Cadillac, but there are a lot of dubious characters hanging around the gaol so it might be better to leave it here. Don't worry about it. Tommy, our doorkeeper, and constable, will guard it with his life!'

Joe was good with people like Miss Murphy, better than I am, thought Patrick. But then he, Patrick, was better with the rough and tough characters down on the quays at night. They made a good pair. *If I get the job of superintendent, I'll insist that Joe gets the job of inspector*, he told himself as he went back over the statements about the murder of Mr Timothy Dooley of the newly erected cigarette factory.

He had started to put away all the statements when the door of his room was re-opened, without a preliminary knock.

'I've just thought of something, Inspector,' said Miss Murphy. 'What happens if she did do it, if she did start a fire and cause the man to die from the smoke? Remember I am talking about a fourteen-year-old girl! Don't you think that we should be prepared for some new evidence to come to light, perhaps another old nosy cat, spying on what went on with these ten girls and a man with a reputation like that Tim Dooley!'

Patrick stared at her. What game was she playing now? His eyes went to Joe who was standing behind, but Joe looked as surprised as he felt. Miss Murphy didn't hesitate though. One of those women who had a solution to every problem.

'He seduced her, of course,' she said in an off-hand fashion. 'Could even have raped her. I noticed his eyes on her that day down in Youghal where they had the *Cork Examiner* taking photographs and everything. I guessed that there would be trouble. The man was a rapist. I knew that. What we need is a newspaper campaign – not to spell it out, of course, but to hint at it delicately, just imply without leaving any room for legal actions or anything. I'll have a word with that girl who was taking down details for the *Cork Examiner*. She looked to be a bright spark. She's the one that we are going to bring, isn't that right?' She lowered her voice to a loud whisper and hissed: 'We don't want that gormless superintendent jumping on to new evidence and sending the poor child to the gallows, now do we, Inspector? But if we have a newspaper campaign going and women going around Patrick Street saying: *"Did you ever? Isn't it a shame?"*'

Patrick wondered whether Eileen could deal better with this outspoken woman than he could do. Perhaps Joe could do something about putting the pair of them into an investigating team. In the meantime, knowing that she was part of the family of the man who owned the factory, he was justified in listening to what she had to say. And there was no doubt that she had plenty to say. By now, Joe had edged her back into the room and had closed the door behind them. She took no notice of that but put her hands on Patrick's desk and launched her attack.

'Why couldn't it have been an accident?' she queried, looking at him closely. 'Why does someone have to be blamed for this death?'

'There was no fireplace in the shed, Miss Murphy,' he said, speaking slowly and deliberately. 'And no need for one, really, I suppose, in a workplace with nice thick wooden walls and the girls busy all the time. I've enquired and there was a rule that no one should smoke a pipe or even a cigarette within the shed, or factory, I should perhaps call it. The fire had to be started deliberately and if the witness is correct – she is a local person who lives close to the factory – if what she says is correct it started a considerable time after the other nine girls had left the factory. The Fire Brigade say that it was started outside the factory, at the back. The shed itself is made from wood, so the wall between caught fire very quickly. And, of course, it was easy to start a fire outside without being seen as it appears it was started just inside the outhouse that had been built for the girls' convenience . . . for the girls . . . the Reverend Mother demanded it of the owner. Of course, these girls were there more than nine hours a day so that they had to have somewhere . . .' Patrick stopped, conscious that embarrassment had caused a flush to warm his face. Joe and he must find some decent and less-embarrassing term for that little wooden outhouse before they finished their report, he thought as he covered his embarrassment by riffling through some papers. How had the *Cork Examiner* handled it? he wondered.

'I understand your meaning,' she said with a slightly mocking smile which annoyed him. 'I can see now how the girl was blamed, but surely anyone from outside could have slipped into that place. Did it have a lock?'

'I believe that the place did not have a door,' said Patrick stiffly. He had inspected it himself, but he didn't see why he had to be interrogated about all the details by this bossy woman. A filthy place, even after the fire, but there was a solid wooden wall between it and the factory, so the smell was probably only noticeable to the girls who used it.

'Apparently a load of sawdust had been delivered two days ago to lessen the smell and that, of course, the sawdust being soaking wet, made the fire smoke badly,' he said, once again taking refuge in his notebook.

She grimaced, but to his relief did not pursue the subject.

He gave Joe an appealing look and slightly jerked his head in the direction of the door.

Joe did not fail him. Immediately he was on his feet and a second later he held the doorknob in his hand.

'Well, we'll be off then, Miss Murphy,' he said, 'We'll pick up Eileen first if we can and then go down to the gaol. You can meet young Maureen McCarthy and you can see what the girl has to say for herself. You'll be interested to meet the reporter, Eileen, too. A very intelligent girl. Studying to be a lawyer, you know.'

Still talking, Joe edged the woman out, closed the door on Patrick. Their footsteps echoed down the corridor and a few minutes later the police barracks car, that humble Baby Ford car, passed the window. Patrick heaved a sigh of relief, shook his head, and went back to his desk. He would have another word with Dr Scher, he decided. His notes on the autopsy would be finished by now and who knows but there might be some interesting details for him. He lifted the receiver and had to wait some time before Tommy condescended to answer. Probably outside, admiring the red Cadillac, he guessed and swore, for the umpteenth time, that if ever he were put in charge of the police barracks, he would order an outside line to be installed in his own office and make sure that there was no way that Tommy could listen into his conversations.

'Get me Dr Scher, please, Tommy,' he said curtly as soon as the receiver had been lifted in the outer office. Dr Scher had conducted autopsies for the police ever since Patrick was a schoolboy. He had been retired from general practice for many years but still was as busy as ever, lecturing in Forensic Pathology at Cork University and giving free medical care to the poor and destitute of the city slums as well as doing his work for the police in a city where death by violence was a weekly occurrence. Patrick had a very high opinion of him and knew that he could always be trusted to be discreet.

'Patrick! I thought that I'd be having you on the phone after our meeting earlier this morning. I can give you the autopsy findings if you're available.'

'Yes, Dr Scher, thank you.' As far as Patrick could tell, Tommy wasn't listening in, but it was best to assume that he was. 'The cause of death was smoke inhalation according to you. Does that still hold?'

'Still holds. Pretty easy to guess with one look at the corpse. He was as blue as the sky in cities where they don't have fog nine days out of ten. Lack of oxygen, Patrick. Even the young fellow not long out of college was able to diagnose that. Did all the usual things, gave him oxygen, pumped his heart, all no good. Brought him to hospital, of course, but nothing could be done. Why don't you pop over and see me? I'm at the convent at this moment, visiting a couple of elderly nuns. I'll be here for another twenty minutes or so, but I have a lecture booked in an hour at the university, so I won't have time to drop into you, but there are a few interesting points . . .' Dr Scher's voice tailed off.

Patrick tightened his lips with annoyance. 'Can't,' he said. 'Joe has taken the police car, driving Miss Nell Murphy to the prison to talk to that girl, Maureen McCarthy, about this case. Picking up Eileen on the way. I don't expect them back for some time.'

There was a silence at the other end of the line and then a stifled sneeze. A moment later Dr Scher's voice came back on the line, sounding his usual decisive self. 'I'll tell you what, Patrick,' he said. 'Why don't I leave a note for you with the Reverend Mother? You can pick it up at your leisure.'

And then he rang off. A busy man and an astute one, was Dr Scher. Would guess that Tommy would be listening in. Probably had caught him at it a couple of times. That sneeze always betrayed a man who suffered from chronic head colds, as did Tommy.

As for the note, well, Patrick knew that Dr Scher had a very high opinion of the Reverend Mother's discretion – had probably discussed everything with her so he doubted whether he would have bothered writing a note, knowing that she would keep his words secret. He looked at the clock on his office wall. Twelve forty-five. As the school was on holiday the Reverend Mother would have slightly more leisure time than usual. Nonetheless, he didn't want to arrive as she was eating her dinner so he might as well go now. He would have to go back into the superintendent's room, first of course.

Common politeness dictated that he should be around when the Lord Mayor and the Chief Superintendent made their farewells, or else he would have to leave the building before they did, having first paid his respects, and now Dr Scher had given him a way out. He would hint at a new and interesting development which he had to probe instantly and take his leave of them. Hopefully that would mean that he did not have to drink any more whiskey or listen to any more of these boring and stale anecdotes.

The Dublin superintendent was very cordial with him. Shook him warmly by the hand, congratulated him upon his many successes during his time at the turbulent city of Cork – a terrible place for murders, according to the man from Dublin. Patrick preserved a discreet silence on that matter and murmured something about how much he had learned on the job since he had joined the Barrack Street barracks so many years ago. To his slight astonishment, his own superior patted him upon his back and murmured: 'Good lad, good lad!'

The effect of all the whiskey, perhaps, thought Patrick. Nevertheless, he was touched and pleased and hoped that he could make a success of solving this crime which by now was the talk of the whole town. To have the matter neatly wrapped up would be a source of great satisfaction to the old man before he retired – a man who had been, in his own way, kind to Patrick since his arrival at the barracks as a tongue-tied young recruit.

TWELVE

No sign of Dr Scher's battered old Humber car when Patrick, after a brisk walk, during which he was forced to greet what seemed like a hundred people, all intrigued by his presence, on foot, in the streets and on the bridges of the South Parish, arrived at the convent gate. The place was strangely quiet without the sound of children's voices on this late July morning and Patrick suddenly wondered whether the Reverend Mother ever went away on holiday, ever escaped from the murk of the city to have a week's holiday by the sea. He put the question to her when Sister Bernadette ushered him into her study, and she laughed at the idea.

'My work doesn't stop when the school holidays begin, Patrick,' she said with a note of amusement. 'Already this morning I've had one distraught woman who has been given notice to quit by a landlord – thankfully a man that I have a certain influence over – his great-grandfather and my grandfather were business partners at some stage. And then I had someone who is having trouble with rats, so I had to see to that for her – and then three shopkeepers who are having trouble with a gang of seven-year-olds who had been caught stealing – oddly enough, Patrick, it usually is the six- and the seven-year-olds,' she said, 'and why do you think that is? You're looking puzzled, well, I'll tell you. You see children don't seem to go in for shoplifting until they are about six years old and then these younger ones aren't very good at it, so they get caught, get a slap probably but the goods are retrieved. And, of course, once they are older than seven, well they tend to be experienced and able to get away without being seen. Some of them, apparently, tie a bit of an old shawl over their faces and hair, or even blacken their faces with burned cork so that they can't be recognized and described, either to me or to your constable. But the children of six and seven don't seem to go in for disguise and, also, they tend to be slower than the older ones and the shopkeepers memorize a description and mostly come around to tell me about the crime. School holidays are a nuisance for shopkeepers, you know, Patrick – one irate man told me that a couple of months ago. He wasn't too sympathetic when I said that teachers need holidays. Went away muttering that he hadn't had a holiday since he was a kid. Anyway, let's forget my troubles. You have troubles of your own.'

Patrick nodded. Face to face with the Reverend Mother he felt quite shamefaced about the imprisonment of a girl just out of school.

'I'm very worried about Maureen McCarthy being in that gaol cell,' he said. Normally, he took immense care never to criticize the superintendent, knowing that in this city of Cork stories were wafted from street corner to street corner; from one pub to another. Nevertheless, the Reverend Mother was safe. He knew that. He had once asked her to keep secret a matter that he had discussed with her, and she had laughed at him.

'Patrick,' she had said, 'my mind is full of closets, each of them firmly closed and locked once a conversation is finished. There will be no chance that any whisper should ever emerge of what you have told me in confidence.'

And so he explained his fears regarding Maureen's arrest, about how she wasn't helping herself with her attitude and refusal to explain what had happened. He told her about the witness statements from the other girls and about the Fire Brigade chief's thoughts on where and how the fire had started in the privy and the hole with the petrol soaked around it.

'So, the fire was started there. What a clever idea using the petrol. And, of course, the workplace itself was made from wood so the fire spread.'

'It smouldered,' said Patrick. 'You see since the . . . the convenience itself was very wet, no roof and filled with wet . . . well, with wet matter, and . . . a big heap of wet sawdust that the owner sent up from his lands in Youghal – left over after some tree cutting, I understand – and then the floor is just earth and . . . the big hole is . . . Well, it's been soaked around the hole with petrol, but as everything else is wet and the wooden walls of the workplace were soaked, of course, not just because of its . . . well, its function, but also from the days of rain and fog that we've had for the last week or two, well – the fire didn't really catch and in the end, there was just smoke, no fire. I suppose that if it were started deliberately, it was expected that the place would have burned down.'

'Possibly,' said the Reverend Mother doubtfully. 'On the other hand, fire attracts much more attention than smoke. My dear Patrick, you must know for yourself that this is a city full of smoke. Everywhere you walk, in these damp and foggy days, with such low pressure, you see smoke drifting from chimneys and often out from open windows and doors. Flames and the noise of crackling wood immediately attract attention, and they would cause a passer-by to send for the fire engines, but smoke is part of the general landscape in Cork – smoke and fog; they blend together over our skies – as you know well, Patrick. But, of course, smoke, when it gets into the lungs, can be as deadly, or even more deadly than fire. The heat and noise of fire cause people to flee whereas drifting smoke is ignored or might even lull the intended victim to sleep, especially if they had imbibed a certain amount of alcohol.'

'I'm sure that you are right,' said Patrick. He took out his notebook and made a three-word note: smoke, sleep, *stocious*. He would not, of course, use the Cork slang word '*stocious*' meaning 'totally intoxicated' in his report when he wrote it up, but there in the privacy of his notebook it instantly evoked a scene of a drunken man, sleeping heavily, and imbibing the fatal smoke . . .

'My concern in this matter, of course, is the child, Maureen McCarthy. I would say, if you were to ask me, Patrick, that she is not clever. It does seem to me that anyone who devised this death by smoke, when the man was thoroughly intoxicated, and getting hold of the petrol, showed a certain evidence of brains and after knowing Maureen for about ten years, I have never seen evidence of any superior plotting on her part. Maureen, I think, got her own way by her influence over her fellow pupils. There are, were, other girls in that class who had superior brain power and I do feel that for a fourteen-year-old, fairly uneducated, and quite untalented, girl to devise the scenario where she started a smoking fire in what you call "the convenience" and then went off without disturbing the man that she left behind, well, it doesn't sound like the Maureen that I knew.'

'Don't you think that it was more likely that she left the shed, the factory as they call it, when he was fast asleep and then lit the fire in the outside convenience,' said Patrick.

The Reverend Mother shook her head. 'You are forgetting Mrs Maloney. Didn't she say something about smelling smoke before she sent for the Fire Brigade? That seems a bit quick, even for Mrs Maloney, if Maureen was just walking away. I don't suppose that Maureen would have a lawyer if it were brought to court, but certainly a good lawyer would make that argument.'

'It's a good point,' said Patrick. 'But you know, Reverend Mother, at this stage I'm not worrying about how things would sound in court. I'm worrying about finding out exactly what happened. I'll leave the court business to lawyers.'

It was a brave speech. And he wasn't sure that he should have said it and was relieved when he saw her head nod.

'You are quite right, Patrick,' the Reverend Mother bowed her head and added: 'My patron saint, Thomas Aquinas, says: "*Veritas super omnia regnet*" – that truth shall reign above all things. By the way, Dr Scher left a message for you.' She fumbled in her capacious pocket and produced, first a couple of rather sticky sweets, fortunately wrapped in paper, which she arranged upon her desk and then a small piece of well-folded paper which she handed to Patrick.

He opened it and it read: 'No sign of recent sexual intercourse.' He glanced, rather dubiously, at the Reverend Mother and to his embarrassment saw that she was smiling.

'A very old-fashioned man, Dr Scher,' she remarked. 'I wonder whether he thinks that I lead my life ensconced within a glass house. It's of importance, though, isn't it? Means there was no rape, no real reason for Maureen to kill a man who was providing her with a weekly wage. Of course,' proceeded the Reverend Mother loftily, 'that's not to rule out that he might have imposed some unwanted – what is it called – "slap and tickle" – is that the expression, or perhaps some other form of sexual amusements, but he obviously did not rape her. Not on that occasion, anyway,' she added calmly.

Patrick made a note and kept his face down for a moment, taking out his pocketknife and sharpening his indelible pencil into the Reverend Mother's wastepaper basket. After a minute, he recovered his equilibrium.

'Not the sort of place for something like full intercourse to occur, in any case,' he said trying his best to sound casual and unembarrassed. He wondered whether he would have to ask Dr Scher to question the girl about a possible pregnancy. It was bound to be brought up by the legal team at the courthouse – that fellow who led the legal team there was a genius at asking unpleasant questions about the past life of unfortunates who were brought to court for some crime or even misdemeanour. To his horror he saw her purse her lips and hoped that the discussion of this matter was not going to go on. She had a thoughtful look about her, but, to his relief, came up with a different point.

'You know,' she said, 'I doubt that Maureen had much moral training at home, and, unfortunately, the home is of great importance in these matters. The girls, when they come to Maureen's age, tend to brush aside what the nuns say and follow the example of their mothers or their elder sisters. Maureen's mother or her aunt would not have proved to be a good example to her daughter. What I can talk about, though, is her character. She had a tough nature and would not easily be led astray if the bribe was not substantial. I honestly, and I have thought about this very carefully, Patrick, and I cannot see the slightest advantage to Maureen McCarthy to plan, execute, or even to go along with a plot to murder this manager, Mr Timothy Dooley. If he had imposed any sexual intimacy upon her, I think that she would have demanded a price, threatened disclosure, but not murdered him. That, in Maureen's view, I would imagine, would have been killing the goose that laid the golden eggs; and could probably be persuaded to lay some more,' she added in a matter-of-fact manner.

Patrick tried not to look shocked. The Reverend Mother, he knew, spoke to him as the upholder of the law in the city area of Cork and as such she spoke openly, and honestly, and it behoved him to reply in the same fashion. He found it very hard, though, to talk about such matters to an elderly nun. He would, he thought, go and have a conversation with someone at the local fire station on Sullivan's Quay. Man to man, it would be much easier to discuss these matters about fire and smoke with someone who must, by now, be an expert on all such deaths in the city of Cork.

It was, though, he thought, imperative to find out the truth about that girl. That arrest, although it had been not his decision, but the decision of his superior officer, should have been, at least, questioned by him, and he felt bitterly sorry about it now. He should not have done it to a fourteen-year-old who was, for all practical purposes, without protection.

'I must get back to the barracks and draw up a list of possible suspects,' he said. He got to his feet, but he was conscious of a tentative note in his voice. And many questions in his mind.

'The trouble is that the man did not come from Cork and I'm not sure whether the superintendent would like me to go down to Youghal just now. You see he has the Commissioner from Dublin with him and he's busy. I don't think he would like me to be absent for a few hours. Youghal must be a good two hours' drive, there and back,' he went on, 'and then there is the question of hours spent finding out about the man and seeing whether there is anyone who might bear him a grudge or else profit from the death in some way. I'll have to postpone that visit to another day.'

'There is always the telephone,' suggested the Reverend Mother. 'Make them come to you. For today, at least. You are a busy man, Patrick, and your first duty is to the people of Cork. I'm sure that Youghal, which I seem to remember is a fair-sized town, will have its own constabulary who should be of assistance to you. In the meantime, I can give you a few pieces of gossip which I've picked up, though I'm very sure that the bishop may not approve of a nun taking part in gossip.' She gave a mischievous smile and then continued quietly,

'But my former pupils always have a large part of my heart

and if I can help you in any way, then it seems to me that that is the right thing for me to do.' She raised a hand – 'No, don't thank me. Causing the death of any human being is a horrendous crime and it is the duty of all citizens to assist in bringing that criminal to justice and ensure that such a person can never take the life of another person. Now let me tell you the little that I know. Here is a piece of paper and you are, I know, always equipped with your indelible pencils so you can write down what I say and do what you wish with the knowledge after I have given it to you. Now do sit here at my desk. It will be easiest for you to write there.'

She stopped and waited while Patrick sharpened his pencil and arranged the sheet of paper in front of him. When he was ready, she proceeded.

'This man, the manager, was not a pleasant character, from what I've been told and from what I observed myself. The most serious matter of which I have heard him accused was the rape of the daughter of the gardener who works in the fields as well as in the gardens for my cousin. The girl was raped and was made pregnant by him.'

'The gardener, that's the man who has been working on the building of what they call the cigarette factory. That's right, isn't it?' Patrick made a note upon the piece of paper.

'That's right,' said the Reverend Mother. 'From what I've been told he was accused of raping the gardener's daughter. Made her pregnant and then said it was at the girl's invitation. Refused to marry her. His employer sacked him but then took him back, saying that it was one person's word against another's, as the man denied the charge. I would guess that the gardener was quite angry about this,' she added. 'He may have even vowed to have vengeance upon a man who had treated his daughter so badly.'

Patrick finished writing and then looked up at her expectantly. It was a moment before she spoke again.

'I think, Patrick,' she said, 'that when you find a person is morally lax enough to hurt a person in one way, that it is seldom that they will not be found guilty of cheating or injuring another person, also. I think that if I were you that I would look into the dead man's relationship with fellow workers –

after all there was a large number of people working upon that estate and you may find that others, as well as the gardener, have a grudge against him, or indeed a mortal hatred. I must say that when I was chatting with the men who were putting up the outside wall of the building, I very much got the impression that the manager, Mr Timothy Dooley was disliked and despised by most of them.' She hesitated for a moment, and then said, 'It was such an easy way to kill someone, was it not? After all, anyone local who observed that this man stayed late of an evening, probably later even than Maureen McCarthy, and that when he left for the evening, before he returned to Youghal in the train, he threw away an empty bottle of whiskey – anyone who had seen him do that would guess that the man would be drunk and from what I understand, drink brings on a desire to sleep. Mrs Maloney is, I think, my informant upon that matter. So, you see, it could have been someone lurking among the marshy plants who might have done the deed without ever been suspected.'

'But not Mrs Maloney, I suppose,' said Patrick with a smile.

There was a silence for a moment. Patrick lifted his eyes from the sheet of paper and looked across at the Reverend Mother. She looked, he thought, very tired and he felt some compunction at continuing to interrogate such a very busy and hard-working person. He got to his feet.

'Thank you, Reverend Mother,' he said. 'You always help me to sort out my ideas; I think that I know where to go next.' He knew that his voice sounded sincere. She did not ask him what he was going to do, or mention the name of the girl again. She just bowed her head.

'I have great confidence in you, Patrick,' she said, and he did think that there was a note of sincerity in her voice. 'I like the way that you progress through your enquiry so very carefully and meticulously,' she added, and he felt proud of himself and determined to earn that praise. Back to the Barracks, he said to himself. He would let himself in by the back door and avoid any further socializing and drinks. He needed to talk with Joe and sort his ideas out.

But first, as soon as he got back to his office, he would

telephone the Youghal police station and see what they could add in the way of information about the dead man and the workers who were constructing the outer wall of the cigarette factory.

THIRTEEN

It was just after lunch and Eileen was standing at the door of her mother's house, breathing in some air, when Joe arrived, and she agreed immediately to accompany him and Nell Murphy to the prison. Barrack Street was alive with indignation about the imprisonment of Maureen McCarthy and Eileen felt a responsibility to do her best to free the girl. Joe was a friend, an easy-going fellow, and she did not have to watch her words with him, and she was, she thought, pleased to have the cheerful, irreverent presence of Miss Murphy, Nell, she corrected her thoughts. The lady had been very emphatic about being called by that name.

'Oh, for heaven's sake, Eileen, call me Nell. I hate being called "Miss Murphy". Half this city is called Murphy,' the lady had said briskly. 'There's "Murphy the Skins", "Murphy the Sausages", "Murphy the Stout" and hundreds of others. And now I suppose that brother of mine will be called "Murphy the Cigarettes". Not too many by the name of "Nell", though, and so I prefer it. I don't need any label attached to me. I'm myself, take it or leave it.'

Quite a character, thought Eileen, and was rather sorry that they were not riding to the gaol in the flashy red Cadillac which was the lady's trademark in the city of Cork. Aloud she said: 'Time the Barracks got a new car, Joe. Every Tom, Dick, and Harry in the place drives one of those Baby Fords. It's a disgrace to the Gardai. Makes you all look silly. You need something that cuts a dash when you roll up at the scene of the crime.'

'Don't tell me. You want us to have a bright red Cadillac,' said Joe, neatly overtaking a horse and cart.

'Wouldn't suit Patrick's style,' said Eileen. 'What sort of car would suit Patrick, what do you think, Nell?' There, she said to herself, I've got it out. It will be easier the next time that I say her name.

'Somehow, I'd see him with a Dodge,' said Nell, thought-fully. 'Nice silent car to drive. I think it would suit the Inspector. Something quiet, but strong, with a bit of hidden power.'

'Or a Packard,' suggested Joe, 'that Twin 6 Roadster.'

'I'd prefer a Hudson Roadster to the Packard,' said Nell. 'There was a new one came out last year, the Hudson 7 1927.'

'Or what about a Willys Overland Whippet?' suggested Joe.

Eileen deliberately cut herself out from the animated conversation. She didn't know much about cars, was not that interested in them. She was happy with her motorbike, and it would do her until she was old, she decided. Her thoughts moved to the girl whom she was about to interview. Fourteen years old, had said the Reverend Mother. Eileen, herself, had been only sixteen when she had left school, joined in with the IRA and lived with a gang of students in a tumbledown, derelict old house on a remote farm in west Cork. She had never regretted that impulsive action, though she had been sorry to have upset her mother. Nevertheless, she had learned a lot from her housemates, most of them now either back at university, or out earning a living as graduates. The old dreams had faded, but the friendships had survived. And so had her ambitions. In another few years she would qualify as a solicitor and be able to help unfortunates like the girl that they were going to see.

With a police sergeant on one side of her and a well-known lady from Montenotte on the other side, the gaoler, though he scowled at her, and obviously instantly recognized her as the origin of a report into 'Gaol Conditions' in the *Cork Examiner*, made no objection to bringing the prisoner, Maureen McCarthy, into a private room, away from the other visitors, and after ceremoniously beckoning to Joe and giving him some whispered instructions, he went grudgingly back to his post.

The girl had been crying. That was obvious, though she put a brave face on it as Joe explained what they were doing and who each person was. She knew Eileen, of course. They were neighbours. In fact, Eileen had a memory of rescuing a two-year-old Maureen who had gone crawling down the steep hill of Barrack Street and inserting herself under the wheels of a horse-drawn cart. An adventurous type, from the start! The type that went looking for trouble. She smiled at the girl but said nothing for the moment. It was Nell who had set up this interview and it was for her to open the proceedings.

She did it well, thought Eileen. Brisk, but not condescending. Explained that she had come at the request of the Reverend Mother and that brought a hint of colour to the white face of the fourteen-year-old. She said nothing, though, just listened and when Nell had finished, she did not reply but turned immediately to Joe.

'Why was I the only one to be arrested?' The question came out aggressively, but the girl's hands were trembling.

Joe, thought Eileen, handled it well. Called her 'Maureen' in quite a fatherly way and explained that there had been a witness to the fact that the smoke had started some considerable amount of time after the other nine girls had left.

And it was then that Nell jumped in. It was a good job that Patrick was not there, thought Eileen. The short hairs on the back of his well-clipped scalp would have risen to quite a height. Talk about leading the witness!

'I know all about that man, my dear,' she concluded after a quick résumé of the manager Mr Timothy Dooley's behaviour with various women and then she looked across at Joe. 'You wouldn't be a dear, Sergeant, and see if you could get me a cup of tea. Something about the air in here – makes my mouth dry. And one for Eileen, too. She looks in need of one, too.'

'You'll get me shot,' said Joe, rising to his feet. 'Still seeing as you are in *loco parentis* . . . that's right, isn't it, Maureen? She's here since your mother is away. She's taking the place of your mother since your mother or your aunt can't be with you just now; that's the way of it, isn't it? Well, I suppose it's all right.'

And sensibly not waiting for an answer, Joe quickly left the room with a suspicion of a wink at Eileen while his back was turned to Miss Nell Murphy who hardly waited for the door to be closed before she went and perched upon the desk and leaned over the white-faced girl.

Eileen smiled to herself, took out her lipstick and a small

mirror from her handbag. She'd give this authoritative lady a chance, she thought, and if it wasn't working, she would take over. Might even try to get rid of her on the pretext that the men might need help with the tea.

'Now tell me, my dear,' said Nell briskly, 'tell me why you stayed behind every evening?'

'To help with covering over the crumbed-up leaves. We put a sheet over them.' Maureen had that off by heart and looked slightly taken aback when Nell shook her head.

'That won't do, my dear,' she said impatiently. 'Use your brains, girl. The police have a witness, a nosy old woman, a Mrs Maloney, who lives nearby and who told them that you stayed behind for at least a couple of hours every evening after the other nine girls had gone home. Your friends would have waited for you if all you were doing was just covering over the dried leaves. You'd have been out in a couple of seconds if that was all that you were doing. Now tell the truth; tell me why you stayed behind every evening?'

Maureen stared at her for a few moments. She had a bewildered look about her. Not too bright, thought Eileen with a feeling of pity.

'Now if that man raped, you or even tried to rape you, we might get a good lawyer to say that you acted in self-defence, that you were afraid that he was going to kill you, that you didn't know what he was doing by trying to tear the clothes off you, you thought that he was doing it so as to stick his knife into you.'

'Yah,' said Maureen, after absorbing these details for what seemed to be a long minute. 'Yah, that was the way of it.' She didn't sound very convinced.

'So, where's the knife now?' asked Eileen. 'If there was a knife, Maureen, we need to know where it might be now. Nothing about a knife being found in the dead man's hand. Remember, Maureen, the place wasn't burned down or anything. It was just smoke that killed him. The lawyer for the state will be questioning you if your case comes to court and that will be bound to come up.'

After all, she thought, as a trainee lawyer she had to antici-pate any possible questions by the prosecution lawyers.

'Good thought,' said Nell, with an approving nod. 'What did you do with the knife, Maureen?'

Maureen gaped nervously at the lady, but said nothing, just sat with her mouth slightly open.

'You're going a bit fast for her,' said Eileen quietly.

'Oh, God, don't say that the girl is half-witted,' muttered Nell in Eileen's ear. Aloud, she asked in an exasperated voice: 'Was he courting you, girl?'

'Wanting to *do a line with you*,' translated Eileen. She, herself, had never heard the word 'court' until she had read it in Jane Austen.

The girl gave a grin. 'What! Him? With me?'

'*Jagging*?' suggested Eileen with a half glance at Miss Nell Murphy.

The girl shrugged. 'He were a bit of a *jobber*, but I didn't care.'

'Paid you well?' asked Eileen in an undertone and the girl shrugged.

'So-so,' she said. 'Better when he was sober. I'd clear off when he began to get drunk – seemed to have a new bottle of whiskey every night.'

'Would he give you a drink of his whiskey?' Eileen slipped that in and watched the girl's face. A slight smile had come over it.

'Well . . .' she said and then, after a minute, 'I knew how to manage him. Get it early – that was the way to do it with him. Get him hopeful. Got a bit narky later on. He had these big mugs and I'd fill up for myself while he wasn't looking. No harm in it,' she said aggressively. 'I was just teaching him a bit of manners. Shouldn't drink without offering around, should he?'

'What was he like last night?'

Maureen paused for a moment and then shrugged her shoulders. 'Good mood, early on. Got drunk quickly. Said he was celebrating. Had a pocketful of money. Ten-pound notes. Kept taking them in and out of his pocketbook. I didn't touch any of them, cross my heart and hope to die!' She had a defiant look on her face as she looked at Nell, thought Eileen, and she felt sorry for the girl. It would be better for her if she had appealed for help from this lady who had turned up to see her, but Eileen thought that in Maureen's place and at Maureen's age, she, also, would have chosen defiance.

'Celebrating? What was he celebrating?' Nell was determined to be of use.

'Didn't say.'

Not too bright, thought Eileen with a grimace. Didn't see the importance of this. What was the man celebrating? What would a man like that be celebrating? Could he have been blackmailing someone? And ten-pound notes in his pocket. She made a mental note to ask Joe whether there had been any money in the dead man's pocket. Or even in his bank account. The police, she was sure, would have the power to look at the man's bank account if they thought that the death might have been suspicious.

'Was he in a good mood, then, Maureen?' she asked, putting in her question quickly before the lady could antagonize the girl. Her own mother's name had been McCarthy, also, she thought, but doubted whether there was any relationship between herself and Maureen. There were certain surnames that were very popular in Cork city – McCarthy, Murphy and O'Leary – the city was full of these names and seldom was there any near relationship with others of the same name. If she were related to Maureen McCarthy, her own mother would surely have mentioned it.

The girl shrugged. 'Gave me a few shillings. I reckoned that was all that I would get out of him that night and so I cleared off.'

'Had he raped you? Don't be afraid to tell us.' Nell was determined to get this matter settled.

'Naa, didn't try anything like that. He'd have locked the door if he was going to have a go at anything serious. In a bad mood. Narky-like – kept coughing and taking more of the whiskey to stop the cough. No one rapes me – not for nothing. I'd make him sorry for ever more.'

Eileen smiled and caught the same amused expression on the face of the benevolent lady.

'*Kept coughing.*' Nell was repeating the words to herself. Eileen sat back with satisfaction and looked across at Nell.

The significance of the cough had struck her, also. Could the fire have started before Maureen left? If she could get a lawyer to represent the girl, thought Eileen, she would ask him to make much of this observation. After all, 'coughing' meant something. Why did someone cough? Could be the fog, but indoors, it was more likely the smoke. If Maureen was speaking the truth, then that fire had already been started and the smoke had begun to seep in through the cracks between the wooden planks. The air within the so-called factory had become clogged with smoke and those within had to cough in order to clear the obstruction to their lungs. She was tempted to ask Maureen whether she also had coughed, but then she remembered Joe, the police sergeant. A much better witness than even the well-off lady with the flashy car. She gave a warning glance at Nell, and then went to the door and called out: 'Need any help, Sergeant?' and when he broke away from his conversation with one of the gaolers, she took the tray from him and nodded at him to go ahead of her.

'The man was coughing, Joe, did you hear that?' she said in a low tone just as she took the tray from him and waited until comprehension dawned. It didn't take him long. He had the door opened and was inside within a minute. He was standing against the wall, leaning on the windowsill by the time that she brought the tray in and set it upon the shelf. Had his notebook out in an instant, also, and she hoped that was not a mistake.

'I'll be glad of a cup of tea,' she said in conversational tones, doing her best to distract Maureen. 'All that talk about smoke has made me feel thirsty. A cup for you, Maureen? What about you, Nell?'

Carefully she poured the cup for Maureen first and then for Nell. Joe had given a quick shake of the head when she raised her eyebrows and touched the teapot and she thought it was the right decision. If possible, he should now fade into the background.

'Did you say that he was coughing?' she asked. It might be leading the witness, but Joe was sensible enough to discard that.

Unfortunately, it didn't work. Maureen just shrugged her

shoulders. Best not to press the question, thought Eileen. She would go back afterwards once Maureen was more relaxed.

'How much did you get paid a week for working in that place, Maureen?' she asked in a chatty fashion.

'Six shillings a week.' Maureen's voice was sullen, and she cast suspicious glances at Joe's back as he leaned upon the windowsill and busily scribbled in his notebook.

'You was robbed,' said Eileen.

'More was promised,' said Maureen. 'Not that I'd ever go back there.'

Eileen shrugged. 'Why not? Not your fault, was it, that the fire was started?' A good job that Patrick wasn't there, she thought, but she, Eileen, wasn't anything to do with the Gardai Sochna so she could say what she liked. Joe would have enough sense not to write down her words.

'Cross me heart and hope to die!' said Maureen, but she said it in a mechanical fashion. There was a slight frown between her sandy eyebrows, and she appeared to be thinking hard.

'I'm not saying any more,' she announced. 'Not in front of him!' She jabbed a thumb at Joe, standing discreetly with his back turned and his body half-turned. 'You can get out, all of you; I don't want any of you,' she went on and Eileen could hear a suppressed sob in her voice. She felt a rush of pity for the girl. A bit like herself at that age, she thought. Always doing the wrong thing out of stubbornness. She had been determined to leave school and to go off to join the IRA, no matter what the Reverend Mother said, no matter how much her mother had pleaded with her. She remembered a big scene where her mother sobbed while she had stuffed a few clothes into a bag and went off to meet the young student who had promised her a seat on the back of his bike and told her that there were other girls in that safehouse on a farm in south-west Cork. He had spoken the truth, though now she thought that she had taken a huge risk. She had learned to shoot, had undoubtedly committed crimes against the state, had not fully realized how she had put her whole life in jeopardy. It had been sheer luck that she had escaped imprisonment and, of course, she had left school without sitting her Leaving

Certificate examination. Something that she regretted even now as it had cost her years of low-paid work and of midnight study to make up for those lost years, but certainly nobody could have, when she was sixteen, stopped her doing what was, to her, a patriotic duty. She did not trust anyone to make decisions for her then and she recognized the same spirit in Maureen.

'Well, there you are; if you are not going to trust us, you have to just go your own way,' she said decisively as she got to her feet. 'Pity,' she added in what she hoped was a nonchalant tone of voice. 'You were the one who was there. You could probably help if we all put our brains together. Why don't you think about it and if you want me to come back, then you can just send a message through the sergeant.'

She got to her feet and walked decisively towards the door. Would this work? Nell was still sitting, looking from one to the other, but Joe had pocketed his notebook and joined her.

'Get out,' screamed Maureen. 'Get out. Let me manage. I can't think straight with you all pestering me.'

She was on the verge of tears and Eileen didn't hesitate. Just opened the door and held it open until Nell passed through. Joe joined her. He grimaced slightly.

'Shouldn't have done that,' he said in a very low voice. 'Patrick will have a fit. A great man for going by the book, our Inspector Cashman,' he said to Nell. 'And he's probably right,' he added.

'Nonsense!' was her reply in a furious undertone. 'Never gone by the book at any time in my life!'

There was something about having money, having had money for your entire life, thought Eileen. She's determined to help that girl willy-nilly, but she can't understand that Maureen doesn't want to be pushed around by a woman with a posh accent. Or by me, either! She knew well that all the mothers on Barrack Street envied her mother when she wore her new coat going to Mass on Sunday. She was considered by all on Barrack Street to be a very good daughter now and was held up as an example to other girls. Maureen was probably sick of hearing about Eileen's success at winning a university scholarship and at the same time earning good money by getting herself a job writing on the *Cork Examiner*. No wonder Maureen didn't want to confide in her.

'In a few years' time she will have some more sense,' she said when she finished her account of the visit after she and Nell had returned to the convent that afternoon to report almost-failure.

The Reverend Mother bowed her head. She did not say anything, but Eileen, herself, as soon as she had said the words, reminded herself that the girl might not have these years. If she were found guilty of murder then she might well be hanged, and if not, it might be life imprisonment.

'Something has to be done,' said Nell decisively. 'She doesn't seem to realize the danger that she is in.'

'Your visit has not been wasted,' said the Reverend Mother thoughtfully. 'I find that a very interesting statement that the manager was coughing. Well done, both of you. And thank you for writing it down immediately, Eileen. One should always do that. The older I get, the more I remind myself to write things down. I developed the habit as I had noticed that elderly sisters, here in this convent, began to distrust their memory as the years went by and so I resolved to start the habit before it was strictly necessary and now that I am elderly, well, I find it to be of immense use to me.'

'Will we be believed, though,' said Eileen with a grimace. 'It's not as if we are lawyers or policemen. We got the sergeant in and tried to get her to say it again, but it didn't work.'

The Reverend Mother thought for a moment. 'Nell, have you got a spare half a crown?' she asked and without waiting for an answer she turned to Eileen, 'I know that you have done well at your first year law examinations and I don't want to teach you your own business, but could you recite for me the name on the door and titles on the door of the office where you are serving your law apprenticeship . . .' She paused, turned back to Nell and explained: 'Eileen is apprenticed to our cousin, Lucy's husband, and as you know he is a solicitor.'

'Mr Rupert Murphy, Commissioner for Oaths,' said Eileen, slowly. And then she smiled ruefully. 'Oh, of course, I forgot!

Of course, he is a commissioner for oaths! I should have remembered because Mr Murphy is always saying that he will never retire and that when he gets to be ninety, and is too old to deal with complicated matters, he will set himself up in the basement as a commissioner for oaths and live on his pensions and buy whiskey with all of these half-crowns . . .' She turned enthusiastically to Nell. 'We can swear an oath, both of us. We can swear that these were her words; neither of us have anything to gain and we can swear it in front of a commissioner for oaths.'

'I went there as an emissary of the Reverend Mother, who is, of course, well known in the city for her charitable works,' recited Nell solemnly, though her eyes were sparkling. 'I wonder why you went along with me, Eileen?'

'Best not to say that she was a friend of the accused. That wouldn't go down well in court – might call her neutrality into question,' said the Reverend Mother placidly. 'Not strictly true, either, is it? What about as your secretary, a part-time job. Very good at shorthand, are you not, Eileen?'

'I've always wanted a secretary,' said Nell enthusiastically. 'People are always accusing me of never answering letters. Yes, I will employ you for a couple of mornings a week, Eileen. Seriously, I mean it, that's if you can spare the time. We should soon clear the mess of opened envelopes on the table in the library. I even bought a typewriter once thinking that it might organize me, but, of course, I never managed to learn how to type, and the thing is gathering dust. Can you type?'

'Yes, of course,' said Eileen eagerly. 'I can type really fast. Someone gave me a present of an old typewriter when I started doing articles for the *Cork Examiner*. I practise every night.' A part-time job of a couple of mornings a week would suit her well, she thought, and it would keep her shorthand and typing in good practice. 'I would love that,' she said. 'I'm quite quick. And I can do shorthand and after a while, when I get to know your style, if you would trust me, I could draft a reply and let you see what you thought of it – just to save you time,' she concluded, feeling somewhat embarrassed and half-wishing that she had never started.

Nell surveyed her with interest and nodded her head. 'That could be very useful,' she said. 'I'm thinking of setting up a business, wouldn't want to engage too many staff until I see how it goes, but this could be a useful stepping-stone for the two of us – for you until you start working as a solicitor, and for me until things started running well and I could engage a full-time secretary.'

'Eileen's studies must come first, though,' put in the Reverend Mother, and to Eileen's relief, Nell smiled indulgently. 'I'll check her homework every day, Reverend Mother,' she said jokingly, but Eileen saw her give a reassuring nod to her elderly cousin and resolved indignantly that there would be no need for anyone to supervise her, as though she were a child. Her aim to be top of her university class with a brilliant first-class honours would still be dominant, still be the first thought in her mind every morning when she woke up. Any time spent working for Nell would be taken from her few leisure hours.

'Good,' said Nell in an offhand way. 'Are you willing, then? Four hours a week. What about that? Would that suit you? I live quite near to the university so that we can find times that suit you. We could even get Mr Rupert Murphy to draw up a contract. That would be fun.'

'I don't think that a contract will be necessary,' said the Reverend Mother placidly. 'One can overdo these matters. Now . . .' The Reverend Mother glanced at the clock on her mantelpiece, before continuing. 'Go and pay Mr Murphy, or one of his underlings, your half a crown and then you can deliver the affidavit to Inspector Cashman. Go there quickly, before they close the office for the day. And, perhaps, while you are there . . .' The Reverend Mother stopped and thought for a moment and then continued without finishing her sentence. 'Yes,' she said. 'An affidavit is just what you need and that is the place to obtain it. Of course, Mr Murphy does employ a large staff, of different age groups . . .'

Eileen lowered her eyes which would, she knew, be sharp with interest. The Reverend Mother was concise and crisp of speech, and it was unlike her not to finish a sentence and most unlike her not to finish two sentences. What would have followed that stray 'and perhaps . . .'? And the reference to different age groups?

Of course, she thought, it would be most unlikely that the owner of the business, Mr Rupert Murphy, husband of the Reverend Mother's cousin, would be the person who would sign off the affidavit and who would collect the half-crown from Nell. No, it would be one of the young solicitors who worked in that busy and prestigious office. All ambitious young solicitors – Mr Rupert Murphy often said that he only employed the 'crème de la crème' – and so it would be very easy to get such a young man interested in this case of a fourteen-year-old girl being imprisoned on the most flimsy and circumstantial evidence. Once Maureen had a solicitor representing her, then there would be a path to freedom opening out in front of her.

So long as Maureen could be persuaded to play her cards correctly and to project herself as an innocent girl, barely out of the school room. It would take a while to coach her, but Eileen thought that she was the person who could manage Maureen. In some ways they were alike. What would have happened to her, Eileen suddenly wondered, if she had stayed on in school and obediently studied for her Intermediate Certificate and then, perhaps, got a job in an office? That bold step of running away to join the IRA and living for a couple of years in a safe house with a crowd of idealistic and well-read university students had made a big difference to her in every way, given her confidence, made her feel that she could talk to anyone. With the help of the Reverend Mother, she had taken up her studies again and had won a scholarship to Cork University, a second chance to lead a life that would be very different to the life that her mother led, scrubbing out the filthy floors of public houses and living in a two-roomed cabin in Barrack Street.

FOURTEEN

'Let's hope for a bit of peace today, some good thinking time,' said Joe as he came into Patrick's room the following morning carrying a folder filled with sheets of paper and holding a notebook and pencil clamped to it by his thumb while he opened and closed the door with the other hand. And then he stopped short of his usual position in front of the desk and stared at the calendar on the desk.

Patrick was proud of that calendar. No pretty-pretty picture, no stupid cartoons to make you laugh, but a solid, respectable cubical lump of crockery with three handles at the side and three open slots on the face of the cube. He never forgot to remember to wind on the three handles every morning so that the face of that cubical calendar always showed the correct year, the correct month, and the correct date. One of those calendars where the date could be seen from both sides, it made sure that he never forgot a day or an appointment.

Joe's eyes had gone to the calendar when he came into the room. He stopped, picked it up and then grimaced.

'Oh, my God, Patrick, today is Eileen's birthday. I've forgotten to get her something. Was going to get her a bunch of flowers. What about you? Bet you've forgotten too, have you?'

Patrick began to feel embarrassed. Joe was a nice fellow but there were times when he didn't know how to hold his tongue. His sergeant was fingering in his pockets now, even turning one of them inside out in a vain effort to find some money.

'July is a terrible month,' he said shaking his head. 'It's my mother's birthday and then it's the twins' birthday and then come two of my cousins. I don't know what happens to my money. And I was going to propose that we go halves on taking her out for a meal. Sorry, Patrick, but would you mind if I borrow something from you? I'd hate to disappoint her.

Girls think a lot about birthdays. I'll owe it to you if you can lend me something.'

'Yes, of course, don't worry about it. I'll stand it – and get a couple of bunches of flowers, one from you and one from me -- nice ones, two different ones,' he said hurriedly, thinking that it would be less embarrassing if both presented Eileen with flowers at the same time.

Feeling his face burn, Patrick leafed through his new leather wallet. He had been to the bank yesterday and it was filled with crisp five-pound notes. In an excess of embarrassment, he pulled out two of them and passed them across the desk.

Joe's eyes had widened. 'Goodness, that's great! Pay for two bunches of flowers and a meal, too, for the poor girl. Looking a bit thin, I thought, the last time that I saw her. Works too hard. Perhaps doesn't get enough to eat. Knowing Eileen, I'd say that she's spending most of her money on books. Well, we'll feed her up this evening. Thanks, Patrick. I won't be long. It's all right if I take the car, isn't it? I'll tell that nosy parker at the desk that I'm off to make an arrest.'

Joe disappeared before Patrick could say anything, so he was left alone with the ten sheets of the girls' evidence and single sheet with the name of MRS MALONEY printed on top of it. He scowled at that sheet. Without the interference of that annoying woman, he would never have got himself entangled with these girls, and with Maureen McCarthy in particular. Why on earth, he thought, leafing impatiently through the identical stories on each of the pages, why on earth should Maureen, or any of the girls, want to kill the manager of the cigarette factory? She wasn't in his power in any way. She could have just given in her notice; said she didn't want to work for him any more. The business would have been shut down for a while if the manager was murdered. She would have lost her job and so would her nine friends. Wouldn't be easy to get another person to take over. After all, it was a completely new idea. Anyway, if she hadn't wanted to work there any more it would have been easy enough to make up an excuse. Say her mother needed her at home, tell the other girls not to go home without her. Really, it was taking a sledgehammer to smash a nut.

What earthly good could it do to any one of them? But then, half of the murders in Cork city did no good to anyone – just happened because of a fit of temper and were mostly connected with excessive alcohol.

He picked up the phone and to his annoyance had to wait for what seemed like an endlessly long time before Tommy picked it up, sounding quite breathless. Out chasing small boys from the sacred precinct of the police station, he thought impatiently.

'Switch the line through, please,' he said curtly. He wouldn't give Tommy the satisfaction of passing on to bored constables what Inspector Cashman was doing about that murder.

'Get me Youghal Garda Barracks,' he said curtly to the telephone woman and then waited impatiently while the various clicks and buzzing noises showed that she was doing her best.

'Inspector Cashman, Cork City Barracks,' he announced when a bored voice with a strong south of Cork accent answered the phone. 'Could I have a word with your inspector, please,' he added promptly. No point in talking with an under- ling as he would either get too little or too much information. Conversations with men of an equal rank flowed more freely. The man at Youghal, Inspector John Davy, he thought as he listened to him, sounded an intelligent person and he extended an invitation to Youghal if Patrick felt the need to go down there in person.

By the time that he had put down the phone he had begun on marshalling his arguments to persuade the superintendent to release that unfortunate child, Maureen McCarthy. Nothing had been heard from the girl's mother and he was haunted by the thought that he was partially responsible for what must be the youngest prisoner ever in the women's prison of Cork city. Picking up his pen he began to record the fight described by the Youghal inspector between the gardener and the grounds manager, Timothy Dooley.

And then he knocked at the superintendent's door and was welcomed cordially.

'Ah, Patrick, how are you getting on,' he said.

'Thought you might be interested in this, sir,' he said and

then read out his carefully chosen words to the superintendent. 'Looks as though there might be another suspect with perhaps much more of a motive than Maureen McCarthy,' he finished, not looking across the desk at his superior, but busying himself with replacing the sheet of paper into his folder with meticulous accuracy.

There was a silence from the other side of the table for some time and then the superintendent said slowly and with a shake of his head: 'That all happened six months ago, Patrick. Not really enough to go on. Not enough for an arrest.'

'True,' said Patrick. But probably more of a motive than that girl Maureen, could have had, he thought, but he said nothing for a moment. No point in annoying the superintendent. He was a man who did not like to be contradicted.

'I thought I might dig a bit more into the man's background,' he continued. 'The inspector in Youghal seemed to think that he was a troublesome fellow. Always looking for a fight. What do you think, sir?'

That worked well. The superintendent nodded his head. 'You do that, Patrick. Always worth looking into the background of the victim. I think I told you that when you were a recruit.'

'You did indeed, sir. I have every word that you said to me written down in some notebooks. You were very good to me,' he added and felt suddenly slightly emotional at the thought that this kind old man would no longer be around to advise and praise.

'Good lad, good lad,' said the superintendent. He gave a wink. 'Joe said that you were going out this evening. Wanted to borrow the car. Important police business, so he said, young rascal. Well, have a good time, all of you. You're only young once.'

And after that kindness, Patrick felt that he couldn't bring up the subject of Maureen McCarthy. If only he could put his finger on the murderer. That would be the sure way of releasing her and would be the most satisfactory as she would be released without a stain on her character and would not have to bear the gossip and suspicion of neighbours and friends.

FIFTEEN

Not for one minute did Eileen think that Patrick had masterminded the magnificent scene that celebrated her birthday. Picked up in a car, driven to a beautiful restaurant where a table, garnished with two enormous bunches of hot-house flowers, had been placed out of doors and just beside a splendid waterfall. It all spelled of Joe rather than Patrick. On the other hand, Joe had told her, very honestly, that Patrick was paying for everything, even for both bunches of birthday flowers.

'What gorgeous flowers,' she had said admiringly to the waitress.

'They're yours, madam, when you are ready to go home, we'll dry them and wrap them again. The gentleman . . .' The girl's eyes went from Joe's face to Patrick's, and she corrected herself swiftly. 'The gentlemen brought their two bunches of birthday flowers here so that they would make the table special for your birthday celebration. We used this table for six guests to give the flowers plenty of room. Now I'll get the menus and open the wine.'

'No singing "Happy Birthday", this place is too posh,' said Eileen once they had given their orders and had all sipped a taste of a sparkling white wine which Joe had ordered. 'And thank you very much, both of you. This will be a birthday to remember.'

'Patrick's treat, not mine,' said Joe. 'I've just been brought along to sing funny songs. But let me do the first toast – Happy Birthday, Eileen! Now your turn, Patrick.'

'Happy Birthday, Eileen!' said Patrick. To hide his embarrassment, thought Eileen, he took a large gulp of wine, and she could see that he felt slightly dizzy for a second. He would hate himself for that, she knew. He was still immensely self-conscious when it came to social events. She hastened to cover an awkward silence.

'Lovely out here,' she said with a smile at him. 'Just us and no one listening in from the next table and the waterfall drowning the sound of our voices. We can chat as much as we please without anyone listening in to three such famous people.'

That made him laugh, she was glad to see. He was beginning to lose the embarrassed air and she hastened to engage his interest.

'Do you know what I was just thinking about, Patrick,' she said leaning across to him. 'I've got such a brilliant idea. Might even have solved that murder case for you,' she added with a quick glance around just to make sure that the waitress was out of the way.

He had, she thought, a lovely smile when he relaxed.

'You're ahead of me as usual,' he said. 'You always were and always will be, I suppose. You know, Eileen,' Patrick paused, looked all around, and then added in a low voice almost drowned by the noise of the waterfall, 'believe it or not, I haven't even got around to deciding that it is a murder case that we are dealing with. Could just as easily be a careless accident.'

'Oh, come on,' said Joe, with an eye on the waitress who had just put down a tray on the table inside the glass door leading to the courtyard. 'It must be the M word. I know you like to be cautious, Patrick, but admit it! M's the word!'

'Mmmm! Smell that soup,' said Eileen ecstatically as the waitress arrived at their table.

'Spiced carrot, madam,' said the girl. 'I hope you like it. We do also have chicken soup in the kitchen if anyone would prefer it – all homemade, of course.'

'No, the spiced carrot is wonderful,' said Eileen, beginning to guess why Joe had that 'swapping favourite recipes' conversation a few weeks ago. She gave him a warm smile. He was, she thought, an ideal friend for Patrick, had managed to winkle him out of his shell on increasing occasions. 'Are you going to try the spiced carrot, Joe? Keep me company . . . What about you, Patrick?'

'I'll have the chicken,' said Joe.

'I think I'll try the spiced carrot. I've never had spiced carrot soup before,' said Patrick and Eileen felt pleased that he was confident enough to make that acknowledgement. He was, she thought, growing more confident every year after his successes in the police force. If only he could solve this strange case of the deadly smoke in the cigarette factory!

She waited until the waitress had taken their orders for the main course, snipped a rose bud from one of the bunches of flowers, tucked it behind her ear, fastening it with a hair grip and then leaned across the table.

'I've got such an interesting little piece of information for you, Patrick,' she said. 'And who knows it might even point toward who could have started that fire and who might have wanted to murder the manager of the cigarette factory.'

He smiled at her. Actually smiled at her in public! Was coming out of his shell, looked amused and happy, she thought.

'What's your good idea, Eileen?' he said in an indulgent tone of voice.

She sat back. 'It has to be someone who could light the fire without being noticed,' she said, including Joe in the conversation. 'So have you checked on who was passing during the time before the fire was noticed?'

'Our usual informant told us that no one passed during the half hour before the girl came out,' said Joe. 'And she saw the smoke then as the girl went across St Mary's Isle.'

'Your usual informant? Mrs Maloney! Oh, come on, Joe! Use your brains! How could she know for certain? Did she explain why she spent a half hour standing at the window or the door and looking across at St Mary's Isle?' said Eileen. She gave a quick glance at Patrick from the corner of her eye and saw that he still looked more amused than impressed.

'Well, she did have quite a good explanation, just to state the facts,' said Joe. 'The lady said that she was knitting and that, as she is a good knitter, she doesn't need to look at the stitches, so she always looks out of the window, and it passes the time for her while she is knitting. My mother does the very same thing – she sits at the window and afterwards can tell you everyone who came in and out of Newenham Terrace, and so I believed her.'

Eileen nodded. She would allow that to pass. It was a

plausible explanation. 'I've been thinking about her, about Mrs Maloney. She's a funny one, isn't she? I'll tell you something that I bet you don't know. Mrs Maloney owns a stall down on the Coal Quay market. A reporter from the *Cork Examiner* told me that.'

'Mustn't do much business then,' said Joe. 'How come she is always ringing us up about whatever might be happening around the St Mary's Isle and around the streets there? I'd have sworn that she spends her days and evenings looking out the window or door or else trotting around within a few hundred yards of her cabin.'

'Ah, but you see it's possible to own a business and manage the business, but not be the one who does the actual selling,' said Eileen. 'As a matter of fact, she has a sister who does the selling for her. According to my informant, her sister was destitute, couldn't pay the rent, wanted to move in with Mrs Maloney, but that didn't suit our lady spy and so she went into business, rented a stall, pays her sister enough to keep her in her own place, and apparently, earns a nice little sum for Mrs Maloney . . .'

'Anyway, it doesn't make her interesting to us,' said Joe dismissively.

'What does she sell, Eileen?' asked Patrick quietly as he sipped his soup with the air of one determined to like it.

'Well, you've put your finger on it, Patrick,' said Eileen. 'Good job there are some brains in the police barracks.' She leaned across the table. 'Well, what do they sell in ninety-nine per cent of these market stalls in the Coal Quay? Well, I'll tell you what they sell,' she continued. She swallowed the last spoonful of her soup and wiped her mouth with the napkin – 'that was delicious,' she said and then without waiting for an answer, she embarked on a list, ticking items off on her fingers: 'They sell old clothes and old shoes that they beg from posh houses, they sell eggs from a few chickens that they keep in back yards, they sell stuff that they salvage from rubbish bins outside the posh houses on the North Mall and such places, but Mrs Maloney doesn't sell anything like that. What does she sell, Patrick?'

Patrick frowned for a minute. 'I don't know,' he said. 'No

reason why I should know. The woman is not a suspect. In fact, it's news to me that she has a stall on the Coal Quay.' With an effort he pronounced 'Quay' as if it had been spelt with an 'e' rather than an 'a'. It was one of those words that he had been practising, one of those words that would have betrayed his origins to people such as the superintendent from Dublin. Promotion, he knew, depended not just on efficiency at your job, but how you looked, how you sounded, who were your friends – all sorts of things like that.

'Well,' said Eileen, 'I know you think she spends her days looking out of her window, and that's probably what she does do for most of her time, but, according to my informant, you won't see her in St Mary's Isle when a ship comes in from Costa Rica and sometimes even when ships come in from Liverpool – all depends on what they are carrying, but Costa Rica should give you a clue.' She stopped and smiled as the waitress came back in: 'Oh, good, I'm starving. And a menu for each one of us. Great! I hate waiting while someone dithers. Now, no talking while I think. It may be twenty-years before I have a meal like this again.'

'I'm sure not, madam,' said the waitress. 'Now, may I recommend something very special for a very special occasion. This is our Hadji Bey menu. You are from Cork, Inspector,' she addressed herself to Patrick, 'so you know all about Hadji Bey, all three of you, to be sure – and you're the lady that writes on the *Cork Examiner*, aren't you? And I think that you were the one that wrote the article about the Hadji Bey family,' she said turning to Eileen before continuing. 'I cut out that article and put it up on the board in the kitchen. Very useful it is to me when I have to explain to tourists about the Hadji menu and how our menu here has authentic Turkish food served with rice and sauces all approved by the Hadji Bey family. I tell them about the sweets, of course, and but I got from your article how the original product was created by an Armenian man and his wife, who arrived in Cork in 1902 after fleeing death when in the Ottoman kingdom. When I read all about that in your article, I said to the cook that we should do something about that, being as Hadji Bey is here on Curtain's Street, just next to us.'

'Hadji Bey!' said Patrick. He smiled. 'Bought a box of Hadji Bey Turkish Delights for my mother for last Christmas and I've never eaten anything so delicious. Makes my mouth water to even think of them. But that would be for the dessert, wouldn't it?' He looked across at Joe for guidance.

'I had the *taramasalata* the last time that I was here,' said Joe. 'But that is fish, and you mightn't like it, Eileen. What about you, Patrick? You like fish, don't you? Or there is the *gozleme*, stuffed with spiced lamb and feta. You might like that, Eileen.'

'Yes, I'll have that. I like lamb,' said Eileen and then looked at Patrick. He might like Hadji Bey sweets – all Cork loved them – but she wondered about this Turkish dinner menu. He was studying it very carefully and then he put it down, quite decisively.

'I'll have a well-done steak and a double helping of chips, and I'll keep the Hadji Bey for the sweet course,' he said with a smile at the waitress.

Eileen couldn't help it. She threw back her head and laughed. It was so characteristic of Patrick. When it came to it, he was a man who made his own decisions. She had known him since they were both children, but he had, she thought, changed so much over the last few years. He had been shy, tongue-tied and hesitant as a schoolboy, though, even then, stubborn and determined – never deterred by the mockery of the other boys when he had spent his evenings and weekends studying – nevertheless, he had been a solitary, shy, hesitant and tongue-tied figure.

But not now, she thought. Now he appeared to be so confident and decisive about so many matters.

Except, perhaps, she sometimes thought, deep down, he might still be same shy, hesitant Patrick Cashman and might need some encouragement . . .

'Well, that steak of yours will give us a good excuse to have a bottle of red wine as well as the white. When it comes down to it, I prefer red wine, no matter what I am eating for dinner,' said Joe to the waitress. 'Oh, and could we have some small plates and forks, please so that we can try each other's choices?'

The small plates and forks so that the Turkish menu dishes

and the chips could be shared was a good idea of Joe's, thought Eileen. It created a fun atmosphere and Patrick's chips were so delicious that she and Joe began to express envy for his choice. They had the place to themselves. It was an expensive restaurant and probably did a good business over the weekend, but on this Thursday evening theirs was the only table occupied in the little courtyard with its sparkling waterfall.

And so, they could talk about the murder.

'Tell us about the ships from Costa Rica,' said Patrick. 'I don't know anything about them, other than I don't remember any trouble when they dock.'

'That's probably because the sailors have no time for fighting and drinking as they are busy earning a bit of money for themselves,' said Eileen. 'The ships from Costa Rica buy our Irish butter, but they bring in cigarettes – and cigarettes, Patrick, are getting very popular. Of course, ninety per cent might be sold to the shops, but the sailors always manage to keep some back and they sell them down the quays.'

'True enough,' said Joe with a grin. 'I've warned my young brother that I will tan the hide off him if I catch him down there on quays buying cigarettes and me a policeman. He was whining that all of the other boys in his class buy them.'

Eileen could see that Patrick was looking guilty – feeling that he should do something about it.

'Stopping people killing each other is far more important than a few sailors making a bit of money on cigarettes,' she said to him. 'Anyway, it's not just Joe's brother and other school-boys who buy them, it's Mrs Maloney, and, apparently, she buys on a big scale, very cheaply, and then she sells them in her stall. She has a few of the usual old shawls and such-like hanging up, just so as not to attract attention, but her regulars know where to come and they spread the news to others. Does a great business, that stall! Not much said about it either. The usual customers love the feeling of getting such a bargain price for cigarettes and so they keep it mostly to themselves and if they spread the news, they do it under an oath of secrecy.'

Patrick put down his knife and fork. 'Goodness me,' he said. 'And she such a pattern of law and order.'

'Quite funny, isn't it?' said Joe with a grin.

'Not so funny if she caused the death of a man by trying to burn down that wooden shed where they are making, or trying to make, authentic Cork cigarettes,' said Eileen.

Joe grimaced. 'She's an old nuisance, but I don't see her killing anyone. Why should she?'

'These Walter Raleigh cigarettes might spoil her business,' said Eileen decisively. 'She's doing a good business now, but that could finish if she got competition. 'You see this new business might put her out of business. That fellow is making the cigarettes on the cheap. Just needs a few of his gardeners to pick the leaves and dry them and then he gets the convent schoolgirls to work for a few shillings in the week – six shillings a week he pays them, so my mother heard from one of the gossips on Barrack Street Hill. What if Mrs Maloney thought that he might ruin her business and that she'd lose her nice little income and have her sister on her hands as well?'

'She wouldn't profit much from killing the manager, though,' said Joe. 'Better to kill the owner, I'd say. But, to my mind, burning the place down might have served her purpose and not been such a risk. The police might not even have been involved, or not very much. Not a big enquiry like there is, now that a man has been found dead.'

'But she may not have realized that the manager was still inside,' argued Eileen. 'In fact, she might have thought that he went at the same time as Maureen McCarthy went. He might have gone out – gone out to urinate or something like that – all right, Patrick – gone out to answer a call to nature – and then went back in again to drink more whiskey.'

'I don't like it,' said Joe, shaking his head. 'Doesn't seem too likely to me.'

'She was the one that reported the fire. Could have saved that man's life by doing so,' said Patrick quietly.

'But she didn't, did she?' said Eileen. 'If she happened to know anything about smoke inhalation, then she could have guessed that and there was an article about it in the *Evening Echo* a month or so ago. I remember reading it and it gave me a shock! Read it out to my mam and warned her about keeping the chimney swept. In fact, I got so worried about it that I called in on the chimney sweep on my way to the university.'

'We're spoiling your birthday party with talking about work,' said Patrick. He said it in quite a decisive way and Eileen saw that Joe looked at him quickly and she understood. That was enough, she thought and rapidly begged a couple of chips from his plate and embarked upon a story of how the university had brought in a by-law that no students, in a 'crowd' of more than one, could go down to the lower grounds of the university where a densely tree-clad stream formed a barrier between the university grounds and the roadway.

'Everyone in the law department – well, most of us anyway – signed and delivered a protest against curtailing our liberty and then the English department students delivered a protest against the grammatical idiocy of talking about a "crowd of one". Apparently, someone told the president that revolutionary students belonging to the IRA, used to meet there. Not true, of course, but other professors didn't like the idea of courting couples going down there in the evening after the dance at the students' club.'

'We lead such boring lives in the police station. Every bit of our grounds is exposed to the general public,' said Joe.

She instantly decided to tell some more anecdotes about the university – to change the subject without embarrassing Patrick. It had been a lovely evening so far and it was important to keep the conversation light-hearted and amusing.

And there was one other thing that she could do for Patrick. A quick glance at the menu had shown her that Hadji Bey sweets were not available and so on the pretence of powdering her nose she slipped into the kitchen and had a chat with the chef about inventing, at high speed, a new and very sweet dessert made from Hadji Bey Turkish Delights. She even offered to pop into the Hadji Bey shop, but the cook produced a box from his cupboard and so she left him to it.

'Gorgeous evening,' she said when they had finished their meal. 'It was lovely to have the car, especially since I was all dressed up, but somehow, I have a yen to walk home by moonlight after this gorgeous meal. Anyone want to join me?'

'Not me,' said Joe instantly. 'I was the one who borrowed the car, so I had better be the one who drives it back to its hallowed spot under the protection of the police barracks. You can walk on your own, young Eileen. Keep away from the drunks. Anyway, why walk when you have a car sitting outside the window of the restaurant?'

'I think she's right,' said Patrick. 'It is a lovely moon, and a walk is just what I need after all that food. I'll join you, Eileen.'

SIXTEEN

The Reverend Mother's cousin Mrs Rupert Murphy had phoned that morning but had not wanted to speak to the Reverend Mother. Sister Bernadette was quite insistent upon that.

'I was just standing by the phone, Reverend Mother, had just replaced it after phoning the butcher about a wrong order that was delivered to us and I'd just put the receiver down when it rang, and I picked it up and it was Mrs Murphy. I told her, Reverend Mother, I told her that I would fetch you immediately, that was the very first thing that I said, Reverend Mother, but no, nothing would do her but that I would take you a message and that was to tell you she would be with you in twenty minutes and not to stir until she came. I wanted to fetch you, Reverend Mother, but she didn't give me a chance. I would have told her that I would see if you were busy.' Sister Bernadette gave a guilty look at notepaper pad, the piles of envelopes and the book of stamps.

'Never mind, Sister Bernadette,' said the Reverend Mother looking rather ruefully at her morning's planned work and at the long list of names and addresses in front of her. 'Just begging letters. I'll see how many I can get done before Mrs Murphy arrives and any that I don't get done, well, I'll finish them before I take my afternoon walk.'

'Well, I'll go and get some tea and cakes ready. Mrs Murphy always enjoys my cakes.'

Sister Bernadette loved dispensing hospitality and she trotted off while the Reverend Mother went back to her letters and accelerated her fluent phrases of flattery, thanks for past favours and hopes for future generosity. It was a task which she hated but which was necessary if the school was to reopen with some fresh paint upon the peeling walls and a few extra desks for the unusually large number of four-year-old children who were due to attend school in the following September. The

increase in numbers was, she knew, her own fault as the
government only paid for children who were over the age of
five. However, she had made it her business to visit the worst
slums in the city and enquire about the ages of the children
there. Once in school, something could be done about these
unfortunate children, but while they ran around sewage-flooded
streets, stole from shops and market stalls, depravation and
even death went unnoticed. In front of her was an article which
she had read and reread: nine thousand unfortunates were
housed in nine hundred tenements in the back streets of Cork
city – roughly a thousand in each tenement. Bodies of half-
starved children were picked up from the streets almost every
week, especially during the winter. The task to redress this
was herculean, but she had focused her mind on getting children into school as early as possible. The government, of
course, would only pay if they were over five years old, but
the younger children were welcomed by her and that gave her
access to the families and their problems. There were times,
and she admitted this to herself, when it seemed as though
the task was beyond her strength, but she had faced the
consequences of turning her back upon the problems and she
knew that while she could manage, why then she would just
carry on.

'I owe you so much,' she wrote, 'and will always remember
how generously you contributed to my book fund for little
children. I am almost ashamed to call upon you again, but I
need to buy a few more desks for the new intake next
September and wondered whether I dared appeal to your
generosity once again. I remember your grandfather so well,
and how he once said to me how moved he was to see such
tiny children, of the same age as his own grandchild – and
that, of course, was you – how upset and moved he was to
see these little children begging upon the streets of Cork . . .'

Every letter, she had learned by experience, had to be aimed
at an individual – not a mass appeal for funds which would
probably be thrown in the wastepaper basket or the nearest
fire, but a personalized letter from Reverend Mother Aquinas
whose family were well known in the city of Cork, whose
tendrils of relations and acquaintances stretched from hill to

hill of the affluent districts of the city of Cork and whose memory was able to produce such interesting anecdotes from the past.

She continued to write even after she heard the jolly ping, ping of the doorbell. Sister Bernadette could be relied upon to display an avid curiosity to hear all the news about Lucy's latest grandchildren and of the health of all of her family and to admire the elegance of the visitor's latest outfit. She had a few more minutes to finish her letter.

'The bishop was so moved by your so very generous donation to our fund for wellington boots for the children that he promised to remember you in his prayers . . .' She wrote the words rapidly before she signed her name to the last missive – the bishop, she knew, always was worth mentioning. A man of power in the city and one who gained the respect of its wealthy citizens. Neatly she printed the name and address on the envelope – addressed to the business place, as was her invariable custom when this was possible. Letters sent to a home got left upon a mantelpiece or pushed into a drawer, whereas letters sent to places of business invariably went through a secretary and as such were tracked until answered and disposed of. And a substantial cheque probably always seemed to be more acceptable in a setting where cheques were part of the business of the day.

'Come in,' she called out as she fed the envelopes, one by one, into a large paper bag. 'How lovely to see you, and so unexpected,' she said to her cousin while discreetly passing the paper bag to Sister Bernadette. The Reverend Mother's letters were treated with great awe and care by Sister Bernadette and a young novice would be instantly dispatched to the post office where the postmistress or postmaster would personally take charge of them.

'Well, how are you, Lucy? And Rupert? And the family?' she said to her cousin once Sister Bernadette had disappeared with the stamped and addressed envelopes, holding the bag carefully with one hand underneath so that the weight of letters did not break through the paper.

'I can see that you have been having a nice relaxing morning,' said Lucy. 'I don't know how you do it. I hate

writing letters – one a day is more than enough for me. That
looked about forty. How do you manage to have so many
friends?'

'Let's hope that I do,' said the Reverend Mother. 'Now, go
on, tell me how you are? Well, I hope. You do look well.'

'We've been to the sea, Rupert and I, and I can tell you
that I needed a holiday after all the hard work of persuading
him that he needed the break. We went to Youghal, stayed
with Nell. The weather was lovely, and we walked on the cliffs
above the sea every day. I feel a new woman, as I said to the
bishop.'

'The bishop,' echoed the Reverend Mother.

'Yes, indeed, he was there, you know. Having a little
holiday, himself, after all his hard work during the year. Very
bad air in Cork city, even up on the very top of Shandon Hill,
the air is very bad, so his lordship told us.'

The Reverend Mother could not help a slight tightening of
her lips as she thought of all the poor who were living in the
flat of the city as the expression went. She wished that they,
like his lordship, could have some fresh air.

'He asked how you are. In fact, it is the first thing he
mentions when he sees me. Something goes click and he says:
"Ah, Mrs Murphy, how are you and how is the Reverend
Mother?"'

'And you say: "Very well, your lordship," and then you both
go on to talk about more important matters.'

'Actually, this time I said: "Looking very pale and tired,
your lordship" – that's what I said, and he tutted. First time
that I ever heard someone do that. You read it in books –
"he tutted" – but I've never actually heard the sound before.
The bishop, you will be pleased to know, did it very well
– two little clicks.'

'So, he's down in Youghal. Funny, I got an answer, by return
of post, to a letter that I sent to the bishop's palace in Shandon
asking for more money to fund our new class. I got a refusal,
an instant refusal – signed by the bishop, himself – well, at
least it's the signature on all the replies that I get from him.'

'He probably leaves realms of signed blank sheets with
instructions to his secretary: "If anyone asks for money, say

no." Rupert does that sort of thing. I've heard him instructing someone to tell a blatant lie – *if anyone wants me, I'm out* – that sort of thing. I hear him saying that to his secretary all the time. Picks up the phone and tells the girl to perjure herself.'

The Reverend Mother sighed. It was not a strategy that she could afford to adopt. If someone wanted her, the chances were that it might well be on a matter of life and death. The risk of a refusal was not a risk that she wanted to take.

'Don't sigh,' said Lucy sympathetically. 'You do look so tired. Tell me about it.'

'It's just that I thought about getting as many children as I can into school at the age of four rather than waiting until they are five,' explained the Reverend Mother. 'The Department of Education won't pay for them, despite the fact that most of its members have sent their own children to expensive kindergarten and nursery classes when they were that age, or even younger. And, of course, most of the children who do go to these nurseries and kindergartens learn to read early and successfully. They get an early start, and they progress fast.'

'And you want the little children of the slums to get that early start. You try too hard, Dotty. You can't take the troubles of the world upon your shoulders. What does it matter if a child learns to read at four or five instead of at six or seven?' There was a slightly impatient note in Lucy's voice.

'Except that they don't,' said the Reverend Mother sorrowfully. 'I'm not sure why, but despite making the teaching as good as I possibly can, many of these children don't learn to read. Some disappear, some die, some attend school sporadically and many leave us without becoming what I would call readers, and some few are, I have to confess, illiterate. Very few are what I would call successes. I got the idea of starting the children a little earlier, trying to get them ahead before they become disillusioned. We've turned an old storeroom, overlooking the garden, into a nursery classroom and I am trying to find money to furnish it.' She passed her hand wearily over her face, feeling the lines upon the dry skin and then she straightened her back. 'I'll get there,' she said as vigorously as she could and was pleased to see a smile of pleasure upon her cousin's face.

'Of course, you will,' said Lucy enthusiastically. 'And I know how you might get a new source of money. Now, don't interrupt – just allow me to explain in my own way.' Lucy stopped, surveyed her cousin's face, and then stripped her gloves from her fingers. 'Don't let me go off without these,' she warned. 'They come from Peru and are incredibly expensive.'

The Reverend Mother surveyed the expensive gloves, soft and warm, she thought, and wondered how much she could get for them if she sold them at the market. It was a tempting idea, but not one that fitted with the seventh of the ten commandments – *thou shalt not steal* and so she turned her attention to her cousin's impassioned speech, which seemed to mostly deal with how pale and tired her cousin was looking.

'And I know what you must do, and I am the bearer of an invitation; our cousin Nell has invited you to spend a week in her cliff-top house in Youghal – wonderful sea air – a complete change,' she ended.

'Impossible,' said the Reverend Mother briskly. 'The bishop would not permit it.'

'Ah, but he will, he does, or he *doth*, as he would say himself. I knew you would say that, so I got him to scribble a note to you. Here it is, written in his own hand, with his best fountain pen. But don't take it for a moment. Just listen to what I have to say. You know that Nell inherited the most magnificent house built on top of a cliff in Youghal, not too far from Walter Raleigh's house where we went that day. Infinitely better though, huge house on top of the hill. Look out the back windows and you see the Blackwater Estuary entering the sea and look out of the front windows and Cork harbour is in front of you. But that is not all. Just listen, don't interrupt. That is not all. You desperately need a holiday, but you won't take one because you think that you have to go on working until you drop, but if you come back with me to Youghal, then you will be working. It won't be a real holiday – it will be a money-raising expedition. That house is full of people who are, collectively, worth millions of pounds. You tell them about your dreams. Nell and I have talked it over.

We know how to handle it. You'll just have to do what you are told, for a change, Dotty. I know it doesn't come easy for you to take a holiday away from your convent, but you will come back to Cork with enough money to fund your dream of a new classroom. Nell is really quite excited about it. She is full of ideas.'

The Reverend Mother thought hard. She looked at the bishop's affable little note. Yes, it was unambiguous. His lordship felt that she should have a week by the sea to enable her to come back with renewed energy for the excellent work which she was doing in St Mary's Isle. She knew how her cousin Lucy would stage-manage everything. Knew, also, that Nell was interested, and a new interest was important for a bored, relatively wealthy woman with nothing to do but to drive fast cars around the city of Cork. And these wealthy friends. Her common sense told her that the cost of a couple of opera tickets would probably pay a carpenter to make a desk for a child. She would give good value for money. She would make them feel good. Make them feel that they had a stake in this new venture, in this new experiment to educate slum children according to the philosophy of Madame Montessori.

Another idea came to her mind, also. There in Youghal, amongst her rich relations, there were the seeds of the murder of a man and one of her own pupils, poor little Maureen, languished in prison, falsely accused of that death. She had to find out the truth.

And there was something else, also. Not her business, she told herself, but her affection for her students never wavered and it was important to her to help them to success, whether they were four years old or grown up and striving to make their way in the world despite their poor and poverty-stricken childhood. Patrick, she knew, could achieve the position of superintendent of the Cork Barracks. He had the working ability, the tenacity and ambition, but his background as a half-starved and barefoot child made him lack confidence. If he could successfully solve this murder just at the time when the position became vacant, then he might have a very good chance to be appointed. If only she could point him in the right direction. There was bound to be a clue to be picked up

once she was there in Youghal and was able to talk with those
who knew the dead man, and perhaps the murderer. She had
a strong instinct that the roots of the matter lay in Youghal.

'I'll do it,' she said aloud. It would probably be a hasty
decision to be regretted quite soon afterwards but, it was, after
all, her duty to obey the bishop. She was seriously worried
about that child, Maureen McCarthy, and it would be important
to find out a little more about the dead man and whether he
had any enemies who might have wanted to kill him.

In addition, she would doubtless be refreshed by the sea air
and by the opportunity to stand back from her incessant anxieties and cares. And there was no doubt but that she was
touched by the relief and affection which she saw on her
cousin's face.

SEVENTEEN

Three days after that astonishing message from the bishop, the Reverend Mother, with a pristine suitcase which dated to the last century, was seated in Lucy's car as the chauffeur drove them smoothly and efficiently through the slum lanes and narrow streets, down busy quaysides and then out of the city and through the salubrious suburbs of the southern side of the city.

The Reverend Mother was now calmly resigned to obeying orders. She had gone through the throes of bitterly regretting her decision. What if there were to be a crisis when she was away, had been her first thought. Some woman on the verge of suicide, coming for advice and perhaps receiving none. She had no illusions about her deputy, Sister Mary Immaculate. whose belief in the will of God might be pious but that doctrine was seldom of little practical use to some unfortunate in the throes of utter distress and often fear. The Reverend Mother had been driven to sharing her anxieties when, after early morning mass in the convent chapel, Sister Bernadette had carried into her study a tray holding her meagre breakfast from the kitchen. Sister Bernadette was quite eager to discuss the exciting event of the Reverend Mother's instruction from His Lordship, the Holy Apostolic Bishop of Cork and of Cloyne. It had been decreed, apparently, that Reverend Mother Aquinas, should bow to the bishop's command and take a short holiday of a few days beside the sea in her cousin's house in Youghal. The Reverend Mother indulged her curiosity for a few minutes, but then turned to business.

'Of course, Sister Bernadette,' she said, striving for tact as well as reassurance, 'Sister Mary Immaculate will be so busy when I am away that perhaps if one of the parents of the children, or one of the children themselves, come with a problem, you might help them yourself if you can – and if you can't – well, often a cup of tea and slice of cake will do as much good as all the talking in the world,' she had said to her, thinking that although Sister Bernadette was a lay sister, far below the Deputy Reverend Mother in status, nevertheless the woman had a practical common sense as well as a warm and affectionate nature – both of which might be of more use to a distraught woman or child than all the sanctimonious lectures about the will of God that Sister Mary Immaculate was so anxious to bestow on all who were suffering.

She had feared that her words might embarrass the humble lay sister but was relieved when dear Sister Bernadette gave an understanding nod.

'Don't you worry about a thing, Reverend Mother,' she had said affectionately. 'I'll be the one that opens the door and I'll do what I think that you would want me to do.'

The Reverend Mother smiled. 'You know, Sister,' she said, 'one of my favourite parts in the Bible is when Jesus spoke of being like a man going on a long journey and appointing his servants each to their work, but the gatekeeper, the janitor, Jesus felt, was the most important – the one who ordered all and who kept watch. You shall be my gatekeeper, Sister Bernadette and in you I will place my reliance.'

And after that brief conversation she had felt somewhat comforted and murmured to herself: '*sicut homo qui peregre profectus reliquit domum suam et dedit servis suis potestatem cuiusque operis et janitori praecipiat ut vigilet.*' Sister Bernadette would be her janitor. All would be well. So, she packed her small suitcase that evening and found herself this morning, sitting comfortably in her cousin's car on way to spend a few days beside the sea.

'Shut your eyes,' said Lucy. 'Keep them closed until I tell you to open them.' The Reverend Mother shut her eyes and hoped that Lucy would give the word quickly. The car was so deliciously warm and the seats were so luxuriously padded that she was afraid that she would fall asleep.

However, a minute later, her cousin gave the word and she opened them.

'There you are,' said Lucy. 'Look! We're out of the city. Sun! No fog! Now you just sit back and relax and soon we will see the sea and that will put new life into you. A week beside the sea and you will return to Cork like a new woman, ready to perform miracles. Forget your troubles. Empty them all out of your mind and concentrate on doing one thing well at a time. Do you remember that governess that we had who was always telling you that? I think you were very clever, even then, and your mind was always overflowing with ideas, and she used to say: "One thing at a time!"'

The Reverend Mother smiled. 'I remember,' she said.

'You were so clever,' said Lucy. 'I don't think that I was jealous of you. I think that I took it for granted that you were clever and that I was artistic. I remember how one of our uncles used to keep saying to your father, "Shame she isn't a boy!" and your father used to get really annoyed. He didn't want a boy, he kept saying. He was very proud of you,' finished Lucy and the Reverend Mother's thoughts turned to the positive influence being thought clever and sensible had been through her life. Perhaps, she thought, the most useful gift that one can give a child is a feeling of self-esteem. Perhaps educating young children in schools was a very bad idea. Both she and Lucy had not gone to school until they were about fourteen and it had been their decision, not something imposed upon them. Up to then, each had been valued for proficiency in different skills and each had their position established in the household as an expert with certain talents and different branches of knowledge to be called upon when needed. And yet, both had lost their mothers at a very early age.

Lucy's father had made the decision that his daughter would be best brought up in Ireland with her cousin while he led a more adventurous life in Canada and arrived home to Cork at regular intervals laden with presents for both. She and Lucy had been sisters in all but name, though, since each had a highly different father as a private possession, they had never felt jealous of each other as far as she could remember.

'Small classes – six or seven girls and boys in each class like those private Montessori nurseries, that would suit young children best – thirty or forty small children in a class is far too many,' she said aloud, and Lucy gave an exasperated click with her tongue.

'Stop thinking about your wretched school. Let's think about the murder. More fun. And don't get all pious. He was a most objectionable and unpleasant man. He deserved to be murdered and so we can have a nice time trying to decide who was the person that did such a public-spirited piece of work. We could put a bet on it if you like. If you win, I'll double the money that I was going to give to you for your latest classroom and if I win then you will promise me to take some sort of little break from the convent every summer.'

'I'll think about it,' said the Reverend Mother. 'And, of course, I must put in a *caveat* referring to the bishop. Let's not discuss him in front of Nell's guests, though.'

'And, of course, I must put in a *caveat* referring to Rupert,' returned Lucy. 'Don't let anyone pester me to know what he thinks about some legal case, by the way – just in case he is involved on the part of the government or of the accused.'

'Of course,' echoed the Reverend Mother. 'So, who do you think murdered this man?'

'Can we eliminate your girls?' asked Lucy.

'Certainly!' said the Reverend Mother sternly. 'I can give you three good reasons. One: none of them had any reason to murder the man. It lost them six shillings a week and nothing has been gained. Two: I doubt any would know that smoke kills. It would not be the way that they would choose to kill if they wished to kill. More likely to steal a knife or to hit him over the head with a metal rod, or even to poison him if they could get hold of some rat poison. Three: I also doubt that any of them would have access to petrol and it appears, from what Inspector Cashman tells me, that the fire was started in the girls' privy by means of petrol being poured upon the wood between the shed and the girls' privy.'

'Well, that's pretty comprehensive, you would make a good witness for the defence, as my dear husband would say,' said Lucy. 'Now let me see. Who is my prime suspect, or who can I rule out decisively? Do you know, I can't think? Who is it that the police are suspecting? Have you any information? Surely your past pupil, Inspector Cashman, has dropped you a hint. No? Not a single one? You mustn't be encouraging him sufficiently!' Lucy leaned back against the cushions and looked idly through the window. They were going quite slowly, through a main road, must be Midleton, thought the Reverend Mother. It was decades since she had seen the place, though it hadn't changed too much.

'I know who it could be!' said Lucy suddenly. 'I've got a suspect already!' She sat up looking quite animated and pulled down the blind in the face of a man crossing the road who had peered in the window to catch a glimpse of the inmates of the expensive car. 'And the interesting thing is,' she continued, 'that we will meet him at Nell's place. He and his wife are quite friends of hers. And guess what his business is?'

'I can't guess,' said the Reverend Mother. 'Please don't ever ask me to guess. I'm so used to telling lies to small children who want me to guess such extremely obvious matters that I'm sure the ability of my guessing faculty to function as an adult's would do in normal circumstances has slowly disintegrated during the years.'

'Well, I'll have to admit that is a very unusual excuse for not being able to guess, so I suppose that I will have to tell you,' said Lucy. 'This man, his name is Douglas O'Mahoney, he has a business making very expensive tobacco pipes – made from the wood from olive trees, if you please. In fact, I would be very surprised, seeing as you are a newcomer to Nell's house parties, if he didn't spend half an hour boring you with the reasons why a pipe made from the wood of an olive tree is worth ten times the amount paid for an ordinary briar pipe. He has spent a huge amount of money buying that place on Patrick Street, furnished it to look like an authentic smoking room in the time of Queen Victoria, and you would faint if I told you how much he charges for his pipes.'

The Reverend Mother tried to listen with interest to this story, but her mind was on money to buy desks and the figure mentioned by Lucy as normally expended to pay for a six-inch pipe was so enormous that it made her feel slightly ill.

'Anyway, he is absolutely furious at the idea of this cigarette factory, because in the first place, women don't smoke pipes, but fashionable women are taking up smoking cigarettes so that immediately doubles the market for cigarettes, and secondly once cigarettes are said to be in fashion that will quadruple their market because, you see, my dear, unworldly cousin, to be in the fashion is everything for people with money. What do you bet, but that as soon as these Cork-grown and Cork-manufactured cigarettes hit the tobacco shops, they become the latest thing – especially if Robert gets plenty of publicity about them being made from the tobacco plants originally brought by Sir Walter Raleigh from the new world. So, what do you bet that once that becomes public everyone who is anybody in the city of Cork will be smoking cigarettes, and pipes will be relegated to old fuddy-duddies?' said Lucy finishing her question with a flourish.

'I never bet,' said the Reverend Mother. She spoke in a slightly absent-minded way. Another idea had occurred to her, and she proceeded to test it out upon Lucy.

'It has occurred to me,' she said, 'that we are all, including even the police themselves, regarding this matter as a murder because a man was killed. But what if no murder, no bodily harm was intended? What if this is a case of arson, pure and simple? After all, I suppose that if you wanted to burn down a business premises without putting any life at risk, eight o'clock in the evening could be considered a time when no one would still be there. It was, perhaps, unfortunate that the man who lost his life was an extremely disliked person and that many would have wished to harm him. But, after all, his enemies were probably confined to a small group of people centred among the family and friends of the girl whom he made pregnant, by rape it was said. But what if your friend with the expensive pipes went around to St Mary's Isle with a can of petrol and a box of matches?'

Lucy looked at her uneasily. 'I was only joking about Douglas O'Mahoney. I don't really suppose that he would go around to St Mary's Isle with a can of petrol and a box of matches – in fact, I hope I don't upset you, but Douglas O'Mahoney is the sort of man whom I just could not imagine going to St Mary's Isle for any reason whatsoever. He's an extremely elegant, beautifully dressed person and I really was only joking when I suggested that he might have a motive for burning down a rival's premises. It would not be his sort of thing at all.'

The Reverend Mother regarded her cousin with a sceptical glance.

'I see absolutely no reason why an elegant and beautifully dressed person should not be guilty of a crime. Nor why an inelegant and badly dressed person should be immediately suspected,' she added. And then honesty compelled her to say, 'But I suppose that the poor usually commit crimes that will instantly supply something to them – as in breaking into a shop to steal food or smashing the window of a dress shop to steal a warm shawl or something of the sort – though I don't think that happens too often – not sure why not – I wonder whether I would take some extreme measure if I were frozen cold and desperately hungry,' she added in a meditative manner.

Cork, she thought, was a city of poverty and disease – diphtheria, scarlatina and typhoid still ran rampant through the overcrowded slums where they killed thousands. Children died of those diseases, but they also died of famine and from exposure to rain and fog. It was amazing that the population endured the conditions without open rebellion. Crime numbers were not high and mostly related to an excess of alcohol. 'Thank God for the religion of the people that protects them against this socialism,' had said the Bishop of Cork. Was it the will of God, wondered the Reverend Mother, that decreed that one man could pay for a pipe what would feed the children of another man for a month? She thought of Eileen and her column in the *Cork Examiner*. It had been signed 'A Patriot' for a couple of years, but then as Eileen became more educated, had started at university, she had become more confident in her own opinions, and the name of the column had been changed to 'A Patriot and a Socialist'. 'Perhaps the answer is education,' she said aloud and then smiled at her cousin.

'Tell me about your rich friends who would burn down another man's premises in order to improve their own business,' she said affably. 'Of course,' she added, 'you've already told me that Douglas O'Mahoney would not soil his soul, or his hands, by going to St Mary's Isle, but is it not possible that someone of wealth and of influence could drop a word in the ear of a more lowly employee – a bit like King Henry

II who had only to murmur, "*Will no one rid me of this turbulent priest?*" and then the deed was done. *Vaulting ambition leads to evil deeds* . . . did I make that up, Lucy, do you think? Or is it a genuine quote?' finished the Reverend Mother, looking blandly at her cousin.

'You made it up,' said Lucy. 'Otherwise you would be telling me who said it. You can never resist educating me. Now let me see. We have Douglas O'Mahoney who might, perhaps, think it would be a useful thing if that cigarette factory were to be destroyed, remember we are not talking about a murder, now. Just a bit of arson, isn't that, right? Is there anyone that might have regarded the factory as a bit of a blot on the land-scape? What about you yourself? Did it block your view of the river? But, of course, Robert was employing your past pupils, wasn't he? So not you. I know who it could be, though. What about that woman who reported seeing that poor child, Maureen McCarthy, wasn't that her name? Well, the woman who reported that she stayed late every day and who threw suspicions upon her caused the police to arrest her.'

'You are talking about Mrs Maloney,' said the Reverend Mother. 'That is a lady who fancies herself as champion of law and order. And, no, I don't think that she resented the new factory building. In fact, I would imagine that it was the brightest thing that came into her life for the last twenty years. Before that arrived, she had to leave her cottage and go out into the streets to find out some gossip, but now she can sit in the warmth and peace of her kitchen and look out of the window and see snippets of gossip every hour or so. It's been a life-saver for her.' As she said that, she wondered whether Patrick had made enough use of Mrs Maloney. A woman who made trouble, a busy-body, no doubt, but someone who was scrupulously honest and all-seeing – that was her impression of Mrs Maloney. And she was certain that if anything odd had been going on that she would have found some means of relating it to Patrick. She would have to direct his attention to the old gossiping woman.

'Tell me more about Nell's guests,' she said aloud. The chances were, she thought, as she lent one ear to Lucy's amusing and compact biographies, that none of these wealthy and important people had any useful information for the discovery of the murder of Robert's manager. Nevertheless, it would be a close-knit community here among the friends and relatives of Robert himself and she could, she told herself, have a perfectly valid reason to visit The Grove and to thank the friendly gardener for the delivery of the myrtle tree and its splendid tub. She turned a smiling face upon her cousin.

'Do you know,' she said, 'I am beginning to quite look forward to meeting Nell and her friends. I wonder at what stage during the dinner party should I introduce the story about my patent invention for trapping and poisoning rats. Nell thought that it would be of great interest to everyone,' she finished with a bland look at her cousin.

'Let's talk about the fire,' said Lucy.

'You sound like a governess trying to distract a child, nevertheless, I must confess that I am interested in the subject. Do you think that Robert has any enemies? It would seem much more likely that a fire was started to burn down the building than to asphyxiate a man by smoke inhalation.'

'You're right, of course,' said Lucy enthusiastically. 'There's no one else that I know of who is manufacturing cigarettes, not in Cork, anyway. But, you know, Dotty, when it comes to it, Robert did come up with a very clever idea. It's not just the making of cigarettes, but this connection with Sir Walter Raleigh and the growing of the tobacco here by the sea in Youghal. He'll get lots of publicity for this and then if the cigarettes sell very well here in Cork, well, he can use these sale figures to engender more publicity. A "sell-out success" – I can just see that on the front page of the *Cork Examiner*. I don't suppose that you take much notice of headlines like that, but I have to confess that it usually sends me straight down to the shop just on the chance that a new stock has arrived. Robert could make a fortune out of those cigarettes if he manages matters carefully. I hope this fire doesn't put him off.'

The Reverend Mother listened with interest. She had, up to now, been interested in the cigarette factory only as a possible employer for her girls, but now she began to wonder whether a well-planned crime may have taken place. It would, she thought, have been quite possible that someone who wanted to burn down the building and, literally, reduce the newly fledged industry to ashes, would have watched the place for a week or so previously. He, or even she, would have seen that the red-headed girl stayed late every night.

Aloud, she said: 'Tell me, Lucy, enlighten my ignorance, does drinking alcohol stimulate your bladder?'

Lucy giggled, gave a quick look at the chauffeur and at the glass barrier between him and them.

'You do ask the most extraordinary questions,' she said. 'Yes, I suppose that it does. Not that I take anything but a few sips of some genteel sherry myself.'

'I'm sure that you would not over-imbibe. I was just thinking that if someone, let's call him or her "our murderer", was watching the cigarette factory on St Mary's Isle, he, or even she, would possibly have seen the girl Maureen visit the outside convenience before taking that long climb to the top of Barrack Street – what do you think? And, of course, the outside convenience would have been an ideal place to start a fire in perfect privacy once all the girls had gone home. It would screen "our murderer" from passers-by, even from the nosy woman who lives in the cottage and who was the police informant, so once that poor girl had gone home, he, or she, could have gone in there with a can of petrol and perhaps some sticks and started up a fire against the wooden wall. All that wood and all those dried leaves would burn immediately, and I would imagine that our cousin Robert would not have the money to rebuild. I believe Nell insisted that he insure it, so perhaps he could set it up again, I suppose, if he'd followed her advice. Nell has a good head on her shoulders.'

The Reverend Mother considered the matter as the car made its way towards the sea.

'But the idea is still there, isn't it?' she said after some time. 'Someone else could take it up, even Nell herself, pay something for the tobacco plants initially, even import them, and milk the idea for the connection to Sir Walter Raleigh. Well, I'm no lawyer, your dear husband would enlighten you about this, but I do believe that there could be no reason why the name "Raleigh's Cigarettes" and a nicely drawn illustration of Raleigh puffing away could not have been used by anyone – unless, of course, Robert had the foresight to take out a trademark.'

'You're very clever about these things: to hear you talk, no one would believe that you had spent your life in a convent,' said Lucy admiringly. 'So, the idea to set the factory on fire and implicate the girl who always stayed late might have been triggered by our murderer's surveillance of the factory and it would, in all probability, have had very little risk to him.'

'Or her,' said the Reverend Mother thoughtfully.

'Good point!' said Lucy brightly. 'I still think that it might be your friend from the cottage, the little old lady who likes reporting misdemeanours to the police, what's her name? Mrs Maloney, that's it, isn't it?'

'Why on earth should Mrs Maloney want to burn down the cigarette factory?' said the Reverend Mother, widening her eyes, while her active brain ran through the possibilities.

'Perhaps she is very pious and regarded the place as sinful – pious old ladies get these ideas, you know.'

The Reverend Mother considered the suggestion and shook her head. 'She never struck me as pious and I've had to listen to her tales about badly behaved children on many occasions. She was annoyed at them stealing apples from the back of lorries, but I never heard her bring God into it. If I remember rightly, she was mostly annoyed about the suspicion that these thefts put the prices up for decent, law-abiding people like herself. And, I suppose that she might have been right,' added the Reverend Mother, thinking that it would be wonderful to live in a utopia where every person was provided with food, clothing and housing and the means of heating their house, but had to earn money for luxuries like cars and fine furniture and perhaps the cinema, though she was tempted to allow free entrance, once a week, to the cinema for children under the age of seven. It would, she thought, develop their imagination, and perhaps lead them on to books to satisfy their craving for excitement and adventure on the six days when they could not go to the cinema.

'So not Mrs Maloney,' said Lucy sadly. 'I wouldn't like to

see her hang, of course, but I suppose that a good lawyer, like
my Rupert, could easily get her out of that, arguing that she
did not mean to cause a death and was purely bent upon
removing the temptation to squander money from the poor
people of the city. That would probably go down well with a
judge. I must run it past Rupert when I get home again.'

'I don't think that it would work – I mean getting rid of
cigarettes,' said the Reverend Mother wisely. 'Surely the place
must be insured. I know that I, or the bishop, I suppose, pay
a large sum of money every year to an insurance company for
my convent. I often think how nice it would be to burn down
that damp, draughty old building and build a lovely new one
with the insurance money, but perhaps Robert isn't insured.'

'Yes, he is, and guess who pays the premium – his sister,
Nell. I told you that, didn't I? And it's no secret because Robert
himself told a whole group of people about it at his birthday
party. He toasted Nell as the best sister in the world. I think
Nell was a bit embarrassed at this public announcement and
she said something about having it so well insured that she
could always burn the place down if it was doing too badly
and then spend the money on something intelligent like a six-
month holiday in the South Pacific or somewhere like that. I
wonder how much the insurance is,' finished Lucy in a meditative fashion.

She was silent for a few moments and then with a hasty
glance to check the partition between them and the chauffeur,
she put her mouth near to her cousin's ear and murmured:
'You know, Dotty, this so-called cigarette factory may not have
been what Nell envisaged when she put her money into it.
That wooden shed on a marsh, instead of a proper factory,
that nasty grounds-manager put in charge with absolutely no
experience of managing a business and, excuse me if I seem
to run down your pupils, but putting a crowd of fourteen-year-
old girls in to do the work with no experience whatsoever . . .'

'That's interesting,' said the Reverend Mother. 'I must say
that I would prefer it to be a case of arson and that the death
of the man was accidental. After all, I suppose if the man were
not completely inebriated and sunk into a drunken sleep, he
could easily escape. It's not like a fire in one of these tall

houses built all over the city a few hundred years ago. They are a terrible fire hazard and when children tell me about lighting a fire upon the floor, I have nightmares about the danger that some of those poor people are running.'

'Why on earth do they do that? Why don't they light the fire in a fireplace?' Lucy was so shocked that her voice rose high, and the chauffeur's head turned in their direction for a few seconds before turning back to face the road again. The Reverend Mother lowered her voice to avoid any further distraction to the man at the wheel.

'My dear Lucy,' she said. 'These old houses have huge rooms. Landlords divide them into two and sometimes into four rooms before they let them out. I've seen a house that had six families in a room that once was the drawing room, I suppose. So, of course, very few have a fireplace and those who do, usually stuff it with paper to stop the draughts from the chimney. The more careful ones might put a piece of stone on the floor before building a fire that the family can huddle around, but if you are shivering with the cold and your children have collected a few sticks, some cardboard from the back of a lorry and even some pieces of coal from a delivery cart, well you light a fire in the middle of your space and get the family to sit around it.'

'Most dangerous,' said Lucy disapprovingly. 'Shouldn't be allowed.'

'No, it shouldn't be allowed,' said the Reverend Mother sadly. 'But, of course, to go back to our fire on St Mary's Isle, that outside privy, which I must confess I was instrumental in getting built, provided an ideal place for "our murderer", or perhaps it should be just "our criminal", to light a fire. I say "criminal" rather than "murderer" because the intention may have been to destroy a business rather than to take a man's life. My goodness,' she said in a different tone of voice, 'is that the sea down there?'

'Well, we are almost there. That's the place where the River Blackwater enters the sea. Don't you remember learning those rivers off by heart with that governess we had when we were small children? I still remember them.'

'I remember Spenser writing about the rivers of Ireland

– and I suppose it was when he stayed with Raleigh.' The Reverend Mother gave a slight sigh. One of the many hard decisions she had been forced to make when she entered the convent had been to leave her precious books behind. Only the Latin version of Thomas Aquinas' teachings had been allowed, its subject matter and the language in which it had been written giving it a sanctified aspect to the Mother of Novices, who had been somewhat suspicious of this unusual recruit to the order. She looked through the car window at the sharp incline leading from the road down to where the sprawling width of the Blackwater River entered the seashore. Was there any chance, she wondered, that she could walk down there without soaking her ankle-length black habit or offending the susceptibilities of her hosts.

'And there's Nell's house, over here, on that hill. She has glorious views of the sea – look there is Ballycotton Lighthouse on that little island.'

'I remember going there,' said the Reverend Mother and decided there and then that there would be no further talk about their youth and their holidays by the sea. She would keep her memories to herself, drink in the sea air and discuss the puzzle of the cigarette factory fire with her cousin.

'Who would want to kill a man like that manager, Mr Timothy Dooley?' she asked.

'Well,' said Lucy. 'From what you tell me the man was most unpleasant, raping a girl, having to be forced to pay some compensation to her, seducing a fourteen-year-old, as far as you can tell, so there may have been other girls and other furious fathers. Other than that, I really cannot say. And, of course, as we were just thinking, that fire might have been started to burn the place down and extinguish the business.'

The Reverend Mother thought about that and then shook her head. 'Unlikely,' she said. 'After all there was only one room in the place and that room had a large window facing south, so that one glance through the window would have shown that a drunken man was sitting at the table, slumped over in a drunken sleep. If someone just wanted to burn the premises, surely they would have checked to make sure that there was no one there. They would have seen the girl come out, go into that outside convenience, and then walk away. It would have been a moment's work to peer in the window and then wait until the man, also, had left.'

'I see what you mean,' said Lucy. 'That outside convenience, as you call it, would have been the ideal place to start up a fire, but if the person who started the fire did not wish to kill the man within the workroom, then, surely, he would have waited. I don't think that it is of any use to check among Nell's guests, you know. The secret of that man's death probably lies in the city of Cork.'

'We'll see,' said the Reverend Mother. She would, she planned, go on some long walks during the few days when she was here by the sea. Walking meant time for thinking and many of her best ideas came to her while she was walking, even in the traffic-filled streets of Cork.

She was, she thought, on holiday – probably her first holiday for over sixty years. It could be used for something outside her normal everyday concerns. It could be used to find the culprit who had lit that fire to ruin her cousin's business.

Or had there been another motive behind that smoke-laden fire?

EIGHTEEN

Nell's house was very magnificent. A huge house, standing on top of the hill with magnificent views over the sea. Nell was a very good hostess and her visitors were shown up to their rooms immediately and told that tea would be served to them, and they could have a rest before coming downstairs and meeting the other guests.

'You've got a room overlooking the Blackwater River,' said Lucy when she came to make sure that her cousin was comfortable. She looked all around and then walked to the window and looked out.

'I know why you were given this room,' she said. 'Nell's house parties are always very gregarious with people popping in and out of each other's bedrooms for hours after the evening has finished. She knew that no one but I would be visiting you and you see, this room has such a good view of that terrible cliff where Robert's wife was killed.' She went to the window and looked out and then beckoned her cousin. 'The car's brakes failed, and it tumbled down there, right onto the rocks. Terrible thing. You can still see the remains of it, though of course it has almost rusted away.'

'Extraordinary that it hasn't been removed,' said the Reverend Mother, gazing down.

'I suppose that it was impossible. I seem to remember hearing that they had to get the body out by floating it on a light canoe at high tide and then placing it on a boat to bring it to shore and even then it was a difficult business. Poor old Robert. A terrible time for him. He was quite ill for days afterwards, not well enough to go to the funeral. Sorry,' added Lucy. 'I shouldn't have told you that. Would you like me to ask Nell to give you another room?'

'Not at all. I shall say a prayer for her and for Robert and then banish the whole matter from my mind. In the midst of life, we are in death,' said the Reverend Mother placidly.

'Well, have a good rest, there is your tea, I do like those tea cosies, don't you? Nell has the best of everything. I'm really looking forward to dinner. She has a wonderful cook.'

And, indeed, the dinner was splendid, thought the Reverend Mother. There were no wine glasses at her place at the bottom of the table, but three different varieties of spring water were lined up for her to choose from. She listened with interest to the conversation about a performance of *Othello* in the Cork Opera House with the well-known Irish actor Micheál Mac Liammóir in the main part.

'Do you ever take your pupils to the Opera House, Reverend Mother?' asked Nell and the Reverend Mother appreciated the effort of bringing her into the conversation.

'How much would the admission price be?' she asked with an air of feigned interest.

'Oh, just about a shilling or so,' said Nell innocently. 'And how many pupils have you got?'

It was so blatant that the Reverend Mother couldn't help laughing. However, now was her moment and she had to make the best of it.

'A penny is what I need sometimes,' she assured her audience. 'A penny will buy a pencil for a small child and a pencil can be the beginning of a new future for some of the children from the slums whom I teach. Give me a penny and I can buy a child a pencil and I can teach him or her to write. Give me a shilling and I can buy a book or better still books. No child learns to read with just one book, not the children who come to me, in any case. It can be very hard with children who have never heard a story read to them, who have never seen their parents read a book, it can be very hard to give them an interest in such a difficult matter as learning to read. And as for learning to write, well, that takes lots of pencils.'

'Is it worth the effort?'

That was a question that she had not foreseen, and the Reverend Mother turned to the speaker with eyes widened in astonishment.

'Yes, of course, it is. If it isn't, then I have probably wasted more than half a century of my life – and,' she added with an effort of lightening the atmosphere, 'that would be a most annoying thought for someone as stubborn as I am.'

'Bravo!' exclaimed her cousin Robert. He picked up a wooden bowl and having removed the apples from it, held it aloft. 'Now who will give the Reverend Mother a penny to buy a pencil, or even a shilling to buy a book. Come on, Tom, you asked the question, and you got your answer. Come on, now and fork out.'

To the Reverend Mother's astonishment, Tom produced a ten-shilling note, but then, to her even greater amazement, this was followed by a pound note from the next person to reach across to Robert and his wooden bowl, and then the mood was set and, within laughter and false protests, notes, pound notes, five-pound notes, ten-pound notes were pressed into the bowl. They all, thought the Reverend Mother, probably had too much of the wine to drink, nevertheless she had no compunction. It did not occur to her to protest, why should she?

She smiled benignly upon them all. From the conversations she had overheard during dinner, these people spent money on all sorts of things, operas, visits to Paris for clothes, a trip in an aeroplane, a new car. It would do them no harm to spend some money on the poor children who lived in the same city as they did. Nell, she noticed, was smiling with an air of quiet satisfaction and her heart warmed toward her cousins. Robert, she thought, had done her quite a service by taking that shallow wooden bowl which showed, so very clearly, every person's contribution.

Nell, she noticed, had tinkled the bell beside her, and whispered an instruction into the ear of the maid who had answered it. When the girl returned, she brought with her an envelope, a substantial envelope bearing the imprint of the Munster Bank, and neatly, one by one, Nell inserted the notes into it. The few pieces of silver left over were neatly stacked and then slipped into a bag.

It would, all, thought the Reverend Mother, be transferred meticulously to her. She was confident about that. It had, she thought, been a very worthwhile visit of hers.

But there was something else that she wanted to clear up

upon this unusual visit of hers. The only problem was that she lacked specialist knowledge.

There was, however, a solution. She remembered well an excellent teacher, whom she had in her youth, had once said something of great importance to her.

'It's not so much important to know the answers, as it is knowing where to look for the answers,' had said that lady and the Reverend Mother, more than half a century later, still remembered that excellent advice. When she went back up to her bedroom, she spent a long few minutes looking from the window. It was August and the days were beginning to shorten. Even so, the tide was in, and the River Blackwater was unloading ships from its placid surface into the broken waves of the sea. A wonderful sight!

She could understand why Nell's mother had built her house upon this steep hillside.

Such an interesting person, she thought when she met her hostess over breakfast the following morning. Nell probably had a hundred and one tasks to perform with a houseful of visitors and expeditions to organize, meal menus to approve and staff to manage. Even so she was amused and interested by her elderly cousin's interest in purchasing a suitable car for the use of the convent.

'You see,' said the Reverend Mother earnestly, 'I wouldn't like to buy a car unless I knew what I was doing, and unless I understood the implications of keeping the car in running order and making sure that it was not an expense upon the community.'

Nell looked at her with interest.

'What, exactly, is worrying you, Reverend Mother?' she said.

She and the Reverend Mother seemed to be the only ones of the house party who had bothered to come downstairs for breakfast. Doubtless the rest of the party had preferred to breakfast in bed.

'When I first became Reverend Mother of my convent, I swore to myself that I would understand every particle of the running of the establishment. I went into the kitchens, I haunted the classrooms, I checked the bathrooms and took the tempera- ture of the convent chapel. If I were to get a car for the use of the community, I would like to be sure that I knew how the machine ran,' said the Reverend Mother, looking very directly into her cousin's eyes.

Nell finished her coffee and looked across at her elderly cousin with a smile.

'Well,' she said, 'you do surprise me, but you are quite right. It's so stupid the way that people buy a car and haven't a notion what goes on beneath the bonnet. Now finish up your breakfast and come and have a look at my car.'

The Reverend Mother sedately drank her tea and munched her toast. Not quite as good as dear Sister Bernadette supplied, but there were, in fairness, a very wide range of supplementary treats available for any who despised the toast. When she had finished, she wiped her mouth on the fine linen of the napkin and then rose to her feet.

'I'm ready for my lesson,' she said, accompanying the words with a smile in case that she had sounded too in earnest. Somehow or other, she could not quite imagine herself buying a car. Still, she told herself, it was good for all, for elderly Reverend Mothers, as well as for children, to have something to dream about.

Nell, she thought, when they were out on the gravel in front of the garages, would have made an excellent teacher. With the bonnet flung wide open, she explained the workings of the combustion engine in such simple terms that the Reverend Mother thought that most of her seven-year-olds could have understood it. A quick lesson on how to test the levels of the oil and change it and how to check the pressure on the tyres, and check the lights – Nell was enthusiastic and firm about the necessity of doing all those things, but then looked at her elderly cousin with a trace of worry in her eyes.

'You might be able to get some young lad to do that sort of thing for you,' she said.

'But you do it yourself,' stated the Reverend Mother.

Nell nodded emphatically. 'Always! I trust myself more than I trust anyone else.'

'You are very wise,' said the Reverend Mother, but she said no more. She was conscious of a great feeling of sadness and of depression. She thanked Nell for the lesson and then went back up the stairs towards her bedroom, feeling that her feet were dragging. On the way she met Lucy and saw, by her cousin's eyes, a measure of concern.

'I'm just going to have a short rest,' she said. 'Don't mind me. You do what you have planned to do, and we will meet at lunchtime.'

She went back up to her bedroom, listening to the merry voices planning boat trips, walks and even, some of the more adventurous, swims in the sea. Everyone, she reckoned, would be happily busy until lunchtime.

Half an hour later she arose from her bed and went to the door. All was silent except for the sound from maidservants sweeping floors and staircase and a clattering of pots from the kitchen. She went down the stairs slowly, feeling glad of her stout, well-soled, laced-up shoes.

No one was in the hallway when she reached the bottom of the stairs and so, after helping herself to a sturdy stick from the hall stand, she went through the front door and down the steep path towards the hillside.

It was not as difficult a path as it had appeared from her bedroom window, but she was glad of her good shoes and of the support from the stick which she had taken to support her elderly footsteps.

Twenty minutes later she had reached the bottom of the hill. She had chosen her time correctly – dead tide, she thought, with satisfaction – the sea had withdrawn to the Youghal front strand beach, and the river barely lapped the entrance to its channel. The rocks were quite accessible and with the help of the stick she should be able to get quite near to them.

She made her way carefully towards the carcass of rusting metal up ahead, a twisted sculpture of dark red spokes and knife-sharp edges. She must seem a strange vision if anyone cared to look down from Nell's house upon the shore; an elderly lady in black peering into the innards of the abandoned, rusting remains of a car.

NINETEEN

The Reverend Mother had passed a sleepless night. It was, she thought, as she yawned and stretched, her own fault. She had requested the book from her cousin who had duly purchased and delivered it within a few days. It had arrived early in the morning, and she could, she supposed, have skimmed through it during the day. Not a book about religious affairs, of course, but it might be said to have had educational value. Although she did have to admit that history was not on that very limited syllabus assigned by the Department of Education to children whose parents could not afford to pay for secondary education, nevertheless, that had never stopped her teaching an elementary knowledge of the subject to the girls who would be in their last year in their school.

But, of course, although harmless stories about Queen Elizabeth and Sir Walter Raleigh might be benignly overlooked by the bishop, nevertheless, the story of the terrible world war which lasted from 1914 to 1918 and the Irish War of Independence which followed it would be, in his mind, far too mixed up with the IRA and their hunger strike. And, of course, the hatred aroused, after the war was over, among the Irish people by the harshness of those unemployed soldiers, nicknamed the Black and Tans because of their makeshift uniform – the dark green, almost black, of the Royal Irish Constabulary and the khaki of the British army – had made the whole subject of soldiers and of the war a cause of strife in a rebellious city like Cork.

And so, the Reverend Mother having received a book about the 1914–1918 war, *All Quiet on the Western Front*, in its discreet wrapping, from her cousin, did not begin to read it until she was in the privacy of her own bedroom, just in case she would be giving a bad example to the nuns whom she led. She would skim through it and find a relevant passage, she planned, read it in the privacy of the night and then slip one of her discreet black covers over the poignant face of the helmeted young soldier and leave it in her bookcase.

But having started, she knew that she would have to read at least a few chapters.

And then she could not put it down until daybreak when the sun rose above the riverside end of St Mary's Isle. It was, after all, the summer holidays, she told herself and she could suit herself. As soon as she had finished her breakfast she went for a walk. They really were having the most wonderful August weather that she could remember, she thought, as she walked towards the convent chapel, entering, in full sight of the convent windows, through the main door and then, after a quick prayer to her patron saint, St Thomas Aquinas, that he might enlighten and guide her, she emerged by the side door and walked towards the deserted building of what had been the cigarette factory. Would it ever be resurrected again? It was, she noticed with interest, almost undamaged. However, its manager was dead, and its owner had not appeared since the day the fire in the girls' privy had seeped through a small hole and had caused the death of the manager.

According to Nell, Robert had now tired of the idea of recreating Walter Raleigh cigarettes, had declared that this year's crop of tobacco leaves had been irretrievably tainted by the smoke. Apparently, he was now deep in a scheme for the manufacture of house alarms. He would, according to Nell, use his experience in the manufacture of alarm clocks to set up a business making alarms for wealthy people in private houses. He planned, Nell thought, to abandon the wooden shed on St Mary's Isle – and to fill in the channel which was to have carried water from the river to the toilet facilities. He would then sell it as a shed for storage and set up the new business in Liverpool where there would be a much bigger market than in Cork city. It was, had thought Nell, quite a good idea. Britain would be a better market than Ireland. There was no doubt but that the war, and the unrest that had followed the war, leaving so many able-bodied men unemployed, had led to great unrest in Britain. Soldiers and even officers, all of whom had risked their lives daily, were now left unemployed and the 1920s had been bad years for them. Unemployment, she had read, had reached a staggering figure of seventy per cent in the north of England. Men who had risked their lives as youths, now penniless and starving, were not averse to taking a chance of being arrested and imprisoned if they could get easy money by breaking into the houses of the well-off and stealing money and valuables. And, also, according to Nell, the threat of violence to women and children as well as the master of the house would make those wealthy citizens invest a substantial sum of money in Robert's new idea. And, of course, continued Nell, he will need a team of workers to lay the wiring and fix the alarm so that the owner of the house has time to phone the police.

'A team of workers,' echoed the Reverend Mother as she listened to Nell's account. She shook her head sadly. 'Not my girls, I suppose.'

'I'm afraid not,' said Nell with an amused smile. 'You'll have to set up your own business, Reverend Mother. Robert would probably sell you that wood shack cheaply. Have a word with him.' And Nell had gone away laughing, but the Reverend Mother had brooded over her words when she was gone.

And now, here she was back in St Mary's Isle, after her relaxing holiday, peering through the window into the large, well-lit wooden workplace. The sacks and barrels of tobacco leaves had been removed but the heavy table and the chair, where a man had died of smoke inhalation, remained. Though the bottle of whiskey had disappeared and the girl, Maureen McCarthy, still languished in the women's gaol.

That, she resolved, could not be allowed to go on, not for another week. The truth, as she understood it, had to be revealed and the matter placed in the hands of the police. The Reverend Mother gave a sigh. She did not attempt to try the door, but walked on past the building, past the make-shift privy and followed the line of the channel dug through the marshy ground from the edge of the river. If the water had been brought and a proper water-closet had been estab-lished, would that death have been averted, she pondered, but then shook her head. It was useless to speculate on the past. Time she was back in the convent and turning idle dreams into busy achievement.

But first she would summon Patrick and open her mind to him. And Dr Scher, also, she decided. He was a man who never hesitated to challenge her conclusions – a useful man to hold the checks and balances.

She walked briskly back. It was holidays but her life work demanded a response from her upon every day and sometimes upon every hour. The children of the parish, and their parents, still often needed her. Then there was the welfare of her community, her fellow workers to care for. The nuns lived in an unhealthy spot – many of them suffered from asthma and bronchitis, they led lives which were deprived of many comforts and teaching could be an exhausting task, especially when it involved children from desperately deprived homes who learned slowly and reluctantly. Perhaps it might happen, some day, that some philanthropist might donate a house by the sea, even a very small house, so that the nuns might, in modest groups, have some chance of breathing in fresh air and taking exercise which did not involve walking through the stench from the river and suffocating fog and mist in this unhealthy city.

When she reached the convent, she made her two phone calls and then went to speak to Sister Bernadette. She would be expecting two visitors, she told her, but on this hot day, and perhaps not long after her visitors had breakfasted, she thought that offers of tea and cake were unnecessary. In any case, she thought they might, all three, go for a short walk. If so, she would rely upon Sister Bernadette to fetch the Deputy Reverend Mother, Sister Mary Immaculate, if any emergency arose.

And so, the Reverend Mother waited outside near to the gate until Patrick arrived with Dr Scher sitting beside him.

'No point in bringing two cars, we decided. Anyway, like this, we can gossip about you in privacy after we have our audience,' said Dr Scher. She noticed that he shot a quick look at her face when he said that. Dr Scher believed in teasing as a remedy for tiredness or for pain and she guessed that her sleepless night had left its mark upon her face. She was, she knew, generally very pale, but a terrible feeling of exhaustion and treachery had come over her and she thought that she would be glad when she had unburdened her soul and shifted the responsibility over onto Patrick's shoulders. She would, she knew, leave him with a deeply unpleasant task.

'Come in and sit down,' she said, adding, 'I have warned Sister Bernadette that you will not need tea and refreshments unless I summon her.' She accompanied them into her room, and as she said the words, she saw Patrick look keenly at her.

'Do make yourselves comfortable,' she said as she closed and then locked the door of her study. Sister Bernadette, she knew, would not come now, but Sister Mary Immaculate was insatiably curious and would be anxious to know what brought Inspector Cashman and Dr Scher at this early hour of the morning. It would be quite like her to give a perfunctory knock and then burst in.

Now they were safe from interruption and without hesitation she began to speak, though she kept her voice low.

'My patron saint, Thomas Aquinas,' she began, 'was a wise man and from time to time I dwell upon his sayings. One has been in my mind during the last few days.' She stopped for a moment and then said: '"*The world tempts us by attaching us to it in prosperity* . . ."

'I have gone over and over these words in my mind and I know they were the key to the truth. Poverty in the family is bad for a child, but so is excess wealth. It accustoms a person to a standard of living which they will always crave if it is not forthcoming. In my own family, a wealthy childhood came to most members because of the good ideas and business ability of one man, my grandfather, but the making of money is not always easy, and the gift was not passed down through the generations.'

The Reverend Mother stopped for a moment and then continued. 'It seems to me, now, that the murder of the manager of the cigarette factory was not motivated by hatred, not by a desire for revenge, but was rooted in an overwhelming desire for riches and an equally overwhelming fear of adversity. It was, I'm sure that you have been finding, Patrick, a crime which had its solution obscured by many false clues. The man who died, who was murdered by a clever and subtle means, was not killed because of his predatory nature towards women, not killed because he made a young girl pregnant by force and then refused to offer what little redress was in his power, nor because he forced his attention upon a fourteen-year-old girl. No, he was killed because he was greedy and because he got in the way of someone who was equally greedy and to whom money was of the utmost importance. Certain matters led me along the path to the truth and I do now sincerely believe that I have found it, though my path wound back to an item of family history.'

The Reverend Mother stopped for a long minute and across her mind flittered images of stately aunts and generous uncles, of the huge pride of family which was felt by all members of her family, from her own very loved father down to the youngest of her remote relations and right back to her grandfather who, according to her father, had arrived in the city as a 'barefoot boy' and had established a business which ensured prosperity for the generations to come. And now she was about to bring disgrace upon the name which he had made to be esteemed in the city of Cork. It was, though, essential that the truth be established and that the guilty, not the innocent, should bear responsibility for the deadly smoke which killed a man.

'The truth,' she said, 'should have been obvious to me. I had only to ask myself certain questions and the answer should have come to my mind. I should have asked, in the first place, not who had a grudge, but who had the means to stage the tragedy? Who had built a workplace from wood, rather than from stone or from concrete blocks? And who had set the scene of a soaking wet privy, attached to the main building, a privy with no roof where the Cork city rain, famous for falling on three hundred days in the year, could drench that small enclosure? Who had ordered the digging of a trench of about a few hundred yards long – supposedly in order to bring water to turn the privy into a proper lava-tory? And who had suggested and authorized the sending up the cartload of sawdust – wet sawdust which when kindled made sure that the fire would smoke and that the smoke would pour into the room where a man lay in a drunken sleep? Who made sure that a can of petrol was delivered to be stored there and who was the person who knew from his own visits and from phone calls from Mrs Maloney that his manager stayed late in the evening and was drinking heavily? I would guess,' said the Reverend Mother, 'that the bottles of whiskey, not an inexpensive drink, were supplied to the victim by the man who planned to murder him. That makes good sense – a drunken man would not be alert to the smell of smoke, and it would not have seemed suspicious as, of course, the man that murdered the manager was not only his employer, but a man whose dark secrets were known – easy for a stupid man like that manager to imagine that his victim was placating him by giving him presents of bottles of whiskey.'

The Reverend Mother stopped and looked from the doctor's bewildered face to Patrick, who was shaking his head.

'But, Reverend Mother,' he said, 'your cousin, Mr Robert Murphy, the employer of the dead man, could not have committed the murder. He has a perfect alibi. He was in Youghal, thirty miles away, when the Fire Brigade phoned him on the night, spoke to him when the fire occurred at the St Mary's Isle. And I spoke to him myself, on the Youghal telephone number, the following morning when he was eating his breakfast.'

'Yes, of course,' said the Reverend Mother placidly. 'Robert Murphy, according to one of my cousins, is a man of brains – set up a business to manufacture alarm clocks – and that was a skill necessary for the success of this murder. Mr Robert Murphy had all the qualifications to set up an explosion, and, of course, a small fire when he was thirty miles away. A clever man – he did very well in the army during the world war, was in the engineers' corps, was promoted because of his brains to a high rank in the engineers, according to my cousin Miss Nell Murphy, and as I understand from this book,' she unlocked her drawer, pulled out the copy of *All Quiet on the Western Front*, held it up and then laid it upon her lap, 'as a high-ranking engineer would have been responsible, during the war, for laying wires for causing an explosion – detonating bombs, I suppose. As far as I could make out, the wires were attached to something like an alarm clock and so enabled the explosion to be fixed for a time when the enemy was returning to barracks or had reached a particular spot on a road, and, of course, the use of the alarm clock meant that those who set the trap could be a considerable distance away from the explosion.

'So the employer of the victim could easily find an excuse for a visit, pretend that he was looking at the possibility of bringing water from the river to turn the primitive privy into a conventional lavatory, arrange to have a trench dug and when no one was near he could lay the wire, attach one end to an explosive device in the privy and the other end to an alarm set for eight o'clock in the evening, a time when he, himself, was thirty miles away down in his house in Youghal. This book,' said the Reverend Mother, passing her copy of *All Quiet on the Western Front* over to Patrick, 'makes it all very plain how to do this – in fact the opening pages show how the experienced officers taught the skill to the young recruits.

'I'm glad that I read this book,' she went on, 'it is so well-written that it made it very clear to me that, after the horrors of war, a man who might have been responsible for blowing up fellow human beings, young men like himself, into small pieces of flesh and bone, would not hesitate to get rid of a man who was trying to wreck his security. You see, Robert, I think, carried a guilty secret and his guilty secret was discovered by this man who, also, served in the Corps of Engineers and knew a lot about engines and such things.'

The Reverend Mother paused. There was, one part of her mind told her, no obligation upon her to continue. The words that were on the tip of her tongue could be swallowed. The man who had been murdered was an unpleasant man, a blackmailer in all probability and also a man who raped and abused girls. A voice at the back of her mind uttered the words: 'Why not just leave the matter to the police and allow the case, in all probability, to be unsolved?' If she spoke now, the family name, a name of which she and her cousin were so proud, would be vilified.

And yet, the truth mattered and if she did not speak now,

that child, Maureen McCarthy, who had grown up in her school, would still be incarcerated in Cork gaol and might even be in prison for the rest of her life – she remembered with a sudden pang that Maureen had been the eldest in the class and was by now within days of being fifteen years old. Could that make a difference to the judge if she were fifteen at the time of her trial? There could be no hesitation, she told herself.

And so, she continued calmly. 'My cousin Mrs Murphy told me this story. It seems that when Robert was a young man, just home from the war, he fell in love with a beautiful girl who lived nearby and who possessed a large fortune. Her parents refused permission, thought Robert was not good enough for their daughter but her parents died because the brakes failed in their car – and so the marriage between the heiress and Robert took place quite soon as the guardians of this under-age girl did not have the same prejudice against him as her parents had.'

The Reverend Mother stopped again, and once again there was a slight struggle within her, but the truth must always prevail, she told herself and so she continued. 'The marriage lasted for a few years, but, of course, for the past forty years, the Married Women's Property Act meant that the young wife had total control over her own money and that, I think, did not suit Robert. And so, another accident was planned by this man, this experienced engineer who knew all about engines.'

The Reverend Mother paused, but only for a moment so that she could set the scene. This was, she thought, an appalling murder of a young wife and the man who perpetrated it deserved to die – should die, as such a man was, like a rabid wolf, not safe.

'There is a very beautiful part of Youghal, where the estuary of the River Blackwater, after flowing over a hundred miles through the uplands of Kerry and Cork, meets the Atlantic waves at high tide. It was,' she said, 'a bit of a struggle for me at my age to go down there, but I was determined to find the truth and so after a morning in the company with my cousin, Miss Nell Murphy, who kindly explained the different parts of a car engine to me, and showed me where the brakes were situated, I managed to go there at low tide and I discovered the car of my cousin's unfortunate young wife which had gone over the cliff and had been lying on the rocks since that day. It was,' said the Reverend Mother, 'easy to find the car – it had been pointed out to me by my cousin Lucy, and other members of the family, but the difficulty was for me, as someone who knows little about cars, to confirm my suspicions about the brakes, but the lesson from my cousin Nell about the different parts of her own car proved very helpful. Suffice it to say that I was reasonably sure that despite the rusted state of the engine, any mechanic would be able to see that the brakes had been completely removed. I suspect that Mr Timothy Dooley, who was reputed to be an expert with machinery – who had been a mechanic when a soldier, might have suspected that the brakes of the young woman's car had been tampered with, so he had removed them, examined them, and threatened his master with disclosure unless substantial sums were paid out to him on a weekly or monthly basis. The whiskey, which may have proved to be his undoing, may or may not have been part of the blackmail.'

The Reverend Mother stopped, gazing across the room at the marshy ground of St Mary's Isle and then she turned and picked up the book.

'There are some words in the last chapter which struck me,' she said, and then read aloud: *"At school nobody ever taught us . . . how a fire could be made with wet wood, nor that it is best to stick a bayonet in the belly because there it doesn't get jammed, as it does in the ribs."* It painted a picture of men to whom the killing of other men became just a matter of selecting the right means.'

Rising to her feet, she handed it to Inspector Cashman saying: 'I shall leave the matter and the book in your hands, Patrick.'

Patrick and Dr Scher, both of them with shocked expressions on their faces, also rose from their seats and nodded their thanks to the Reverend Mother as she unlocked the door to her office and led them down the corridor to the entrance to the convent. There were no words exchanged between any of them now, not even the customary teasing from Dr Scher.

This was not the time for that. The Reverend Mother needed peace to find the resolve eventually to tell her cousin Lucy of this humiliation to their family name. Patrick needed to work out how to proceed in his investigation and this new line of enquiry. It would not be a simple task to question and arrest such a prominent member of Cork society and the superintendent was not going to be happy with this turn of events. Perhaps it would even jeopardize Patrick's chances of promotion and stain his future career.

But whatever happened, in the words of Thomas Aquinas, '*Veritas super omnia regnet*' and here the path of truth really had to reign above all else, even to the detriment of so many people, both past and future. The Reverend Mother sighed as she returned to her office and sat back down at her desk. She would arrange to meet with Lucy tomorrow, but for now she had some letters to write.